WHAT BOOKS PRESS

AN IMPRINT OF

THE GLASS TABLE

COLLECTIVE

LOS ANGELES

ALSO BY ROD VAL MOORE

Igloo Among Palms

BRITTLE STAR

ROD VAL MOORE

WHAT
BOOKS
PRESS

LOS ANGELES

Publisher's Cataloging-In-Publication Data

Moore, Rod, 1952-

 Brittle star / Rod Val Moore.

 p. ; cm.

 ISBN: 978-0-9889248-1-9

 1. Criminals--Fiction. 2. Exiles--Fiction. 3. Escapes--Fiction. 4. Outer space--Fiction. 5. Planets--Fiction. 6. Science fiction. I. Title.

PS3563.O645 B75 2013

813/.54

What Books Press
10401 Venice Boulevard, no. 437
Los Angeles, California 90034

WHATBOOKSPRESS.COM

Cover art: Gronk, *untitled*, 2012
Book design by Ashlee Goodwin, Fleuron Press.

BRITTLE STAR

for Lisa

But for this rock, its shadow says, *I could get at the sun.*
—James Richardson, *Vectors*

WE LANDED. Stood up in the crowded aisle and sighed. Shuffled forward.
Exited the spaceship like we exited Earth: sour candy shaken from a tin.

And the first thing to do after such a long voyage, despite the shock of
heat, was to bend and stretch, straighten out the kinks, all the while sipping in,
cautiously, as if through a straw, the alien and maybe sickening atmosphere.

But, no time to think about that for too long, because regimentation
began right away. Time to heed orders, the first of which was:

"Select a uniform in your favorite hue!"

And we did, though in fact there were only two colors, with only a
subtle difference between them: one that you might call celery, the other
possibly celadon. However, both were nice enough, even beautiful in
context, given that here, in this new bone-yellow landscape of ours, on this
parched little planet we'd been sent to, with a sun much larger and more
stinging than ours, there was nothing visibly green or alive, besides us, in
any direction. So we each plucked up a green uniform, and gripped it to
our chests childishly, not bothering to compare hues, happy that both had
an organic quality, and that none were prison-striped, or the blood orange
of the reformatory.

Knox, on the other hand, could not decide between colors. After
most of us had fished one out, our exceptional Dr. Knox, future dance

instructor, moved forward gracefully, but then stared down in paralysis at the remaining two uniforms. The celery, he might have been thinking, was just as nice as the celadon, or was it, illogically, the other way around?

"There will be no color or charm on our new home. So think of it this way: we will all be bringing our own private idea of life to a previously sterile world!"

So suggested the in-space magazine, which of course we had all read a thousand times in the course of the interminable journey, with nothing else to do but sit there, strapped in, and read it, and jam it back in its slot, then take it out and read it again. And again and again. Knox, perhaps recalling those words, maybe wanting to make exactly the right impression on such a naked world, went on hesitating, squinting down at the remaining uniforms and then up at the drab, scabby surface of this planet where he had been, we had been, deliberately discarded.

"Pick one, pick one," scolded a voice that came booming out of the interior of the ship. But Knox still wasn't ready. We watched him, irritated with him, from where we had retreated to, in the shade of the ship, clutching our new garments to our chests.

"Do not touch the exterior of the spacecraft!" the same voice squawked. In fact we weren't touching it at all, nor did we want to, given that the surface had an unpleasant liquid quality, a general runniness that had allowed the ship to flow, or drip, at unbelievable speed, through space. Still, obediently, we moved further away from the ship, and more into the heat of the day.

And perhaps that was the moment when it occurred to a few of us that it was never too early to think about escape. Dr. Knox, maybe moved by the same consideration, at last picked up the celadon, only because it was ever so slightly a deeper green—only because the darker fabric might help one blend into certain shadows, become a little less visible to the authorities?

The authorities being the trustees who made the long voyage with us, merely in order (per the magazine) to "render assistance."

"Just like," it read, "you once circulated around the classroom, offering help to your own students."

———

True, we all were academics—professors or adjuncts or deans at a one-year college—and we had all been sentenced in the same way. There were no sadists or psychopaths among us, as far as we knew, but it was true that we had all committed serious crimes. We were all guilty of depressing, work-related transgressions, or so the judgment panel had ruled, and here we were, somewhere in the stars, somewhere, according to the in-space magazine, near the Horsehead Nebula. Here we stood, tongue-tied as students, clutching our prisoners' uniforms, or *unis* as we came to call them, savoring the unbelievable heat, tasting the air for traces of arsenic, or ultramethane, wondering if our first few minutes of exile could end in heat stroke or toxic shock.

If knowledge of history serves, the ancients banished their felons to stony islands. The convicts of our day and age, as we saw first hand, get sent to nakedly mineral planets, and though the one we found ourselves on appeared agonizingly dead, blasted by a sun that was too huge to block with an outstretched hand, or two outstretched hands, we understood that all prisons are featureless, and meant to be. That way the inmates become the features, the contents, the landscape. That way everything one looks at, or touches, or falls in love with, is first a reminder of guilt, then maybe a lesson in redemption.

———

Knox, after finally picking up the celadon, walked off with an expression of triumph, though he then simply walked in a loop, and, when he found himself back at the pile, there remained a single, unclaimed unifom in celery, obviously larger than the others, too big for him. But, after checking that everyone was already provided for, he snatched up that one too.

———

Then what? We all milled around a while, moving in silence, each of us with a uni folded over one arm, like waiters with towels, Knox with his two unis, one per arm. After a time, a trustee came into view, slowly and ceremoniously descending the ramp from the ship, walking in that peculiarly mincing way they had, especially in the beginning: toe first, heel last, reminiscent of barons in coattails in some torchlit performance or other.

"All right, then, here we are, and that's great, everybody," the trustee began, speaking into a mike wand held so close to his lips we could hear the snap of his saliva. In fact, you could see it too, threads of spit stretching from tooth to tooth each time he opened his mouth.

"Okay," he continued, wetly, stringily. "Now everyone has a uniform selected. Is that correct?"

We nodded. Already aliens, we were intelligent, but not quite ready to speak.

Then, in a sharply condescending tone, he went on to explain that now it was time to put them on. The hour had come, as he put it, to discard the out-of-date togs of the old world and make our debut in the new world in appropriately space-age uniforms—which, as he explained, were designed by professionals in the penal planet apparel industry, and manufactured specifically for the conditions of this particular planet.

Still, no one moved. There was some throat-clearing, some background chattering, but it had more a tone of grousing than of defiance. We were not very rebellious yet, not even Dr. Knox. It was just that the more we thought about it the more clear it seemed that, in order to follow this particular suggestion, we would have to strip down to the skin. Did he mean for us to do that then and there, in front of each other? Inside the ship, in the course of the voyage, there had been a degree of privacy, a row of cramped bathrooms that allowed for physical discretion when needed, when appropriate, but there was nothing out here on the surface—just us standing around, shuffling our feet in the soft, sticky dirt, feeling the heat rising up around us, all of us a little shabby and spectral after days and days of confinement in the hurtling ship. There was no question about the unsuitability of the clothes we were wearing. Such tweedy and earth-toned Earth outfits were growing more uncomfortable by the minute, so taking them off sounded, in a way, like a great idea. All right! But still we paused. There was more clearing of throats, more tugging of ear lobes. Some of us laughed. Others laughed at the laughing. The edge of dull dark shade provided by the ship was, we understood, the only privacy we were going to get.

"Yes, that's right," the trustee shouted, reading our minds probably, gesturing in a way that was meant to seem carefree, even liberating. "Rip those old rags off and pile them up, please. We're going to burn them to a crisp right here in the here and now."

"Even our shoes?" questioned Knox.

Dear Knox. He was always the one, in the beginning, to cry out things.

"Oh yes, everything," said the trustee, tracing a large circle in the air. "Haven't you ever heard the maxim, *Give a man a uniform, and you give him a new suit for his soul?*"

No one answered that because yes, of course we had heard that one before. Or read it. The in-space magazine again.

Still the silence continued, but then, a moment later, there was a disturbance. Somebody in the crowd was being a little hysterical. We were a mixed lot, men and women about half and half, young and old, and of course this gender mixing, age mixing, added some discomfort to the idea of public nudity. Then it was noticed that four or five among us had already obeyed orders, and had become perfectly nude while not appearing to move, as if their clothes slipped themselves off without a trace of fumbling.

"Very good!" cried the trustee, pointing out these pioneers.

"Will you be changing too?" cried out Knox.

"You're referring to me?" asked the trustee, who, like some of us, was wearing a full business suit with lapels, a thickly patterned scarf, rubber shoes, a diminutive hat. "Why yes, that's right, I suppose." He looked back into the ship and seemed to follow some instructions conveyed from within. "Yes," he said, turning back. "We are all slated, as I understand, to get new uniforms."

And then, despite his years, despite his dignified appearance and his relative girth, he proceeded to set an example to the rest of the world, and methodically removed each and every piece of clothing. In the end, pink and bare as a seaside toddler (Bless his soul, said someone out loud), he carried his bundle of clothes down the ramp, where he dropped it in our midst, designating that spot, as we backed away from the spectacle of his nakedness, as where to begin the burning.

"Who brought a match?" he asked, chuckling, but looking around at the rest of us a little cautiously, placing one hand over his genitals, as if it had occurred to him that they were not entirely safe in our midst.

In the end, what else could we do? Follow suit. Follow unsuit. With a great deal of jerking and stumbling, everyone squeezed their bodies out of their old outfits like paste out of tubes, and in a matter of minutes, longer for some of us who were older, we all were blinkingly on display to one another, members of the same penal nudist camp, a highly sober and asexual one, with lots of squinting and shading of the eyes, as if bare skin were, like snow, blinding to the eyes. As quickly as we could then, though there were awkward delays, we slipped into the new outfits, with several attempting to get into their unis so rapidly, so casually, that they got tangled up, and fell, making their exposure that much more indecent, though none of the rest of us could summon a laugh.

And finally there we all were, newly suited, and, perhaps, theoretically at least, newly souled.

Certain people who happened to be standing next to each other that morning never spoke to one another again, while others became husband and wife.

———

Again, from the magazine: *In your new home, it is in everyone's best interest to conform to the loftiest standards of style and comportment. To comb one's hair like a gentleman is to become a gentleman. To sip the air as slowly as a peaceful man is to live at peace. But to continually palm one's forehead in apparent shame—that begins to smack of grandstanding.*

———

The unis themselves, once we had them properly adjusted, were, as promised, cool and yes, even stylish. Everyone seemed pleased with such clever one-piece coveralls, as indeed they were very au courant, very outer space, the kind of thing that surgeons might wear in the most expensive operating room, or acrobats in a futuristic circus performance. Shoes, it turned out, were no longer necessary, because the fabric extended down, pajama-like, to cover and entirely enclose the feet as well. And the best part was that everything was so easy to do and undo! Extending from the neck to the groin was a single, gracefully curving zipper with teeth so soft that skin could not be pinched, only tickled a little in the act of zipping up. Meanwhile all our fusty old crime-tainted clothes and shoes had piled up in the designated spot and now formed a little tower of unappealing Earth tones and Earth textures. The trustee, mincing and bouncing, the only one still naked except for the top hat, which he put back on at some point, rushed back into the ship, and came back a minute later wearing a celery uni, the only difference being that he had also put on a kind of tie, the same celery color, quite skinny and almost unnoticeable, though we understood in a flash that this was how we were to recognize the trustees and appreciate them as our friends. As the fellow tiptoed down the ramp, accompanied by scattered applause, bowing to left and right, he produced out of nowhere and fired up a little flame-spitting wand, and as soon as he reached the pile of old clothes, he reached out and torched it gently around its perimeter.

Soon enough it made a quiet and strangely cool bonfire out of our pasts, out of our vanity, and that felt gratifying, though the smell of burning rubber shoes was at first unpleasant.

"You'll find that everything burns poorly here," said the trustee. "It's because of the toxins in the air."

Knox must not have heard this last comment, or he would of course have started crying out questions. Toxins, you say. Well, it was true that the air, perhaps as in Hell, tasted of something citrus and metallic, with a gelatinous quality in the aftertaste, coating our throats like phlegm, or lemon ice cream. But for one reason or another no one among us really thought much about it at that moment, because after all there was also a kind of numbingly pleasant sensation to the air we took in, and perhaps the toxins, whatever they were, acted more like apathy-inducing drugs than poisons.

So rebirth felt okay, rebirth was pretty good. Exile had its little advantages. We weren't remade as something new, but we weren't precisely what we had been either. To think that the earth under our feet wasn't Earth! To think, as we thought then, that we were the first and only humans to find themselves there. So what to call the place, if indeed we had the naming rights? It was said that the planet had never had any name, that it was merely one of many penal outposts, perhaps designated by a number, or an icon. We'd thought of various derogatory names on the voyage out, but once we looked around our tongues refused to repeat them, not out of respect but out of a sense of our own insignificance.

So how to describe where we found ourselves? We found ourselves on Planet. That made us, presumably, Planetlings. Not long before we'd been sarcastic, academic Earthlings. Not long before we'd been malefactors, at least so it had been judged, but better now to stop using such language. Now we needed to be sentence-servers. Apologizers. The idea was that we were to be gently flattened, until we were like coins with all the details hammered away. Barely recognizable, but not in pain. Flip us at the end of our sentence and the answer will always be the same. No heads, no tails. Resistant to all temptations, evil or good.

"Hurrah," we all shouted, or someone did, probably not Knox this time, and the rest of us, some three hundred or so, simply echoed him, half in mockery, half serious. At length we began milling around, finally finding our tongues, breaking the silence, able in a way to talk to one another, which came as a relief. Sometimes, during the voyage, weeks had passed in utter silence. But now you couldn't shut us up. Of course what we went on about at first was the gift of the unis. How smooth the zippers were, how well the fabric draped in some places, clung in others. Also especially nice was how our new clothes cooled us without making us cold, absorbed sweat without making us dry. In retrospect, it may even be that the unis were made of a material that absorbed and weakened our mental powers, and turned some of us, at least, into fools.

Anyway, we talked and talked, not knowing what else to do, not wanting to look very hard at that landscape, even though the open aridity constituted a welcome relief from the dark stickiness of home. The trustee rushed back inside the ship, leaving us to our chatter, our walking in circles, our laughter, our banalities. There was some talk of gravity, as everyone sensed it was a trifle lighter than at home, so much so that some tried jumping up and down in place, while others got down on hands and knees to measure the jumping, seeing if the feet went any higher than at home. It did seem a *little* higher, but in the end it was pretty hard to say for sure.

As for Knox, he never said a word the whole time, and just sat down as near to the liquid skin of the ship as he could without being accused of touching it, not ready for that silent stage one of exile, let alone the chatty stage two. But as he was about to close his eyes he became aware that someone, a gray-haired but not elderly woman, had plopped down next to him, and was knitting her enormous black eyebrows at his clothing, fingering the sleeve of his uniform carefully, while for his part he focused on her swollen cheeks, wondering if she had food stored in them like a chipmunk, as he was hungry, as we all were, and even thought of asking her for some.

"There's stripes," she muttered, cheeks deflating, not looking up at him.

And yes, to be sure, though no one else had commented on this, when she held his sleeve to the light, at exactly the right angle, subtle stripes became apparent, though more in the weave than in the color.

"Ah, ah," he murmured, debating with himself if the stripes were meant as a subtle reminder of old prison outfits, or were simply a point of style, like, say, a pin-striped business smock. Then the woman looked up and pushed silver clumps of hair out of her face and burst out grinning, blushing, cheeks empty, and Knox was astonished to see that she appeared to have no teeth, and he had never heard of or could have imagined someone not having them.

"And it crackles," she added, eyes wide, speech distorted by the missing dentition, and, as Knox shifted about in the dirt, and stood up, half to move away from her and half to test her claim, the fabric made a distinct noise at the slightest movement, something he hadn't noticed before. Had it been designed that way on purpose, to give the trustees a way of staying aware of everyone, monitoring everyone, by setting up ultra sensitive microphones, maybe, in order to listen to the subtlest movements?

But in the end, he laughed at the idea, and the woman with the mop of gray hair turned away to speak to someone else, apparently on the same subject.

In time, with the temperature ever rising, a few more facts were revealed.

The same popular trustee ventured out again. Could this be the only one, we wondered? When we first heard about trustees, we assumed there would be a board of trustees, a group of them, and indeed there were rumored to be quite a few, confined to some first class compartment of the spaceship. So, it was reasonable now to expect them all to emerge with some drum roll or other drama from inside the ship.

But no one dared shout out such questions, even Knox.

"We trustees are not a branch of any government," the fellow read from a scrap of paper which was obviously not the magazine, because we hadn't heard that statement before, and had all along assumed that they were connected to the government. The trustee had several such scraps of paper to read from, and kept fumbling, dropping, re-arranging them. At last he looked up, quizzically.

"Now," he continued, "I shall read some maxims. Does everyone know what those are? Maxims, people? Aphorisms? Remember that there were a number of them in your magazine."

"What are maxims again?" someone shouted.

It was Knox, asking a rhetorical question, because of course he knew and we all knew a maxim or two and who does not. Clearly it was his way of having a little fun, Knox playing the smart aleck student with the trustee, who didn't project airs of authority, but did react impatiently to the question.

"Maxims! Adages!" In the end, he looked cast down by his own words.

"I remember one from the magazine," said someone else, raising his hand. This was Krell, a fellow prisoner whose name we already knew, since he'd made a point of trolling the aisle, introducing himself to everyone on board, and the flight had taken so long that he ended up repeating his introduction many times over.

"*A life,*" recited Krell, "*can only be successfully managed one liberty at a time.*"

"That's it," laughed the trustee, with a note of falseness in his laughter, while several animal groans, voices from an abyss, could be heard rising from the crowd. After all, we were mostly professors, or had been, and were not at all unfamiliar with that type of student, subject to ridicule after class, who insists on showing off knowledge even when the answer, like the maxim Krell had come up with, serves as a reminder of one's subordination.

"And here's another," said the trustee.

But the prospect of even a very short speech made the heat hurt more.

"Hold on a minute," said Knox, standing, taking a step closer. "We can't memorize these things unless we... unless we know our teacher's name."

"Oh, very true. Yes. It's Chemo. My name is Dr. Chemo. And, as I always tell everyone I meet, prisoner or not, you may think of me as your chum."

He smiled broadly at that, but with the look of someone who had been taught to smile mathematically, turning a straight line into a curve one micro angle at a time.

"I know that it's a strange name," he continued. "But then again, I'm a trustee and you'll find trustees are strange all around, and deserve to be locked up, ha ha, more than you."

"You got that right, Chummo," came a nasal voice. And though we laughed, we never discovered the speaker.

It was one of many things said that day that some people would come to regret saying.

Not because of punishment, but because of love.

But such regrets were months away.

At the moment Chemo stood there with his mouth puckered as if to suck from a straw, his eyes watery, as if the strangeness of his name, or the shouted reaction to it, had touched his heart, had nearly brought him to tears.

———

It was a planet with two suns. *Two suns are twice the energy and excitement,* read the magazine, with a picture of two smiling shining orbs eyeing each other a little lasciviously. That was a lie, like so many others, because one sun was almost always positioned in front of and obscuring its partner, like the ham in the school play. As we watched, disappointed, this one sun kept climbing higher in the sky, as all suns do, and always kept its partner behind it. Meanwhile the shade cast by the ship shrank in correlation, so that most of us were no longer in it, and were exposed now to what two suns, no matter their relative positions, must result in: excess rays. However, to tell the truth, the unis were superb at blocking most of the heat, and keeping the skin cool, at least where they covered the skin. It was the uncovered areas, such as the neck and hands, that were most affected, and immediately everyone started wishing they had more magic fabric, out of which to fashion berets and scarves and gloves. It was noticed from the start that Knox had ended up with an extra uni, and people around him began touching it, in this way subtly asking for it. Maybe if they had said something out loud he would have given it away, but this pawing offended him, and he yanked it away from several outstretched hands and stuffed it inside the zipper of the uni he had on, down near his gut, where it made a theatrical protrusion. Still some people came up to him and patted it, as if it were his pregnancy, and he twisted himself to yank that away from them too.

Others, the not-so-highly degreed among us perhaps, ran in circles around the ship with their mouths hanging open, thinking they'd find relief that way. Then the last centimeter of shade vanished, and all we could do was to surrender, just as one had to do on Earth once in a great while in the heat sinks of the great sticky cities.

"I've never been more miserable in my life," said someone, and everyone laughed to hear it expressed so inadequately.

"Lies, lies, and more lies," someone else muttered, and there was a general, cautious murmur of assent. The magazine had deceived us. Either that or its author had been misinformed, because one of the articles claimed that our new penal world was known for its climate. That could be read in many ways, of course, but after all we'd virtually memorized the thing as it was the only reading material during the voyage, and everyone vividly remembered that one word used to describe the climate in that same article was the word flattering.

"More like flattening," was one remark. But now the time for joking was past. We were prisoners, after all, and believed we could get used to most extremities, but on the first day of our exile we were expecting something a little easier. Was it because we were academics? Some criminals are hardened, but so far we had only begun hardening. We had reached the mental stage of accepting punishment, but not the stage of accepting pain.

"Let go!" someone screamed, thinking the heat was grabbing her, dragging her off somewhere, but no one moved to lend a hand. We stood around, silent again. Breathing was difficult. It felt like gargling with boiling water, and after a while, even later when we had gotten inside the new structure and cooled off, something like a sticky bolus or wad of something remained, half stuck in the throat for hours afterward.

But Dr. Chemo, maybe because he could see so many of us holding our hands to our throats, or maybe because he was holding his hand to his own throat, spoke gently into his pencil-thin amplification wand, his saliva gone now, and explained that this difficulty in breathing, this swollen effect in the throat, while we might think it was the heat, was presumably a result of the poisonous atmosphere.

That shut everyone up, of course.

Again we reviewed our memorization of the magazine. But no, no mention of a poison had appeared there.

"Then we are to be executed?" inquired Knox, smirking, holding up a hand. It seemed he was the only one, besides Chemo, able to speak.

"No, no," laughed the trustee. "I'm sorry that everything hasn't been carefully explained."

We waited.

"The atmosphere," he went on, complacently, waving his tie around as if ameliorating the air that way, "contains a few toxic elements."

He coughed for a while, then recovered. Unlike his fake laugh, it didn't strike us at all as a fake cough.

"I won't bore you with the science. But don't worry, because we won't stay outside for any length of time. As it turns out there isn't a great deal of oxygen either. You know, you'd have to be exposed to this stuff for several hours before getting any serious effect from it. You know that, right? Look, people, you've been outside for less than an hour."

"Then, before the several hours are up, we go back inside the ship?" someone asked. It wasn't Knox this time, but someone who was imitating his style.

"No, no," Chemo answered back, looking anxiously behind toward the open door of the ship, as if expecting more information. "No. I must tell you that...no one is allowed to."

"So now what?" It was Knox again, and yes, we could all hear a note of panic in his voice. Then it was time to panic, it seemed, if he was leading us in that direction.

Without answering, the trustee twisted, turned, and, still waving his skinny tie, clattered up the ramp, back into the interior of the ship.

"Are they really going to kill us now, Dr. Knox?" a woman asked, politely, holding her hair flat against her skull, like she thought it might come off in the brisk wind that had come up. But hers of course was the question we all were asking, meanwhile holding not our hair, but our breath, the best we could, then realizing, no, don't hold it, there's a lack of oxygen, so the more you breathe, maybe, the better, but then the more you breathe, the more toxins you possibly take in.

"Or are *we* going to kill *them*?" someone muttered.

"Who said that?"

"I did."

We couldn't see who it was, but at any rate, there it was: an idea that had now been planted, a seed of murderousness in one or two minds, at least, that had at least once been known for good manners.

———

During the endless voyage all Knox had been able to revolve in his mind, like a ball bearing, was the moment of departure. At least we've learned this much by now: that the mind pushes away pain by obsessively replaying the memory of the moment of loss and so deferring any review of the moment after loss, more painful by far. We've learned, in short, that hard mental work is performed primarily to shirk harder mental work.

For Knox this meant recollecting the moment of lift off from the spaceport. Strapped in, there he was, sentenced, done for, squashing his head against the window in order to look straight down at the roof, to squint down to get a glimpse of Mhurra.

In other words, a glimpse of the wife he might not see again. And after a moment there she was, barely visible through the skylight glass as the vessel hovered above the building. In truth, all that could be seen were her wrists and hands, all ten fingers wriggling under the glass, like anemones in an aquarium, but he knew it must be her because she was making the same rapid cryptic movements she had often made, her funny and bad imitation of sign language, an old joke with her, not very amusing really, but this time it was as if she were trying to send him some sort of actual message, as the movements were very specific, and repeated the same way over and over.

He watched, hot tears in his eyes, wanting badly to understand her message, but he couldn't. They'd never actually communicated that way before, only pretended to, and he spent the subsequent days of travel, strapped into his seat, arms barely free, imitating the movements that he remembered perfectly, drawing the attention of us other passengers, but ultimately boring us, as he continually revolved his hands and splayed his fingers in silence, moving his lips as if to read his own hands aloud, but unable to make any sense of anything. But concentrating on it, and so insulating himself.

And for him those were unprecedented moments of physical grief, the sensation of emotional vomiting, the feelings of amputation and eruption.

Deferred, deferred. He made himself remember, in order not to remember, what he saw right after Mhurra's hands were lost to view: that is, the expanse of that city they'd spent their lives in, that city that spread out to all horizons in colors of dark rum or beer or illuminated molasses, a liquid city, with thin towers, dark as chocolate. That city that told the story of the impermanence of modern architecture, skyscrapers jutting up as he watched, and then maybe even melting or retracting back into the general goo. But then the ship veered away, and the city, and the wife, were gone. Replaced by an empty nothingness. Replaced by a sea of chocolate, or of ink. Something full of life and full of knowledge of him was down there, but irretrievable, drowned in darkness.

Then came the painful shift into space, and then the tedium of the interstellar voyage. And then, weeks later, arrival, arrival, the landing on what looked from a distance like a solid orb of nothingness. A planet that had no name, no meaning. Tragic to some, a shrug to others. *If you want to see life on this world,* someone said, or he thought someone said, at the moment they first stepped foot on the new world and squinted out over the yellow landscape, *look in the mirror.*

And so it began: our penance, our time to be served, all of us so far removed from Earth that we also felt far removed from any sense of either innocence or guilt. As Knox might have put it, if he were asked, or if he wasn't, it was the beginning of his narrative of amorality, as well as his narrative of detachment.

Nothing good can last, he might have said, bitterly, taking in his new surroundings. *But nothing that does last can be all that good.*

And on this new world then, there were few clues as to how to behave as exiles.

We had lost the Earth, and so lost ourselves, since we were made of earth.

Here, on the new planet, there was little to experience besides lacerating heat, and the company of criminals.

And poison. All the time we were breathing in air that was reportedly fatal after an hour, or maybe after two hours. Prisoners in olden days were directed into chambers in order to be fumigated, gassed. We all knew that. We were educated, up on things, nothing if not rational. Hardly necessary to put us on board a rarefied spacecraft and send us to another world, light years away, in order to effect the same hideous, tedious result.

Remember how Earth has plenty of its own chambers.

So we rolled our eyes at each other uncomfortably, showing the whites, acting out our deaths ahead of time, some with their hands over their mouths, heaving, as if about to vomit. Others arched their brows at all this, perhaps sarcastically. Others wore expressions drawn from tragedy, faces tilted up toward the double sun, like self-sacrificers. Dark is the day! An outside observer—the proverbial man from Mars—might have cried out to stop it, to put us out of our misery. How long is mortality supposed to last? One or two people on the edge of the group let out fake death rattles that seemed to go on for minutes. Others staggered, their brains and blood maybe already curdled by the heat. Life is a tragedy for those who feel, a comedy for those who think. We had all understood from the moment we received our sentences of one-year exile, that we were to be regarded from then on not as modern humans, but as throwbacks to some earlier time, unspecified, unimaginable. Human but with some recent and essential aspect of humanity removed. That, and not exile, was, in short, the punishment, and the subtraction had taken place before we boarded any ship. The rest of the sentence was to go down the drain, into the anonymity of plumbing, society having found it convenient to shit us out. Still, some of us took solace in the recollection that our exile, as promised, would come to an end. That we'd be redigested!

Meanwhile one of the heavily sighing souls among us, near us, was blurting out a sentence. We all were trained to listen well, and the sentence felt like quite a good one, but incomprehensible.

Still it seemed as if the words, *I'd rather die than,* were in there somewhere.

Knox undertook, then, to split himself in half, so that one half of himself could talk to the other half about the possibility of death.

Is it possible?

Yes.

Is it welcome?

In some circumstances.

"So if all do their duty," someone nearby muttered, "they need not fear harm."

Is it possible to move forward through such darkness? Yes, when there is the faintest possibility—oh, very faint—of soon reuniting with the light, with the beloved. For days Knox's fingers, as they retracted from touching what wasn't there, were spastic and crooked, but at least there was something to imagine recoiling from. If Mhurra were there she would bring with her her own bents, her language, and that made it easier to imagine a caress. What he had loved to touch, when first within an inch of her, were her eyes. When shut, of course. Two cold orbs, humor-filled, connected by nerves to the occipital lobe. She'd improve her posture then.

"I'll kiss your eyes a little," he told her, "as that's the closest one comes to kissing your brain."

———

Outside the spaceship, some were craning their necks, not peering upward, and when it was understood that they were trying to breathe the highest possible air, the rest followed suit. If the toxins were heavy, they'd linger near the ground. Meanwhile, the idea of a cleaner heaven was logical and soothing. Also, to look at the sky was to not look at the planet. To gaze upward was to apply celestial eyedrops, or locate the god of the new planet, if there was one. But, after a long time of looking, our eyes would falter, fall, and mutely take in again the landscape: cinnabar and sulfur, poorly lit, sketchy. The sun, hot and huge as it was, was oddly dim, lower in wattage than what we were used to from our home sun, making a distant line of hills seem flat, painted on, repetitive, like cartoon scenery that revolves behind a galloping and wisecracking animal.

"I don't like the look of those hills," someone drawled, a cowboy accent, as in ancient skits. Whoever it was, was making a joke of things. But all of us, sheeplike and mostly from the humanities, or the soft sciences, were at that point humorless.

Later it got dusty, nodules and swirls of yellow powder arriving out of nowhere, not like a cloud of gas, but moving in slowly, thinly, until the world was delicately blurred with dust.

This made it hard to speak. Soon we all became coated with it, like it or not, in the form of a face powder, a light flour the color of turmeric. Still, we breathed and lived. An actual feeling of increasing strength came with it. In the end, we looked at one another and laughed. My friend! You are beautifully made up today! That sort of thing.

"Look!" a woman's voice cried out, and wheeling around we discovered that it was nothing more to shout at than a trustee, a new-to-us trustee, descending the ramp.

He didn't walk the same walk, and wore a uni that seemed to hover somewhere between a celery or a celadon. But no, it was definitely a celery.

He was bald, and in his case that was a plus, because though his head was soon as covered with dust as everybody's, he was able to easily wipe it off with the sleeve of his uni.

"You mustn't worry," he said, speaking reasonably. He was clearly someone you could easily work under, like a dean who only supports, and never undermines. "Don't get upset, because we are going to erect a shelter for everyone."

"Hurrah!" we shouted, sincerely. For some reason his baldness gave him an air of superiority, of one who might quickly become popular, with his non-mincing bearing, his very white face that suggested something lopsided and primitive, something carved hastily, not finished.

"And will the shelter be poisoned too?" someone joked.

"No, no," laughed the new-to-us fellow, his top row of teeth tilting up like a friendly, scary skull.

"How long?"

"Another hour."

"But the dust storm!"

"It's over."

"And you're saying we can't go back inside the ship."

"No need!" said the congenial, or at least congenial-for-the-moment, trustee. "No need to worry, as we are addressing that, getting things done on that. Working overtime."

"Working on what?" By this time we were speaking almost as a group, almost in unison. Fear of injury had momentarily brought us together, but it was not to last. Any kind of real camaraderie was hard to muster. Like all malefactors, we were destined to splinter.

"I told you what we're working on. We're preparing the shelter for you. It was supposed to be a surprise, but we knew you were worried about the air."

"Tell us more about it. About the shelter."

And so, taking a quick glance back at the dark interior of the ship, then sitting down on the ramp and wrapping his arms around his knees, the fellow explained that we were all soon to have and live in a new city of our very own, where every man could count himself a king, or at least an authentic bourgeois.

"At least tell us the name first," ordered Knox.

"It's Dr. Fermat. And yours?"

"No, the name of the city."

"Oh, no name yet. But what is your name?"

"Knox."

"Okay, Knox. The surprise is this: it's a domed city. You will be domed inhabitants. Call it the City of the Domed, if you like that. And here is the best part. It can be built, it will be built, within a matter of minutes."

Hooray for noble Fermat. A trustee to be trusted. Had somebody actually said that?

"Listen," he continued, holding a finger to his lips.

In the silence that followed, and then the noise that followed, we realized that something tremendous was in fact about to transpire. There was such a vague and visceral buzzing emanating from the belly of the ship that we thought it was going to take off and leave us stranded forever, castaways rather than exiles. Instead it seemed more to sink than rise, to sag into the soil, like a deflating dirigible. What was worse was that the liquid skin poured completely off, onto the ground, where the fluid sank out of sight, absorbed by the dirt. The ship that had once seemed nearly alive with currents and eddies, now appeared made of iron, or some very primitive metal, bare and crusty, derelict.

"No! No!" went up the cry. We had cheered the prospect of a domed city, then been crushed by the prospect of losing our transportation home. Without the liquid, how were we to drip through space again? But there was no time to meditate on this apparent disaster. The nose of the ship gave a shudder, something like a sneeze, then split a little, opening a kind of stoma, which in turn gave birth to a tongue or tentacle that burst out and immediately plunged itself into the soil, and continued plunging, as if the ship were programmed to probe deeply into the inner organs and glands of the planet.

There was an unpleasant sexuality to it all. We kept backing away.

But Fermat went the other direction, advancing right up to within centimeters of where the probe kept snaking down endlessly into the dirt, a colossal ovipositor. There was to be much more dancing on that planet, but here was the first instance: Fermat turning toward us and jigging triumphantly, holding his ribs, winking, and by way of any number of gestures, giving us to understand that celebrations were in order, though all we could feel in ourselves was an itchy mixture of bewilderment, embarrassment, and loss. A moment later Knox went forward to join Fermat, and it will never be forgotten how each of them bent down to watch the probe, each of their profiles beautifully shaped, each sticking out a finger at the same time to feel the tentacle as it shot down, each retracting that finger, and examining the nasty friction burn, and both next dancing in pain, or exhilaration. Though in either case it quickly appeared that Knox was by far the better dancer.

———

Of course Knox was by far the worst of us in other ways. Some crimes achieve a gleaming and forgivable clarity over time, and others don't. We weren't supposed to know the nature of each other's wrongdoings, but in Knox's case we were all quite aware of the sordid facts. His crime had not consisted of, as with most of us, some genteel misappropriation, or misrepresentation, or forgery, or defalcation. It went beyond all that. In our cases, we were heartily ashamed of what we'd done, and ready for rehabilitation, anxious for it even, ready to be straightened from bottom to top, ready for a reconstitution of heart and soul. But it might have been the case that he, Dr. Knox, had gone too far to achieve any real correction. His crime involved the spectacle of assault, and it had been reported any number of times, at least on the cheaper news channels. It was impossible to imagine, looking at him, that this man who set his lips together so mildly in the act of dancing, whose arms were thin and fluid, whose fingers had the long wistfulness of an amateur musician, was capable of violence, of actually attacking and roughing up one who was superior to him in rank. But that is, so we understood, what he was guilty of. And our knowledge of it made us wary of him on the one hand and fiercely admiring on the other.

Give us a disposition as ferocious as that displayed by Dr. Knox, as a maxim-esque comment went at the time, *and we could throttle, well, not another person, but at least our inner malefactors.*

Also, on the voyage out, Krell, the sometimes very voluble Dr. Krell, in the course of all his kibitzing, had readily recounted details of the Knox case, moving from seat to seat, whispering so that Knox, a few seats up, wouldn't overhear. And we welcomed the details! Oh, if he did that (reasoned every mind that listened), then our own crimes were whimsical, wispy, barely worth mentioning. Knox, in that sense, was our ointment, a strong fragrance that masked our own stink.

Later, on the planet, we heard the story from the perpetrator himself. Eventually he explained to everyone who would listen, especially when he was later giving dancing lessons and had a captive audience, that despite being the worst criminal among us, he was not a bad sort by any means. But, like all of us, he had performed duties that were vaguely academic, intellectual, or managerial in a particular school or department. The one-year colleges happened to be where most of the arrests were being made in those days, but his was not a story of everyday corruption, as was so common elsewhere, but only of responding to an injustice, the type of routine circumstance in which the just are granted less power than the unjust. Nothing was different about Knox other than a resentment of high-handedness, and the turning point came when, one morning, as a joke, more for the benefit of some students in the hall who were watching, he abruptly grabbed a hold of the throat of someone, a dean who'd been lording it over everyone for days. And lording it over was the worst crime of all on the Knox scale: it was the unpardonable crime of swaggering, throwing one's weight around, answering but never asking questions. Finally Knox, at his wit's end, grabbed hold of the dean's throat, still with a sense of sarcasm, of theater, wondering frankly if that's where his fingers were supposed to be. Unfortunately, he continued to hold onto the poor man for longer than necessary, if only as a way of extending the joke, turning it into a moment to be relished by all like-minded observers, making it sharper, funnier, wiser. But the dean, a former professor of syntax, with zero sense of irony, fell down, collapsed in a lopsided and deflated way, hitting his head against the floor, where it gave out a sound like a tin bell, followed by a golden ring from a real bell that this dean kept on his key ring. So, there he was on the ground, and to Knox it seemed almost as if the old administrator had secretly wanted to fall or flop, wanted in the worst way to turn the joke into a disaster for Knox. The fact was, he was injured slightly, with a slight concussion, but this was obviously a result of the fall, not the strangulation, and if you yell an insult from across a room, and the insulted party falls pitifully down, are you guilty of assault and battery?

Such were the milestones, millstones, shared by us all, though to lesser degrees. We were not really the types to commiserate with Knox, not at first at least, because most of us kept our own counsel, believed in the old adage that a dog must have its bark, but train it so that its bark has the sound of a feckless, friendly inebriation. Enough of swatting and strangling. These are our modern times. That was the general belief, at least, and so it was not that easy to get into trouble, yet people managed to mess up anyway, and show up in court, facing the exile panel.

And so. Here we were.

As for Knox, what he told us eventually was that as he gazed down upon his victim, watching him contort in pain on the harlequin-tile floor, he had a clear and sudden vision of the future: he saw himself, saw all of us really, in some dreary penal landscape or other, standing around in our sleek uniforms (how could he have known about the uniforms?), looking out over desert scenery. But that was the part he got wrong, because in his vision the landscape had been the color of blood instead of what it turned out to be, which was brass, and yellowed paper, and urine.

————

After a time we grew tired of waiting to see what the subterranean probe would accomplish, and sat down on the ground. Another thing was, what if the poison was lighter than air, and drifted two or three meters off the ground? Maybe better to breathe the bottom layer, breathe in the actual yellow dirt if need be. We'd been promised a city, but there was no sign of one yet. So we lay prostrate, humbled, everyone's face and uni filthy now, steeped in the dust of the day. Some lay on their backs to watch the clouds, then lay on their stomachs to watch the dust. What was the program, what was the agenda? Dr. Fermat had retreated back into the ship, with no further explanation of the construction process, so there we were, strewn like crash victims, and it may as well have been a crash, since the ship now seemed destroyed.

True, one year was the official sentence. One single year was what they handed down. But everything—the way the *Antibody* settled like an abandoned vehicle in the yellow dust, the green uniforms that cooled our skin in the heat, the theoretical city, the theoretical dome—all this suggested that we might be in for a longer sentence. And so, like fallen angels, we lolled at the bottom of our new realm, some pressing their eyes into the ground and realizing that here, even at this close-up level, there wasn't the slightest sign of life. No stalk of weed, no bug, no mite, no microbe.

A lifeless planet, except now we were the life, and shouldn't every world be blessed with that? In that sense our exile was not a punishment but a reward. It was possible to see ourselves as missionaries, sent to rescue this world from its humorlessness. Alternately, we were sent to infect another world with our humanity.

———

The first and more theatrically stern of the two trustees, Chemo, emerged once more to say that they were making great progress, that indeed within minutes (though they had said the same thing minutes ago) a great translucent dome would arise, wherein all would dwell, and within the dome there would also arise a nicely appointed and comfortable city, although it would probably be better to refer to it as a town, given its relatively small size, just the right size for a group like us, three hundred all together. It would have to feel like a very small town, he explained, though actually the dome would be larger than necessary, simply to give a sense of airiness and calm, a sense of freedom.

"Are you saying we can't leave the dome once we're inside?"

It was Knox again, naturally, standing up, Lucifer in his little lake of fire.

Chemo seemed surprised by the question.

"Why would anyone ever want to leave?" he asked, rubbing his voice wand over his mouth, as if applying lipstick. "Look around. It's ugly! And the air is no good out here, as you know. Oh, sure, run outside if you like—no doors will ever be locked—but come on, chums, think how soon you'll want to go running back in, back to healthy air and water and lots of good eating and good friends. Am I accurate? Am I logical?"

Chemo came off as more congenial than before, perhaps only because he had mastered the trick of speaking into the voice wand without spitting into it. Still, everyone stayed put on the ground and didn't appear to pay attention.

"Look," he said, putting down the wand for once, and walking among us, speaking quietly, normally, nearly inaudible, a comfortable hiss in his voice. "Here is the main point. None of this is meant for permanence. No one wants to stay here past their allotted time. Trustees..."

"Yes?"

"We trustees are sent here too, you know. We didn't volunteer for this."

Hearing that, disgusted, Knox stood up, walked a few steps towards Chemo with his hands stretched out, as if with the intent to strangle.

We all laughed, but maybe it wasn't meant to be funny. Knox stopped, and laughed with us, but we couldn't help but understand what he was suggesting— that we could now commit crimes with impunity, just as souls could sin forever in hell. Because, think about it, where else was there to be sent?

Chemo laughed too at last, though artificially.

"All right," he stammered, backing away, clutching at his tie, but maintaining a smirk of authority. "In the meantime, get to work."

What work? There was work?

True, prisoners often did perform various types of manual labor. But the magazine hadn't mentioned anything about that. We wanted to ask for more details. Did he mean academic work, such as we were all used to? But we said nothing, kept our thoughts to ourselves. Every thread of life was different now, everything torn apart and re-attached, and here there was so much to get used to. What degree of authority, for example, did these trustees actually have? Could they force us to do things? Nothing was clear. As for work, there wasn't any task at hand, and so the command had to be purely rhetorical, but it took a while to understand that, and a few people actually stood up, shifted around, cleared their throats, wilted in the heat, got up again, and even walked out a ways into the harsh landscape, as if their jobs might be located there. And out there, as the rest of us watched, we noticed how miniature dust tornadoes, shaped like martini glasses, would come up and envelop our wandering comrades at times, as if on purpose. But they were harmless, and when these souls came back to the group we saw that the little storms had brought about an opposite effect from what was expected, and both their faces and unis were clean, polished to an extra bright luster.

Knox didn't venture out. Still, we wished he would, because he was clearly agitated. His ears slowly seemed to stick out more and turned a deeper red. He looked taller than before, like a brief whirlwind would do him good, polish him down to size.

"I'd like to make an announcement," he said out loud, eyes closed, but only loud enough for two or three people near him to hear. They turned away, and his speech was never given.

Later, we were all, including Chemo, lying in the dust again.

Knox stood up again, and it was surprising to see that he had picked up the trustee's voice wand, and was monkeying with it.

"Testing, testing," he said. Testing what?

No one moved to take it away from him.

"There's far too much of me here," Knox declared, with the volume turned way up. "Ladies and gentlemen," he continued. "It will be a question of coming to terms with the surplus."

Then, again, someone screamed, as if attacked, and, jumping to our feet, we witnessed the emergence of the dome. Some dozens of meters out on the plain, it began to rise, like a great surfacing bathysphere, before our eyes. We had begun to doubt all the promises, but there was definitely something round and epic going on out there, something birthing and crowning. As it continued to push up, white in color, corpse-like, it had a gummy and insubstantial look, not so much a pleasure dome as a fancy bubble-gum blower's trick. And yet, after a moment's hesitation, it spread wider, and wider, and wider, until it had broken through much of the dirt of the plain, and reached the size of a stadium, or an enlarged tumor. And now we noticed how it sometimes shrank a little, as if it were being breathed into existence by underground lungs, though always to enlarge to even greater size on the next exhalation.

"Hurrah," someone said, but only someone. The rest of us watched in silence. Whatever it was seemed a miracle, though an evil one. When the explanations came we learned that it was all science, all logical. The underground probe snaked out by the *Antibody* achieved all this by first collecting various waxy or semi-viscous minerals in the soil and concentrating them first just below the surface. This accretion was next inflated upward, where it composed itself in air, shaping into a larger and thinner hemisphere, ever more lucid, finally on the verge of bursting. At that point, we naturally cowered, sure that it was about to break and cover us in its goo. But it stopped, and that was it, that was the promised dome, perfected.

A moment later, as if to answer our unspoken question, there came a series of lesser inflations, balloons within the balloon, but these were more squat and confined, curvaceous yet slightly boxier shapes that swelled and even squeaked as we watched, splitting like cells, agglutinating rapidly until, in less than half an hour, behold a cellular complex, a town, as promised, of paraffin-white buildings, with sweeping roof lines topped by radish-like spires, light-bulb turrets, and, most delicate of all, thin arching bridges that soared like spider threads from form to form.

Several now could be heard applauding, but slowly, as if stupid, or reduced to the state of children. After all, what were we looking at but a toy on the grandest scale, a grow-your-own-crystals set gone out of control, but dazzling even to adult eyes—even to sociopathic eyes.

"This is for us? For us?" someone muttered. There were those among us, perhaps the ones with the most critical minds, who rubbed their eyes as if to grind away all further incredulity. There were others who turned away, ashamed of their lifelong defeatism, and wept.

And then there were those who clapped harder, blurted out kudos, and began surging forward, firm in their faith in the trustees, because now, well, of course we had an emerald or at least an alabaster city, a pellucid beehive, a force field. A cheery science fiction prison.

"Maybe the greatest city in history!" someone shouted, and while this was too much, hardly true at all, no one offered a contradiction.

"When they hear this back home," announced Krell, his words amplified because now *he* had the voice wand, "They'll go on a crime spree."

There was general laughter then, nervous, as was natural in a mix of relative degrees of sociopathy. A note of weeping could be heard underneath. Then, at the trustee's signal, we simply shut up and ran, and ran, resisting the poison atmosphere, boycotting it, going so far as to fake cough, nearly fake die, all the while earnestly grasping at the promise of refuge, in love with the idea of a futuristic dome. Chemo and Fermat were up front, trying to lead the way, running backwards and narrating in gasps, but we paid no attention, and soon ran right past them.

Knox, for his part, hung back, listening to the crinkling of all those fleeing uniforms. Dear Knox! He was always the one to hang back—the one to always relish space that suddenly emptied of people. What he did in this case was march, inserting a degree of duty into it, breathing not gasping, back in the direction of the ship. A moment later he came up short, and reached out solemnly to put a friendly hand on the tentacle, the instrument that had pushed its snout under the soil to fabricate the new town, scumming everything from elements and spirits somewhere below. Poor hose, finished with its masterpiece, hung down from the flank of the ship, spent and wrinkled. Not at all to his surprise, what he was thinking about and afraid of, all during the vast inflations, now came true. The silver kidney, which had drawn us away like bile from our homes, looked horrible. The portholes, out which we had stared like sullen children during those weeks of travel, were squinted shut, and the whole middle of the craft sagged like an ancient couch cushion.

"Death, death, death," Knox said to himself, and was weighed down by the words, by the parallel. Exile could be as permanent as.

But did it mean they meant to keep us here? No, no, there had to be other ships like it back on Earth. Another ship would be sent out to bring us home at the end of our sentences. Of course!

So, dear Knox turned on his heels and walked, full of questions, toward the dome, no urgency in his stride, ambling and slouching, rocking his hips. If he had been breathing the bad atmosphere all afternoon, he reasoned, he could breathe it a few minutes longer. So he interlaced his fingers behind his back, slowed more, and mentally strung out a letter to Dr. Mhurra, to the wife, speaking it out loud as he went, though he knew no word could ever reach her along any normal or comfortable avenues.

What is uncomfortable for us? Unexplained avenues.

We were both crushed and comfortable with the fact, found in the in-space magazine, that no correspondence with home would be possible during our stay, because that broke the laws of physics. Knox composed then, supernaturally, and it helped so much to imagine a tendril thin as gold, microns, stretching from brain to brain, his and hers tied in secret knots, careful how you move so as not to break the thread. It wasn't the first time he imagined it, and had mentioned it to Mhurra before he left.

No, she hadn't wanted a tendril. The unphysicality of it meant it was a dead idea to her, and in fact she grew increasingly taller, shaking her hands near her cheeks when she spoke of it. There it was, as far as Knox was concerned, not just knotted to some hook of his brain, but tied deeper inside than that, even knitting the brain together, lobe to lobe. Still, he wasn't sure of any of this, and wondered if, like a snake charmer's rope, his ephemeral string would only go up part way, to where, if you climbed it, you would disappear, rays lingering in the emptiness you'd occupied.

The religion of letter writing came easily. He continued to compose, and speaking aloud as he walked, made it verbal and more memorable, saying, "Dear Mhurra, you are so far away it feels like you're on another planet. Just as legs go bifurcate more after a long walk, souls split apart after a long space voyage, and I feel cut in two, living on two penal planets. Climbing the tendril and maybe worming their way to you, are fragments that aren't all numb, or split, not yet."

"All right?" asked Knox, continuing the letter. "No, not all right. Yours truly on the Brass Planet.

p.s., called that for its color, but close enough to yellow that it feels like brass, though fake brass. If you were here you'd see a red tinge, drops of horse blood I guess, or, if you like, clumps of paprika. Dirt to sprinkle on food. You, because of biology, would call it Dead Planet, or New Thanatos? So please don't come! Come here but please don't come. Two adds up to worse than one, just as three hundred (three hundred of us) is also worse than one. Help me out. Another thing is coral reefs. Those polyps that only open when under water, at certain high temperatures, makes me think of space polyps. We only open on dead planets. A stronger spark of life than all others."

It is true in exile, as it is true anywhere, that, when dividing labor, some will view the more mentally challenging jobs as more desirable, while others will hate the idea, and rush to take on physically grueling tasks that the more thoughtful shun. We were anxious to get to work, but none were anxious to work at tasks that contradicted our nature. This sounds like logic, but sometimes logic is our strongest emotion, and rational views are taken up angrily.

The minute we bent down and squeezed through the incongruously narrow door of our dome, our igloo, and before we had a chance to look around or learn where we were to stay, we were herded, like a holiday crowd, down avenue after avenue, each bathed in natural light, infused with a mood-changing, wax-candle smell. In the end they assembled us in rows in a plaza fit for a capital city.

Time to learn about your jobs.

Hooray for jobs.

It's difficult to remember everything that was said exactly, but those were the sentiments.

From the inside, the great round arching dome above us more or less disappeared, and became, to all appearances, the sky, though a milky one. Underneath it was our town, a jumble of angles and curves, high rises and low rises, a dazzling construction of multi-formed buildings, all exactly the same material as the dome, everything tinted in the same neutral pale frostiness, a white bakelite translucency. There was something Art Deco about the whole town, with its parallel lines and flowing curves, that invited touching, but when we reached out to touch a surface it felt warm and pliant, as if not yet quite set.

"Please take care not to cause any damage," said Krell, as if he had been promoted to trustee. But several ignored him, and, like kids with wet cement, started trying to write their names in the pavement. The material, however, was self-correcting. Any line drawn in it would persist for a second, and then heal.

"Exactly like us," observed Krell.

"Please don't cause any mental damage." This was Knox speaking to Krell, and for a moment their eyes locked, while one smiled and the other did not, then vice versa. One exuded a relatively warm irony. Some sense of the tragic. A tendency to rub his hands over his face to keep a clear picture in his mind of what he looked like. The other did not.

———————

Chemo stood again before us and, twisting his tie, began doling out the aforesaid and unexpected jobs.

Some of us were assigned to the fabrication rooms, there to direct the production of food chunks, as well as synthesis of drinking water, likewise derived from the raw materials of the planet.

Others were given less menial positions, and though there was no logic to any of the designations that we could see, it seemed in the end that everyone was satisfied, given the circumstances. A sociology professor was assigned the job of regularly placing her ear to the ground to listen for subterranean shiftings. Some former admissions directors got more lofty posts (e.g., maxim collator, nutritionist). Knox, who'd once been a voice coach, more recently an assistant dean—and what could he expect after such inversions?—was startled to learn that he had been appointed to the position of dome dancing master.

This confused everything. Knox, out of synch, one or two seconds behind in his reactions to everything, knew only that he had never taught dance. Then, one or two seconds forward, he danced something impromptu on the spot, expertly, though not noticeably.

One prisoner did happen to notice his steps, as she was standing next to him, idly staring at his legs just at the moment he slightly twitched and scissored them. It was the same gray-haired woman who had fingered his uni earlier, except that now she looked a little older, as if the wait in the heat had aged her, and this time, when she smiled at him, she unveiled a perfect set of teeth that had not been there before. What could it mean? Maybe he had only imagined her as toothless. Either that or she had the ability to extend and withdraw her teeth when desired, like certain snakes, or was it sharks? Again she was fingering his uni, although this time it seemed to be her way to see if he might still be dancing.

"Why do you do that?" he asked.

"Check the fabric. I wondered if jumping—is that what you were doing? I wondered what happens to the fabric while jumping."

"I have another uni," he answered. "Do you want to take it and study it?"

And he pulled the extra one out from where he'd been stashing it, and pushed it hard into her stomach, as if to gift her with it, or injure her.

"Put it on over the one you're wearing!" he barked, laughing at himself, out of the moment again, embarrassed.

"Shut up," she whispered. "They're coming to my name."

And though a few more names and positions were called out, Knox couldn't tell which of the names was hers, and saw no change in her expression during the reading of the list. Later she wandered off to somewhere else, taking his spare uni with her.

———

Several of us were provided with long and super sharp ceramic knives, and sent off immediately to take on the job of substance carvers. Since the manufacturing process was only able to blow and shape and decorate bubbles in varying sizes, and because nothing was allowed to go to waste, the task of these carvers was to slice out rectangular doors and windows everywhere, rapidly creating entrances and ventilation for the bubbled up structures visible all around us. Also, after a few quick strokes of the knife had produced a horizontal window, they would, as per their instructions, cut and assemble the long white slab of removed material into a piece of primitive furniture: a table, a set of shelves, an oversized arm chair, cups and plates, and, in at least a couple of cases, as they became more skillful, a perfect ping-pong table, with a very thin slice of material for the net, and two paddles, and a ball.

Once the slicing was accomplished, going inside the cells to make everything comfortable would be up to the inhabitants. Naturally enough, as the carvers proceeded with their work, the rest of us could hardly wait for a chance to wander around and investigate our freshly dissected cells.

They looked so interesting, so novel and inviting, at least from where we stood, that it was hard to remember that they were prison cells.

No one actually shouted out a hurrah this time, but the overall mood was one of gratitude. Why? Maybe because this was a planet more raw, less lived in, than most? Maybe because we were, if not stupid, at least critically out of our depth.

Dr. Krell was appointed to the position of defense coordinator.
Defense against what, we wanted to know.

Someone asked it out loud, and Chemo stepped forward to explain
that we needed to be ready for conflict with the inhabitants of another
penal colony, exactly on the other side of the planet, which might sound
geographically rather far off, but on such a small planet, it wasn't really all
that far, as our patient trustee explained.

But who were they? This was surprising and terrible news, in a way.

They were prisoners, we were told, who had arrived at the same time
as us, more or less, but were actually people of a much lower order than
ourselves, in that they had been convicted of much worse crimes. In
addition, because they had lived for years in wretched industrial precincts
of Earth, where the atmosphere was barely tolerable, they were immune to
the effects of the poisons in the penal planet's atmosphere, and were known
to roam the landscape, highly religious and psychotic, looking for us,
because yes they knew all about us, as we knew about them, and they were
another reason it was a good idea to stay inside the dome.

"So they're our polar opposites," joked Knox. "Our antipodes."

It seemed odd, though, that the magazine hadn't said anything about
any of this, and we looked at each other sideways, and then looked at
Chemo to see if it was all a joke, but he stared back sweetly, babyishly, and
someone in the crowd sighed deeply, erotically, as if already in love with
either the man or his power, despite his piece of disturbing news.

Other trustees showed up at that point, and it turned out then that
there were only six of them, dressed all alike in unis and ties, one trustee
for every fifty prisoners. They stood, elbows locked together, in a line in
front of us, as if prepared to block us from moving further down the street,
or as if preparing already for the invasion of the Yoohoos, as they called our
brutish neighbors. But no, it was only in preparation for a performance.
The ones we already knew, Chemo and Fermat, had taken their places
among them, and now we could see that half of them were women, as more
or less corresponded to our own gender balance. Surprisingly, they now
began addressing us in unison, and were good at it too, as if they had been
practicing during the long voyage.

"Your attention please!" they began. "Please. Your attention please. A maxim is to follow. Maxim number one. *We are always twenty percent less unhappy than we suppose.*"

Having delivered the message, the trustees unlocked arms, broke rank, shook hands with one another and, having mingled with us in the crowd for a moment, more out of confusion with the layout of the new town than out of good cheer, marched off.

Nor were they often seen after that, and though each had an apartment in the same buildings where we had ours, with walls as presumably translucent as anybody's, they became strangely elusive, and there was even some speculation that some of them had been transferred to the dome on the other side of the planet, due to possible problems there.

And because everything was all so new and dazzling to the senses— meaning our elaborate village, the tremendous and milky dome that arched over the whole, even the sweet fruity smell that seemed to waft up from the soles of our footed unis as they slid along the wax paper slickness of the sidewalks—we lost the ability to think out our situation, our abjection. In retrospect, we were as complicit as any in our own lowering, but that wasn't obvious back then. What we embraced about this luxurious-looking punishment of ours was its implication of renewal, the knowledge that not only were all the old charges to be wiped clean, but even the little charges—the tiny errors in life that the state knew nothing and cared nothing about—were to vanish as well.

Here is a magazine title: "Our Promise is to Partially Erase Your Past in Return for Time Served."

We loved that. Not one person piped up and said they wanted to cling to the felonious part of their past. But was that what they meant by "partial?"

"Attention, your attention please for maxim number two: *Misdeeds are easy to forget, but great moral acts, as well as great funnybone acts, are often alluded to in conversation.*"

It was the chorus of trustees chanting together again, but this time they were out of sight, and it took a moment to realize that their voices were issuing from small round holes in the fabric, sliced earlier by the carvers.

A speaker system, then. We had a built-in maxim broadcasting arrangement ("Oh, hurrah," said someone) and the new maxim suited the situation well. It meant that the good things you did in life lasted.

At least until dinner. Or maybe it meant that goodness and comedy are similar forces. Or that in order to be good you must undertake the goal of memorizing what you have done and will do, not simply acting it and ignoring the act. In all cases, keep yourself a secret, don't mention your crime, don't confess. That way it never happened, and after all we now lived in a world that was crime-free, so let it be free of criminals as well, starting now.

Or starting now.

———

A Place to Call Home, was the title of the magazine on the spaceship. One of us later penciled in, on one copy, *No Matter Where.*

And then Knox, we were sure, was the one who later crossed out the last three letters of the addendum and changed it to *No Matter Who.* That copy of the magazine circulated to every seat on the ship, and in the end helped us feel more structural, more rooted and planted. We started to believe we could grow innocent and trembling leaves in our new home. Spring flowers.

It was a very long trip.

Good for us! We hadn't been shaken off Earth like bad candy, but ejected out clean, like mooncalves, and once true outer space was reached, we were given to know that our course involved falling or dripping down, as they put it, toward the Horsehead Nebula.

"May we call the planet Horsehead?" someone inquired.

"No, that's taken," was the disappointing response.

Never minding the name, it was a world devoid of life except for criminals, and that implied responsibility and innocence and blandness. The dome was a non-judgmental bracket, a parentheses arching over us, a space where it was easy to hate not so much our friendly trustees as—the distant Yoohoos. Empty for us, no matter who.

———

Our weight was less.

Some said that we were much lighter. No, no, that's not it, someone else explained, it's only red blood cell expansion (each one ballooning slightly) that causes a sensation of lightness. It's atmosphere, and air pressure, and has nothing to do with gravity. Some of us were scientists, or had worked in science departments, and so of course the specific gravity got measured to the figure of point nine five. Tiny, but more disorienting than a big difference, which you get and adjust to immediately. So yes, here was a slight bounce to the step, a stroll down the street had optimism to it. Later, Knox tried to take advantage of his lightness, whether real or imaginary, in his dance classes.

Then a new maxim:

Whatever landscape surrounds you is constantly rotating, with you as the axis. Use this fact to locate yourself, use this fact to find home.

———

But you must move away from studying the causes of things, Knox announced one day in class, and go to the next category, namely, the effects. This may take a long time, but listen with a hand over an ear to get the full effect. The secret of happiness will become clear, but only while you are being punished. Therefore, you must write in order to focus the punishing. As you write, picture all the millions and millions of writing animals, us, over as many years. Do what others do, think what they think, but do it with pen in hand, and the pen is the tongue or tail of the soul. Holding a pen in one hand, or one in both hands. Yet on this penal planet there were no pens, no paper either, no obvious antique stores, but that was all right, he could learn, was learning, how to write in his head, using the paper that resulted from ironing out his thoughts, finding coinciding moments. To prove this to himself again, he squinted and hummed and at last constructed another letter to Mhurra, and this time what a nice feat of discipline to see it, as he saw it now, centered and whole in the middle of a whiteness that blossomed, spilled out horizontally like milk, as he pushed away all other distractions:

You were angry, and angry with me for leaving, or not, all for an act (one act of strangulation) that entails leaving. At the spaceport you made vicious signs with your fingers. They spelled, maybe, *don't come back, strangler,* or possibly *stranger.* Or something less, or more. Do you read this letter? Try to picture a dry lake bed, white sand, with writing in the middle. Send your eye here to see it, send your hand (I picture it on an arm stretched out to a spider filament's diameter), to flash more sign language.

―――――

Inscribed and framed in the mind that way, Mhurra became something on another planet to him. She had a fuzzy outline in the dust of distance, and appeared to him long-limbed, ashen, heavily made-up, as if their separation were to be performed on stage. Pity them both, and next, despite the pity, there would be screams and old-fashioned gunshots heard from off-stage.

"You mean you will be lost without me," he suggested one day, not long before departure.

"No, I'm lost now. Maybe I'll be found without you."

"How encouraging."

She nodded her head in silent-movie gestures of agreement, moving her lips without making a sound, eyes going blank as dust clouds. Then she dropped the act and went on to remark that she would first hire, then hang out with, then sexually exalt a violin teacher she'd easily find in the classifieds.

"Oh yes," he said. "I'd like to meet him too. Call him right now, since it would be better for my peace of mind."

"I'm coming too."

"Coming where?"

"To your planet. It's not that hard to do. If it's where they send criminals I'll become one. How hard could it be? Teach me to commit crimes, and we can walk to the launching platform hand in hand."

"There's a fractious side to you."

"Ah, that's the ripping process," she said. "Rip a big heavy book in half. That's how it feels. Your departure. The violin teacher's departure. Any one of a million inner beings comes marching out of me. Or, I should say, out of you slash me slash us."

And in retrospect it was possible she was signing to him at the last minute the news that she had decided to commit the crime and would be showing up on the next transport drop. It was true that there was room in the new city, that three hundred exiles hardly filled it at all, so more might be on the way. And picture another craft landing and Mhurra floating regally down the ramp, making the same enigmatic gestures as when last he caught sight of her fingers.

Write with the pen of the mind and tell her to be sure to make the crime a misdemeanor, or she'll end up on the wrong side of the planet, under the wrong dome. Dome of the apes. His mental penning was getting faster, and now when he made mistakes, he could delete them, as on a computer, and he even forgot to sign his name, he was in such a hurry, but of course she would know immediately who it was, and understand how stupid he was being, and certainly decline the suggestion to commit a crime for the sake of love.

———

That first day under the dome, before we were assigned suites, all we could think of to do was to stretch our legs and walk the newly minted streets, touch our cheeks to the smooth and still warm walls, dash down alleyways, turn corners to discover more plazas, more radish-shaped domes, and triangle-topped towers.

At last the loudspeakers came on again and instructed us to make our way up various flights of stairs in order to claim our new suites. Once there, however, some few murmurs of disappointment were heard.

"I thought the rooms would be larger."

"There really won't be any privacy."

"It's not transparent. It's semitransparent. Not paraffin, but metaffin, they said. Something like that."

"Right, but we'll be able to more or less see each other all the time."

This last complaint was the one most commonly heard, until Krell, ever merry sycophant, stepped forward to point out that it was, after all, a penal colony, and how could one expect, therefore, total privacy?

"Please," came a snotty sounding response, "can't they at least give us a dark closet to sit in once in a while?"

"My friends, my friends," Krell expostulated, already a politician, though one without an ounce of power. "Privacy would work against us! You see why, don't you? What would you do with your privacy? Maybe backslide? Return to crime? This way we can all keep an eye on each other and come running to help if we see something weird, or inappropriate. Isn't that right?"

"Yeah, but what about sex and intercourse?" someone else called out, and everyone within earshot laughed.

One of the exiles, holding her hands behind her head, as if to display a subtle wantonness, said, "Don't worry. If sex is healthy and loving, it deserves an audience."

"That's a good position to take," came the rejoinder, but this time no one laughed, because what she said sounded like a kind of wisdom, and somebody earnestly suggested that, if the maxims ever took a turn toward conjugal advice, it might be a good one to begin with.

Knox, having conquered his disorientation, was in the crowd by then, and felt sure that he recognized the speaker.

"Who *are* you?" he asked, out of breath, when he finally got near enough. She turned to look at him, and he realized that, yes, this was definitely her, full of teeth this time too, and now, as she looked him up and down, he noticed a darkness around the eyes and a crook to one side of the lips that suggested a kind of wonderment, a kind of skepticism. Like his own, he thought.

Then, appearing to lose her teeth again, she said, in a creaky but fake old woman's voice, "I am the oracle of this world."

"Ha ha," he answered, tentatively.

And then, giving him a peevish glance, she turned and squeezed her way into the crowd and was lost in a sea of unis, some celadon, some celery.

All right. He got it now. It was an act. She could stretch and suck in her lips in such a way as to make it look, very convincingly, like she had no teeth, as in a put on, an odd comedy, playing on some cliché or other that on every planet there has to be one witch or ancient crone who utters bits of wisdom and prophecy. What, he wondered then, might she predict for him? For the hell of it?

"Wait!" he shouted, but it was the wrong moment, because just then the crowd of people had gone utterly silent for a second, and his voice rang out in the hallway, and everyone turned to look at him with an arched eyebrow.

"Wait for me!" someone laughed.

But then there was a rustle of movement and surprise in the group.

"Our names, our names," they were insisting, and sure enough, when Knox craned his neck to look, it was apparent that each of the suites in that particular hallway had the names of designated inhabitants carved above the doorway, as if we were donors, or famous dead people. But the handiwork was crude, the letters childish, as if to emphasize the cave-like look of the arched and permanently open entrances.

And coincidentally, the first door Knox looked at had his own name above it, misspelled *Knock*, as if to say knock before entering. Scratched in below, also improperly spelled, was the name of his roommate, *Krill*, but of course he understood that that would be Dr. Krell.

———

One day, because he knew how to hold the pencil of the mind to the paper of the brain, he wrote the following:

Philosophers tell us that love is only true love when it doesn't matter what planet you're stuck on.

What struck him at first was the amount of white space around it, and he was about to try to fill it in, with more words, or art deco doodles or something. But then he realized that he had written a maxim, an untrue and terrible one, but that at least it looked like one, and would do very well as an inscription on a monument way out in the desert, or a note left on a table.

———

The maxims, the official ones, kept on issuing, in chorus, from the little black speaker cavities found all over the city, so that no matter where we went, we were sure to be blessed with, or subjected to, depending on the mood, another little gem, including such acceptable and even encouraging aphorisms as *One should judge a man not by his noble qualities, but by his use thereof,* and such rather disheartening observations as *Philosophy masters us through theory, but only those who act become the master of philosophy.*

There was something familiar to him about these tidbits, but it was impossible to say where they came from. On one occasion Knox, running into Dr. Fermat in the street, asked if he knew the author of the maxims.

"Oh yes," answered the trustee, running his palm over his baldness. "They were written by someone from olden times who inspired millions. You know, to self-improve themselves, I guess. Don't know his name, but I know there's talk of naming the planet after him."

"How's that possible? If you don't know his name, I mean."

"Oh, just that they'd call this the Planet of Maxims, Maximworld, Maximia, something like that."

There was a pause. Fermat smiled, stretched his two elbows backwards, then leaned so far back that his stomach protruded forward. It looked ugly and lumpy there, like a bag of potatoes, but it was a temporary effect.

"Speaking of maxims," Knox let out at last, stepping back an inch.

"Go ahead."

"Would it be possible to submit new maxims? You know, say I write a few, then put them in to be broadcast?"

"So, everybody's a writer now."

"I don't know about that. I think I know how to write maxims. I've got one or two that are more about surviving separation from one's loved ones."

"Well, sorry, but they say we have to stick with the classics. There's hundreds of them to get through, I guess. Maybe in months to come, who knows? But wait, did they assign you a position yet?"

"Yes."

"As what?"

"Dancing master."

Fermat rubbed his chin, frowned, and kept fiddling with his tie, as if he wanted to put it to some kind of use.

"I only ask because in fact we're going to hire someone to read the maxims. You know, we're tired of doing it in unison. Too bad you're already committed. Did you start the dance lessons yet?"

"Not yet."

"In that case, start them tomorrow in the multi-purpose room. I plan to be there, if you don't mind. I mean as a student."

Knox, on his way back to his room, disappointed, trying to reanimate himself, composed another one.

Every maxim is a kind of dance, every dance a maxim.

Next day, Knox was shocked to hear his very own maxim, the first one he composed, coming across the airwaves, not via a chorus of trustees, as in the past, but in a deep and exaggeratedly wise female voice, something like that of a cartoon owl.

Philosophers tell us that love is not love that alters when you find yourself stuck on another planet.

It took him a moment to recognize his own sentence, or something very close to it, and his first thought was that they'd found a way to read his mind. No, that's absurd, he concluded. But not impossible. More likely, the sentence, so close to the one written in his head, must have been a repetition of something he had read or heard long before, something from the works of that same ancient author whose name could not now be recalled. No matter.

The maxim that issued the next day was definitely not familiar:

Anyone who has made serious mistakes, and then honestly wishes to be angelic, should always be addressed as Angel.

Mildly insulted, not only by the owl's pretentious voice but by the fact that the thoughts weren't coinciding with his anymore, Knox took up the writing of maxims again, not worried if they came out of his own head or someone else's, though he made every effort to be original. Such composition, he understood, constituted rebellion, first against himself, second against the trustees. What mattered most was that thought was medicine, that words were steady intravenous drips.

Hatred puts us both above and below them whom we hate.

Not bad, but the *them whom* part sounded awkward. Too many ems.

The more throats you strangle, the weaker your own voice.

A little too personal.

Then he got better at it:

Falsehoods, or fakes, are oxygen for truth.

A penitent is one who finds penance more difficult than it is for others.

Few know the size of their own shoes.

Worse is better than worst, better worse than best.

For Knox, it turned out that an empty geography and an empty spirit are a good match, as memory scars one, and embroiders the other.

Oh, but that too turned out to be a maxim.

Sometimes a sentence would come to his head that he couldn't make much sense of. *He who has a mind to beat a dog will easily find a stick.* What could that mean? Other times the words he wrote brought him to tears, and so he wrote about the tears. *When we learn to cry we become more flexible, like robots that learn how to lubricate their own brains.*

———

Knox wasn't the only one. Everybody started to speak in maxims. Maximese, we called it.

"Every savage can twist," sniffed one student to another, on a day in dance class when everyone was out of sync, and half were waltzing while the other half were extravagantly free-form.

"Please try to move as I showed you to move," Knox hissed to the whole room, not sure who had spoken. "Dance, dance, dance, and do it, if you will, in the recommended way. Even savages have choreography."

There was a general shrug. No movement of feet.

"Remember," he went on, not at all sure that he was qualified to teach the course. "Remember that I'd like you to dance as you'd like yourselves to dance, within the form. I'm not a tyrant, but I do ask for discipline and concentration."

There was mumbling around the room, some confusion. As for those of us enrolled, we didn't understand at first what dear Dr. Knox meant by saying that dance could be more stern and splendid, please, than merely shimmying randomly about. All we wanted was some music and some simple ways to arrange our limbs, in some easy-to-remember sequence. Here, put your right arm in the air like this, and then start shaking it. Like that. And proceed to your left leg, making it kind of crazy. But Knox's expression at the moment was that of the headmaster, of the one in possession of by far the best mind in the room.

"Come on, Professor," somebody yelled out confrontationally, and what could be worse than a classroom full of former professors? "You've got to go about this differently. When are you going to give us a chart of all the steps involved?"

"I do it in my head, and so can you," grumbled the instructor.

"In my case," came another voice, "I *will commit* my class time to the discipline you propose." Of course it was Krell, in the front line of dancers as always, and naturally we smirked a little at his style, his blandishments. Like our buildings, you could watch things going on inside him.

"Good," nodded Knox, since at least it was what he wanted them to think, if not say out loud. "That's the stuff, Krell. Everyone feel the same?"

"Yes," was the wheezy chorus of response, with a falling intonation meaning resignation.

And then we took up the position that Knox was already modeling for us: body sideways, feet pointing in the same direction, arms shot out to the sides like clock hands.

Krell immediately, precisely, followed suit.

"Dance of the Warriors," Knox informed us. "Dance of the Agitators."

We all looked pretty good in our green unis. Agitators if dance students could be called that.

Also present was the prematurely gray woman, her teeth visible all the time now. It had to be that she was showing them off, agitatingly, gasping and laughing as the dance steps clarified for her, taking a toothy joy, like we all did, in barbarity, as long as it was precise.

Often, while trying to shout instructions, a glimpse of her teeth would cause Knox to lose his train of thought, as the gleam of them hit him right in the eye sometimes, like someone signaling with a mirror for rescue, and his response was to move instructively among the dancers, but often to weave his steps past hers.

Fermat, as promised, was there, arriving late as always, wearing only his uni, sans tie. We guessed he'd discarded his badge of trusteeship to get some freedom in breathing and movement, and really he was the best among us, moving articulately, and, as always, we watched him more carefully than we watched Knox. Thanks to Fermat's example, Knox got the discipline he wanted, and all at once we'd move with a burst of agility, and fancy ourselves ready for our prison spotlight.

And, from the beginning we had an audience, and this also was a motivation to do a decent, nervous, even semi-excellent job. We were not on any kind of stage but, as mentioned, the walls of the city were nearly transparent, not opaque anyway, so that anyone passing by the multi-purpose room could at least see the blurry outlines of our bodies. Residents would linger outside to watch, and even sit on nearby benches for a while, while the rest of us, inside, aware of their gaze, would definitely put more into it, get down on the floor (if such were the dance master's instructions) and whirl and crawl (slowly, slowly, like a lizard, he'd insist), even turning our heads (unprofessional, he'd hiss), to check if people were still out there, still watching and maybe approving. Maybe singling out.

"All eyes on me!" Knox would cry out at such moments, and then satirize how our chins bobbed, using spastic exaggerations of his own chin. So we'd settle down, and he'd end up moving more coolly among us as we repeated a particular sequence, sometimes even grabbing an arm or a foot or a chin to force it into its proper alignment. At such moments, despite the pleasure of giving instruction, Knox felt a pressure, as if an entire planet were pressed up against his neck, shot-put style. Laying his hands on people, straightening them, molding them just so, made him feel queasy inside at times, other times glorified. Probably it was the nausea and recognition of something holy in the human body that can result from competing brain cells.

But the image that never left his mind's eye was that of the *Antibody* collapsing. Instead of one year, as promised, he considered as he taught, as he adjusted us, we faced extended uselessness. It wasn't possible to shake the premonition that there would be no end to dancing, to moving our muscles and bones around this room, merely finding out that there is a limitless variety of human postures. And he knew that we knew this about him, because of course we all felt it deep inside, though maybe not to the same agitated degree.

In the meantime, we were dancing! Every savage should be dancing, a maxim might have said, but didn't. They were precious moments when exiles joined the in crowd. From the outside our movements must have had the character of a failed skirmish, but inside we had a sense of sacred clockwork, as if our feet were guided by stars, and communicated something across light waves, light years. We had no audience besides our neighbors, so why not turn it, for both their benefit and ours, into a ghostly egotism, a synchronized shadow-puppet show that might well blast forward on Earth's vid screens in years to come. That was all there was for the moment—to go a little animal in the time left to us before falling prey to less flattering forms of madness. In years to come we might be dancing, but unrecognizable as such.

———

One time, before the day's lesson began, Fermat took over at the head of the classroom for a moment to inform us that we were required that day to step outside the dome and head out to the ship again, for a demonstration guaranteed to impress.

"But what about the poison atmosphere with its toxic fumes?" the students whined. Some others mentioned the threat of those others, those Yoohoos, wandering the planet and planning antique atrocities. Someone even brought up the rumor that a body, maybe one of ours, had been found out in the desert, preserved in a giant beaker, so that the victim would stay recognizable, floating in solution, for centuries.

"Okay," said Fermat, "Maybe there's some truth to that. I hear the same rumors you do, but I don't have any more facts. Anyway, what counts is that our defense minister has determined that no Yoohoos have been spotted anywhere near our dome. Don't correct me if I'm right, Dr. Krell."

Krell stepped forward then, and made a tiny bow.

"And as to that poison atmosphere thing?" continued Fermat. "Here's the solution to that."

Grinning, salesman style, he whipped out an object, an elegant white tube that looked much like a voice wand, but shorter and more slender. He stuck this instrument in his mouth and proceeded to slowly inhale through it, then exhale, even introducing a jazzy hand movement into his demonstration, like a conjuror. Then, with a number of lively and expert leaps in place, wiggling his toes as he rose, he demonstrated that it was an easy-to-use gadget, even when engaged in strenuous activity. The tube, kept squarely in his pursed lips, began to make a nasty wheezy sound, but he arched his eyebrows to show that all was fine, that he was getting all the breathability he needed.

Plucking the thing out of his mouth then, and passing it among the students, he was inspired to do a few more dance moves, bending his knees and elbows, just to show off his relaxed and fluid artlessness.

"You see?" he announced winningly, a slight man in a celery uni that bunched awkwardly at the ankles. The truth was, Fermat had a meager and curved-forward musculature, much like a circus star, or a robot, that made it hard not to place in him some degree of trust.

"See what?" asked a young prisoner, a skinny girl really, very young to have been in academia.

"See, the device you're holding," smiled Fermat, "it's called—can't you guess?—the breath wand. Listen carefully. It's a new development, and it works for everybody. Everybody's lungs, I mean. We'll all get one on the way outside, trustees included, so calm yourselves, there's no favorites."

"Frankly," put in Knox, stepping up to stand side by side with Fermat, taking advantage of his teaching position to establish a rough equality between them. "Frankly, I don't have much confidence in it. What if someone loses theirs while we're out in all that toxicity? Or drops it, and it breaks?"

But Fermat at that point seemed to have exhausted his topic, and a faintly glib embarrassment settled over his face and hovered there.

"Oh, you know," he shrugged, no longer exuding any trace of charisma, only a kind of self-amused defeat. "Just, you know, be careful with them."

"Anyway, now that we've got these," Knox observed, with no show of emotion, "it seems we should be free to travel around the planet as we like."

Fermat hunched his shoulders a little, screwed up his lips, but then his expression cleared, and he made as if to put his hands in his pockets, forgetting, as we all always did, where they were on the unis, and then locating them, settling in.

"I'm sorry," he said. "But the answer is no, and I agree, it does seem a shame. But they told me these units are only good for a few hours. Travel around the planet?—think about it. You'd need dozens of the things? And I'm afraid there aren't that many. Sure, you could set out walking away from the dome, but after a while you'd have to turn around and come right back. So there would be no point."

We went silent. The topic was awkward. There was an unpleasant expression on every dancer's face. The atmosphere was inimical to learning. Knox must have felt this, because, after retreating to a corner for a while, he stepped out, abruptly raised his arms above his head, and in this way ended class early.

And we poured outside into the street just in time to hear a new maxim:

Don't forget to remember that remembering is one way of forgetting.

Later, Knox and Fermat and all the rest of us advanced outside the dome, out into the pale yellows and red, and there we were instantly reminded of the suns, or at least the one out in front for that portion of the year, which, when its effects on that first day were painfully recalled, someone christened Blister Star, and the name stuck. Meanwhile we had all been given one of the new breath wands, and we inhaled on them the way deep-sea divers once inhaled through rubber hoses. One flaw was that the steel exteriors heated up so much in the sun that our lips were nearly burned. Still, more worried about the poisons than the heat, we sucked and sucked, putting up with the scalding surface in order to enjoy a degree of insouciance. Gazing out over the flatness of the plain, the distant line of hills now seemed closer, more crumbled and sharp, like masses of broken brown egg shells. Now, maybe to all our minds, the interstices among those hills looked like interesting destinations for runaways.

"If we just had enough of these things to last us on the way up there," someone was heard to mutter, though it was hard to understand people when they had breath wands in their mouths.

"What do you mean?" someone answered.

"I mean the air on those peaks might be breathable. We might not need any breath help once we got to a higher altitude."

Or then again, we might. But an interesting fantasy took hold of a few. It could be worth the risk, because the height would give a chance to look back and regard the world from the top of a beetling cliff, make out and point to our milky bubble home in the distance, subjects of the cover art of a science fiction paperback. At the edge of such precipices, such separate planes, one could wave to confined comrades as if to say, look at me, the one who is set apart from you, who is with you but not of you. As one maxim goes, *No man is a planet,* but right now I am the only soul on the cliff. Then let me launch myself from the edge, and discover whether the lighter gravity will provide a tender landing at the bottom, soft as the landing of a billiard ball in the palm of the hand, or a scrap of paper floating to the floor.

Or not. Such were some fugitive delusions.

Meanwhile Chemo had climbed back to his old position on the ship's ramp, and there he posed for us, achieving something new for him by sweeping his breath wand out of his mouth at intervals and pointing it at us casually, movie-star-style, as he spoke.

"Dear chums," he began, "we are gathered here today for a christening."

"Chummo!" someone shouted.

"Hold on," barked the trustee, then remembered to get his wand back in his mouth, then took it out, stared at it, and laughed.

"Hold on," he repeated. "Hold on. Like I say, it's a christening. And I hereby christen this planet... that is... the name of this Planet, may all men know by these presents, and so forth, the name of the place is to be Mars. Is Mars."

"What?" someone cried out.

Knox.

"You know...Mars. As in, I hereby christen it The Planet Mars."

No one spoke, not even Knox, except for one or two calls from the back of the crowd to repeat the statement.

But Chemo, seeming to want to repeat it, had a sneezing fit, which lasted a long minute, entertaining to watch. On the first sneeze his breath wand went flying, and someone—not Knox—picked it up and put it in his own mouth, along with his own, then turned to the crowd to mug, and flex his biceps, pretending that the two white sticks in his mouth gave him great strength. So we laughed through our wands and waited.

Then Chemo said the same thing again, named the planet again, and again no one spoke, and this time really no one, as we were all silenced by the peculiarity of it all.

Mars was a famous planet, as planets go, of course, but it was uncomfortable to have a second one. Mars Two, or New Mars, those might have made more sense, but the general feeling was, let them call it what they like. Not our home. Our own names didn't feel like our own names anymore, so let someone else have them.

There was a slight dip in the temperature, a tiny relief. It felt like a cloud had come along, but no, the sky was a monotonous, spray-paint blue, as before, as forever. Then the heat came back, like gas from the planet's intestine, hot as before, as forever. Chemo tightened the zipper of his uni, wrestled the knot of his tie up. Again, we all wished for uni hats and uni gloves. Or that they would pass out painkiller wands as well.

"Mars it is," he droned on. "Beloved *Mars*...because it's not unlike the first Mars...in redness."

Yellowness, really. Maybe some strokes of orange. Flecks of red.

"And someday...visitors will choose to come here to reminisce on the long ago days of old Mars...and be brought to tears by the rusty tonalities of the soil...the wide rocky plains...the craters...even the icy poles, because, yes, though you people haven't seen much of this world, it does have those exact features."

Finally the crowd murmured disapprovingly, hummed really, because while none of us wanted to stop breathing through our wands, no one was in the mood for speeches. However, the mention of icy poles, it had to be admitted, was a welcome reference, but only because of the heat, and it was true that day that merely the mention of ice instantly calmed any exposed skin.

"The only thing it really lacks...to become a satisfying replica of old Mars, is...can you guess?"

"Martians?" someone said, and of course that provoked prolonged laughter—though, due to the wands, it came across more like a choking sound, as if laughter were a kind of strangulation.

"Well, yes, Martians, that's true," admitted Chemo, all smiles himself, waving his wand around his head cavalierly, immediately putting it back in his mouth, then snatching it out again to ask, seriously, squintingly, "But where on earth would we get Martians?"

"Here we are, Dr. Chemo," said Knox, in his best wise-guy style, because he had figured out that he could let the wand dangle from a far corner of his mouth and still more or less breathe through it while speaking. "That is, if you want to call us Martians."

"The only thing lacking," answered Chemo, shooting Knox a dirty look, but quickly imitating his corner-of-the-mouth technique, "is, as I was about to say... listen to this now... are you sitting down?... No of course you're not. Anyway, what I say we need is... a... network... of... beautiful... canals."

There was more laughter, insulting in tone this time, but Chemo didn't seem to hear it. Then there was silence.

Naturally, everyone knew that faraway Mars, however much people might get nostalgic about it, had no canals. But it's true that it once was thought to have them, or willed to have them—by poets or early visitors. All this before it became just another Earth, another catastrophe, with its crust of chocolate-dark city mostly smothering its supposedly red surface, and canals if there ever had been any.

"But, Dr. Chemo, are we supposed to do the digging?" asked Krell, obviously bewildered by the drift of the whole ceremony.

"You?" echoed Chemo, rising on tiptoe, wiggling his hands at his sides like they were wet and he was trying to dry them. "You want to know how to dig them? Here's how." And he nodded his head meaningfully toward the ship, as if signaling toward somebody inside.

Then there was more waiting. He waved one arm up and down madly.

"Here's how!" he sputtered, nearly a madman now.

And then things began to transpire. A process began. Better, better, better, was possibly the general mood among us.

First there came a profound buzzing from below our feet, as if the core of the planet was hollow and filled with grinding gears or breaking wine glasses, or gargantuan wasps. Then our ship, poor *Antibody,* lurched into a similar buzz, and the tentacle that still lay buried from the building of the city began to repeat those same kinds of erotic agitations. Perhaps this time the tentacle did not move quite as intensely as before, but did appear to go deeper, like a robot worm, a constructive genius probing and complaining but succeeding at its task far under the planetary surface.

Then all eyes turned then toward the dome, all of us imagining, naturally, that our town was now going to grow in size somehow, or divide like a cell and end up as two identical towns, or burst into pieces, or be sucked back down underground. But nothing of the kind occurred.

"No no, you big dopes!" screeched Chemo, always the sulky martinet when given the occasion. "Don't look there, look over here!"

So all eyes turned to where our giddy little man was gesturing, to a spot not far off across the plain, where already there was something going on, not a whirlwind of dust, but a turbulence or bubbling right at the surface, and by reflex we huddled together closer and reached out hands to neighbors' elbows for greater steadiness, and though this time it was tempting to suppose that a new something was about to rise there (though what it could be was hard to imagine), instead there was more of a sad surfactant effect, a *drooping* taking place. Concavely.

There came a rushing sound then, as of a million toilets flushing, a million bathtubs draining at once, and some later swore that they heard orchestral music in the air as well, as if in a film score or a dream. Meanwhile the snaky tentacle coming out of the ship, the root of it, was writhing as if in anger, shaking *Antibody* like a tail wagging a dog. Apparently this time the purpose of the snake was to reach down again to the bones of the planet but, instead of exhaling, it inhaled. Instead of constructing, it undercut, and we could see now how its purpose was to collapse and subtract.

Worse is better than worst, was the only maxim Knox could bring to mind, and his indigestion, or nausea, or anguish, whatever it was, got worse, or worst, or in other words came creeping back, painful as bonecrack flu, and he remembered times on Earth when, because he was feeling exactly this same way, Mhurra would turn her heels on him and shut herself in her room, claiming that she couldn't *abide* a sick man. But would he please be sure, the day that he got well, to knock gently and persistently on her door and give the shibboleth?

Which was *Abide with me.*

But the little earthquakes underfoot brought him back to the moment, and he thought it might help things if he were to express himself out loud.

"All planets are born mad," Knox announced, given to bouts of despair once in a while, a fake Diogenes when wanting to impress.

"And some remain so," grumbled the woman with the shock of gray hair, standing next to him, something he'd been aware for a minute or so. All the while she kept a mercurial and almost imperceptible grip on his elbow, but didn't seem to mind when he gripped hers more substantially, and that together they achieved a triangular stability.

But the rumbling was a terrible roar by now, drowning out all else. The feathery pressure on his elbow disappeared, the crowd shifted nervously, and when his hand went out again to grab an elbow, it belonged to somebody else.

Thus stabilized again, looking out over the head of his fellow convict, focusing on the featureless plain, Knox grasped that there were now about to be features. He'd regarded the old blankness with a blank stare, and now felt a nostalgia for it, but understood that if its prior condition were to be altered, in fact it was prior conditions in general that he felt instant admiration for.

So is it always with exile. Now that the trustees, or whoever was the boss of the trustees, was calling the place Mars, and altering what it had been, re-engineering, re-signifying, he understood that up to that moment it had been his, ours, a landscape that he could inscribe however he wanted, with any emotion or narrative he chose. But best to examine and comprehend it quickly, he thought, for it is about (like Earth, like Earth!) to become unrecognizable.

What would maybe best anesthetize the hypercharged criminal mind? Nullity, he supposed. But the authorities might have suspected that being zeroed out might engage and enchant such minds, or at least the minds of the worst of the worst among us, and now, they concluded, nothingness must be filled with somethingness. The whole planet must go from blank to embroidered. Knox's insubordination, vaguely conceived in the last minutes before planet zero became planet Mars, was one of silence and surrender. Nullity of mind, like an empty journal, a lake of spilled milk, a featureless world, demanded ornament. Dendrites of resistance also formed canals. So here was a new maxim for them, if they dared broadcast it.

If the heretic can embody a world, a world can embody the heretic.

"Step closer!" bellowed Chemo. "There's absolutely no danger to you or to me. Step up and take a look at our super remodeling job."

Moments later, the roiling whirlpool of dirt shut down, and noises ceased. The music, if there had been music, turned into soft static. There was a tongue-biting silence, punctuated by faint ahems. Several individuals fainted simultaneously, affected by heat and noise, or by the bombast of it all. Then, casually, like something left in the sun, we could feel, under our feet, how the planet seemed to slightly shrink. Then it cracked, and then it crackled. Everywhere on the surface thin fissures moved out slowly, but amok, in three or four directions. It felt in a way like we all were going to die, that the cracks were horizontal lightning bolts that would strike us dead. In fact one of them came straight at the ship, at us, but veered at the last second. Another one shot toward the dome, but instantly veered again.

"Wait a sec, wait a sec," murmured Chemo, in the searching tones of a connoisseur, an expert on craquelure, but wearing as he spoke an expression, like the rest of us, of jumpy, itchy terror.

"We are safe! We are safe!" came the optimistic chant.

But it was over, and fear turned to jadedness. Your cracks are very nice, someone yelled, but we wouldn't call them canals. Thank you for the demonstration. Some turned away, their heads down, starting to worry about the one-hour limit of the wands, and glancing up frequently at Chemo to see if he wouldn't bow or bless us or give some other signal to head back inside our now extra-appealing dome.

But the project was not finished. There came a few more earthquakes then, small ones, nothing to worry about, tremors only strong enough to shake the dust off our unis. And then we could see how the cracks were turning into ruts, which then turned into ditches, which turned into sloughs, which turned into channels, and those channels straightened and dropped and squared until they had become stupendous excavations, ten meters across, ten meters deep, sides and bottoms lined with an opalescent material that closely resembled, in its alabaster smoothness, the miracle fabric of the dome and city. And there we were, standing on the very edge, peering down into this immediately astonishing and anguishing earthwork, only to watch while one of us, an idiot, a criminal, jumped in, apparently believing that the lower gravity of Mars would prevent serious injury.

"There ought to be ladders," hissed Knox, but Chemo triumphantly pointed out that, not far away, there were steps already emerging and forming in the near wall of the canal, and he instructed several to descend and take care of the one who had jumped, fortunately not hurt very badly, due to the malleability of the as yet unhardened material.

"So what do you think of your new home now?" laughed Chemo, and everyone spoke at once because everyone had an opinion. Some called it a triumph of planet art. Krell said that the canals constituted, as a whole, a graceful inscription on the plain, perhaps a web embracing the whole orb, and how sublime it would be, this enthusiast pointed out, to be high above the surface at that moment, and see this abstract art, this delicate intaglio written across the great topaz curves of the previously drab planet.

But what was the point? Why replicate another planet, was someone else's question. Why replicate the *fiction* of another planet? Oh, but the canals will be filled with water or another fluid some day, said another, and then we shall all go in for some health-giving swimming, comrades, and even, can you believe it, water skiing, as long as we find a way to detox the atmosphere. Oh no, others claimed, the canals will remain pristine and dry, and presumably be put into use as a highway system. Each of us will get a high-powered automobile, air tight, to aim down these precisely straight and slick new thoroughfares, and a fellow could drive right around the circumference of the extra small planet, and be back at the dome within an hour.

Knox hung back, determined not to join in the speculation, as again he was more concerned about the ship than the spectacle. As everyone else crowded along the edge of the canal, he turned back to examine the once detested but now cherished *Antibody*. It had been used to build the city, and had seemed to recover from that, but now, having formed the canals, it looked wretched, like a kidney that has been pushed to the brink of failure by disease. A trickle of thick liquid the color of half-and-half slowly ran down the empty ramp and then evaporated in the heat, like water spilled on a skillet, leaving a white tongue of stain behind.

So our ticket home was torn up, and it did not then, and would not ever, come shuddering back to life. That much was clear, and naturally it was hard to avoid the conclusion, staggering as it was, that the thing had never been intended for a round-trip at all. Here it lay where it lay, and for now, even though the remainder of the one-year sentence still stretched far ahead, the vehicle had at least served as a reminder of eventual return, and now Knox's feet began to grow, to stretch the fabric of his uni, to turn heavy as liquid, as if loss caused swelling, or made his feet step forward in time, ahead of the rest, to the swollen condition of old age. The fear was that the fabric would have to be sliced open to let the flesh out, and he sat down heavily in the dirt to reach and try kneading them back down to size.

But feet wouldn't be necessary in the new situation. It was the presence of the ship, the landing platform that led home, the idea of home, that resulted in dance, teaching others to dance.

And a few of us, our backs to Knox where we stood at the edge of the near canal, executed, for his benefit, a few moves we'd learned from him that very day.

———

Normally Knox avoided contact with his roommate Krell. No need to speak more than a few words since moving in together. Krell had his way of injecting his thoughts everywhere they did not feel lacking. and that was most of all at home, his body occupying room after room, rooms Knox thought he ought to have had to himself, given how many buildings around town sat empty. But after the sapping of strength of the *Antibody* it occurred to him that maybe buried there in Krell was the most rational outlook of all. You could see laser beams of light streaming from his eyes spelling surrender, spelling celebrate. Or celery, or celadon. Krell always emphasized the hopeful side of things, the textured side, and in a room he had a surface effect that, like a new coat of bright paint, enlivened the talk, set the walls at new angles. Or so he seemed to think.

Two cellmates among dozens of pairs, then, sat at their dining table, licking and chewing on dinner chunks in silence, as was often the case, and Knox found himself staring at Krell without thinking, just admiring the full head of hair, most of it pulled back into a ragged ponytail. His red cheeks hung down, overlapping, like melted wax or candies.

"Your hair is so long," Knox commented.

It was a bent and silly way to start a conversation, but too late to take it back.

"Oh that," shrugged Krell. "My Earth wife liked it that way."

"Hmm. What's an Earth wife? I don't know what that is."

"My wife on Earth, silly. Did you think I meant a wife made out of dirt?"

Knox laughed at that. Krell could be funny. For a moment he wished for a dirt wife.

"No, no, I mean, I'm sorry, but maybe she passed away?"

Then, seeing the look on Krell's face, "Or maybe not."

"Certainly not."

Krell was testy now. This was better. Knox had begun by wanting to explore hair, or idealism, and now this.

"I only mean I hadn't heard the term before."

"I call her my Earth wife because she's on Earth, not here, where I hope to one day have a Martian wife."

Knox laughed again, picturing a green woman, with antennae. But then considered how Krell was already acculturated, already calling it Mars. This is a third planet, Knox wanted to say. This is the planet that is neither one.

"You published articles about space travel," he said instead, at that point remembering something he'd read by Krell some years before. "So maybe you have some idea whether a new spaceship could be built here, or whether it's more realistic to wait for a second craft to arrive."

"Does any of that make sense?" answered Krell through a mouthful of chunk.

"Assume another ship will come along. One that can take us back home. Picture yourself climbing the landing ramp."

Krell relaxed in his chair, sliding down almost to the point of collapsing to the floor. "Already thinking about home, I see. You must be one of those who keep imagining that they're not guilty."

"No. I accept my sentence. I want to serve it, and then I want to go home. Right now, if you look with your eyes, and not your idealism, the *Antibody* has died."

So Krell admitted then that though he was only a journalist he did know something about engineering, and explained in some detail the state of spaceship technology back on Earth, how the engines functioned, how there were fleets and fleets like so many raindrops dripping through the galaxy at any given moment, and how stupid to worry, because the trustees already said something about more convicts coming in the not-too-distant future.

"No, no," said Knox. "He said visitors, not convicts. Maybe by that he means tourists. That could be why there's so many empty rooms here, you know—that they're anticipating a lot of paying guests here."

"Tourists who've committed crimes?"

"No, no, you don't understand."

And so on. Start over. But it didn't work out. Night came and went. Knox felt worse in a way, more sugary and demoralized, and went off to his narrow bedroom cell to lie on his platform and dedicate the middle part of the morning, as usual, to—now he knew what to call her—his Earth wife, dirt wife. All flesh is grass, after all, and all humans made of Earth.

———

Mhurra appeared to him then, in his asleep and awake state, in the form of a fountain. He had gotten good at calling her up. In the dream, a hose had been left on, and as it sprinkled flowers, the water, rising vertically, took on the female form, which soon resolved into a nude ghost of her, a paraffin replica, with her long stomach, stretched out belly button, and short knobby knees. He found that if he pushed his hand into the fountain near the bottom, it disrupted the whole form, but if he removed his hand, she gathered back, resolving from horizontal to vertical, and if he lightly touched the water at that point where her bottom rib curved away from him like a quarter moon, the form remained shimmering, persistent, complete.

But the vision turned sour, because then he became aware that there was a knob that one twisted to turn off the fountain, and someone else was moving slowly toward it with an outstretched hand. But then that changed too, because the hand quickly turned the knob the other way, and while the fountain doubled in size, the shape of the woman disappeared from view.

———

But surprise, he snapped out of that vision, and, not surprising, his eyes were full of tears. Twin tiny fountains. He felt strongly the convenience of visualizing her and weeping over her with the same organs. Quickly enough he dried the tears, knowing that in theory he could be observed at any time, and it wasn't that he felt the eyes of authority on him, but the eyes of his peers, of Krell in particular, as there was still something slightly belittling, in the end, about an exhibition of self-pity. Wasn't there?

So jumping up, barking a severe command of self-esteem to himself, looking left and right, up and down, yes, unquestionably, he could see, and truly allowed himself to see for the first time, the outlines of fellow prisoners moving about in their cells, in the same way that they, if they wanted to, could see him. Were any of them sobbing? Hard to say. Stuffing themselves? Yes, it appeared they were, as he could make out the movements of hands toward mouths. Were any of them drifting into the arms of a newfound sexual partner? A Mars wife or a Mars husband undressing in silhouette, as in a peep show? Impossibly possible. Not all the movements he saw could be interpreted, and for the most part it was difficult to sort out individuals in the mess of dark forms he saw hovering everywhere, like a host of spirits, the sight of which was subtly comforting to him. How could he ever forget that here they must live like infant bees in their little hexagons, and what a thrill it gave him for a moment, this sense of unity and confinement and colony. Better, perhaps, to take up the pen of the mind again, and use it to express this odd acceptance. But words wouldn't come, and all he could bring to mind was the face and hair of the woman who kept showing up next to him, who was maybe watching him from not too far away at that moment, like a boy poised over his see-through ant farm. Maybe she was focusing on him, watching him fail to write, watching him fail to make progress, and not at all forgiving him these failures, because to forgive is inhuman. He thought he remembered such a saying from his childhood. But what about this one: *Everything that is forgiven is a deferral of things that are harder to forgive.* Write that down, put that in storage for his future career, if he could just get the job he coveted: keeper of the maxims. If it brings tears to his eyes, it will bring tears to theirs.

He went further into language, and composed something that was neither maxim nor letter, but actually some lies that came to mind about the two suns, about how Blister Sun has hands, but can't reach them through the barrier of the dome, so *it's cool inside.* But listen how the other sun, the so-far unseen one, can be heard overhead cracking and tinkling, as if clearing its throat before its grand appearance.

But that was it. Despite a desire to keep writing, creating a whole book perhaps, Knox lay down again, fell asleep completely this time, and again, despite himself, dreamed of his wife. Earth wife! Not much of a dream this time. First she was seen pointing to a hole in their house that a careless workman had made. Then, there she was walking toward him to wake him from a nap. And, in the delicacy and lightness of this dream state, he woke up, felt sure that he really did hear footsteps, and opened his eyes a crack to view her coming toward him. Oh my dear. For one second of time between sleeping and waking, of stupefaction, he was convinced that in his room, on this planet of the expelled, she had magically arrived, and was walking straight toward his bed, carrying a little suitcase in both hands, ready to spend the rest of her life with him, no matter where.

But then it wasn't her. As a matter of fact it was Krell, holding a ping-pong paddle in both hands, positioning it in front of his mouth like a mask. But he backed away swiftly when he saw Knox fluttering his eyes open.

"Sorry," he said. "I came in the wrong room."

Knox turned away, feigning agitation, then feigning sleep. A moment later, turning back to stare through the wall, he could see the outline of

Krell sitting on his bed a few meters away. And so, though knowing that Krell could equally see him, he let out a scratchy sob, and then the tears came out like pus, and his body kept moving, revolving there awkwardly, like a bumpy log.

———

Next day this came over the speakers, choppily, as if the reader was a little sick.

We are all of us in the same canoe.

———

Once he'd canceled the dance classes, Knox wasn't sure what he was supposed to do with a body that didn't dance. Sometimes he wrote. One small surprise, after several days of this, was that he'd been allowed to quit his job with impunity, but he still anticipated that Chemo or Fermat might climb the stairs to his rooms at some point to stress the idea of returning to work. But trustees, he had come to realize, didn't stress ideas. Their procedure seemed to consist more in abstract inspiration. They broadcast maxims, celebrated education, wore skinny ties, speechified. There was nothing harsh, nothing in any of it at all—just room for absorption that curved you around to the elaborate and diamond-shaped facts of the guilty self.

So what else, then, in the meantime? There was always the possibility of ping-pong, and Krell was an enthusiast, nearly at the professional level by his own account, always persuading his roommate to play. But better, thought Knox in the end, to get out, to try exploring and seeing. Better to learn the details of the town.

So he began by walking the streets like an itinerant, a prisonless prisoner, not sure why he went where he did. He began by peering around corners, climbing dead-end stairways, crossing slender bridges, sleeping on a bench in the plaza, all the time wondering why the rest of us showed so little interest in that kind of thing, leaving the streets largely empty except for him and maybe one or two others. Sometimes he stopped very still in the middle of the boulevard, only to stand with his head lifted, watching us in our cells, wondering how long and hard he could stare without being impolite, and deciding what he would like to see and what he wouldn't like to see. Many details of penal behavior were revealed to him in this way. Prisoners had the habit of sitting around, stretching, eating, sleeping, all of it punctuated by outbursts of push ups, or arm wrestling, or, on one occasion, two roommates getting into a fight and, like silhouette figures on a pulled shade, first slapping at each other, then coming together for a kiss, followed perhaps by sex, if he hadn't moved on to avoid seeing it. Another time he recognized one of the trustees, and watched for hours as she drifted through the motions of her day in the same absent manner as anyone.

After a few days of this, he thought, yes, he could do this for the rest of his sentence, even a life sentence. Maybe they'd give him a new job title: Existence Monitor.

But what could he do with these observations, mildly interesting as they were? There was no like-minded cellmate to confide in, no students to share anecdotes with. Who was left?

Only Mhurra.

"You won't miss me," she had said, unforgivingly, just before departure. "You'll think you do miss me, but you won't, really. Part of you is me, and look, there that part will be, snug and permanent, loitering under your lungs or your pancreas somewhere. How can you sit around and miss what you haven't lost? Let her out, and she'll perform daily miracles for you. She'll talk to you, and believe me, it will be me talking, and you talking back."

But no, she didn't quite know him, at that. She didn't see how without her he would turn rather frail, a moon calf really, pale as moon milk, like he'd been hung upside down and the blood all drained out into the sand, leaving a trace of red among the yellow. And her leftovers inside him? Maybe sometime during the long voyage they had fallen out, in the same way that a wallet falls out of a pocket, or a ring falls off a finger. Or maybe a thimbleful of her was still there somewhere.

So he tried to see with Earthwife eyes. He supposed that, maybe like Blister Star eclipsing its companion, her eyes could eclipse his weaker ones, blink and absorb them, but it was in those moments, seeing as he hoped she would see, that everything went fuzzy and dark.

"You're not inhabiting me at all," he said out loud to her, despite the terrible distance he felt. "I'm not a scientist. I can't see as you see. It's like, and it's not funny this time, it's like you're on another planet."

70

Although there never could be any wind under the dome, Knox thought he felt the slightest tickle of a breeze on the top of his head, as if someone very tall, a woman on stilts maybe, was standing behind and mussing his hair with a couple of lively but gentle fingers.

And at that moment yet another maxim came over the speakers, vaguely relevant.

You can't keep your secret escape tunnel, comrades, by bringing the door to it with you.

But still. Reconstruct. Keep the view another way. Some people have perfect pitch, so train yourself to have perfect vision. Do this on your own.

Whatever Mhurra was, wherever she was, she was first a scientist, and as cautiously poetic, gangly, and analytical, as any proper scientist ought to be. She struck people as imperious but that was only fierce curiosity that made her eyes burn into you that way. She carried herself, slouching, like a madwoman, or a modern dancer, and flinched a little in the face when spoken to. And yet, in the end, she was someone you'd go to a party with and find out later she'd made friends with everyone in the room, while you hadn't met a soul. Mhurra, instead of Dr. Mhurra, was how she'd introduce herself, and how she liked to be called. Sometimes people heard it wrong, and called her Merla, but it was a feature of her curiosity to note the error and never correct it.

She worked for the state as a biologist, more as a researcher, but also occasionally as a teacher. This meant she knew the pitfalls of academia, the distractions of self-satisfied deans, and gave her husband endlessly subversive and even semi-violent suggestions, narrating the details in a deep and dangerous-sounding voice. Once she'd recommended shifting, or as she put it, configuring, the dean's office chair in such a way that he would fall comically to the floor. Later, she instructed Knox to replace the sugar tablets at the coffee station with sleeping pills.

At least it was clear that Mhurra disliked the dean more than he did, and to Knox this was comical and endearing.

"Is that what you do to your supervisor?" he asked.

"Yes, once, but not lately, because we traded places. I'm her supervisor now, and she hates me instead of me hating her."

One time he came home with a long story about how the dean in question had committed yet another blunder—using the master key to take a certain piece of equipment out of Knox's office, giving it to a member of a completely unrelated department, then shrugging when asked for a replacement, as if such things were out of his hands.

"Why don't you choke, but you know, just fake choke him," Mhurra offered, pouring two more drinks, speaking in her dry, faintly inebriated, maybe perfectly serious way. Maybe, he thought to himself, he didn't know her that well after so many years. Fake choke?

"Teach him, however you like," she concluded, "not to monkey with his equals, his peers."

But when he took her advice and acted the monkey, really did do some fake but disastrous choking, she claimed she'd said the word joke, not choke. Fake joking.

"And how would that work?" he wondered, speaking to her through the bars of the local precinct, several hours after the incident. "What the hell is fake joking?"

"You know. Where you call him a thief for taking your equipment, and then say, only joking. But you're not. You're fake joking."

———

One day he heard a maxim that reminded him not so much of his crime as of his misunderstanding.

Anger is a wind that sculpts a face very poorly.

———

In the end, the strangling episode proved to Knox that he was the one with the loss of restraint, the one with the ape-like hands, the one who could take what was flippancy to others, and turn it into catastrophe.

Yet not to forget Mhurra's own tinges: her vertical gloom, the frequent indispositions and subsequent thickness. Some days she'd seem enveloped in a crust of dirty ice, delicate but opaque. Her procedure most days was to follow what came to her mind first, as long as she could construct a rationale for it: go to her lab, study her lizards, breakfast later, if that's what seemed better at the time. Or, alternately, loll with him in the morning, erotically or childishly, and skip going to work altogether, if that was the mood.

When taking over the day she'd do it with a kind of manufactured spontaneity, telling him what they ought to do that day to achieve happiness—almost, it seemed to him in retrospect, as if she were following a secret set of maxims—then succumbing, strangely, to long stretches where all she could say was shut up, shut up, shut up. Physically, at such times, she had a needling way of buttoning her buttons, then unbuttoning them, braiding strands of her hair, unbraiding them, upbraiding herself for idle habits, gathering herself as if about to stand up and do something heroic and herpetological, though she'd often end up staying in the same chair for six or seven hours at a time, sometimes with a book, sometimes with the invisible but very thick book of her own reveries.

Now here she was, in that dream again, but not turning into Krell this time. No, in this version Mhurra was sliding across the bedroom floor, barefoot and bare naked, languorous, her skin flashing like aluminum panels. It seemed that her feet floated an inch above the floor, that her whole body was weightless as dust, but then she perched ponderously on the edge of his bed, leaning over him in such a way that her thin breasts and thin hair hung down at the same angle, parallel, dull, becoming horrible. There were strings or tendrils of spit hanging from her lips, and he saw in the dream that this was her way of talking, that the tendrils weren't spit, but whole sentences, whole explanations, and that he needed to put the ends of the strings in his ears, like little speakers, in order to hear what she was trying to say.

————

When people squint at us we think they are focusing, thinking hard, flattering us with intensified interest. Probably it was a result of his bad eyesight, or poor memory, but when Krell squinted at us we tended to think of him as an extra-attentive listener. There was also the fact that he was said to be a writer of some sort, and maybe he'd want to write about you, after all, and that required a narrow concentration on both his and our parts. Maybe because of a severely slouching posture, it was also as if he were constantly scrutinizing the street, the planet, and constantly thinking, how bad can it be?

Except for the single strangling incident, Knox thought of himself as one who was immune to all effects of personality, but during dinner one night, after an hour of Krell's squinting and slouching, he started liking his cellmate a little better than before. Together they held up food chunks in order to compare who had been given the larger one, and then traded, and laughed. At one point, much later the same night, Knox stood up, feeling almost as if he had the flu, and leaned over to embrace Krell awkwardly where he sat.

"Yes, I would like some coffee," was Krell's unexpected reply to the hug.

Knox, unaware of any rudeness, rushed off to answer the request. Rummaging in one of the cupboards, looking for the powder that wasn't at all actual coffee, but served as an acceptable substitute, Knox came across a bottle of what looked like alcohol. To his surprise, when he turned it around, the label read Victory Verymouth. That was it. There was no picture of any particular victory, or text of any kind to explain the difference between vermouth and verymouth.

"Where on earth..." he began, holding it up for his cellmate to see.

"You have to know the right people here to get even fake vermouth," grimaced Krell, fraternal, but shrugging. "Go ahead and pour a couple. The ersatz gin will appear later, maybe out of thin air, maybe filling the canals."

As if verymouth were the real thing, and didn't taste, as it did to Knox, of first mint candy and then watery blood, Krell was suave, asking Knox questions for the first time about life before a life of crime, not saying a word about himself, wanting to know only about such as books, educational views, children on Earth, all the gratifying probes, but with Krell adding a touch of hauteur to his droopy face and his squinting, the questions had a studied, on-screen mood.

"Now what about you?" asked Knox, lazily changing the subject, getting used to the flavor of the drink, refilling their cups. He was, at last, interested in Krell, at last outside of himself.

"Hmm?"

"Tell me about your Earth wife."

"Mars wife."

"I don't follow."

"You wouldn't think it to look at me right now," yawned Krell. "But I'm getting married. An exile wife. Didn't I tell you? We got undressed standing next to each other that first day. A feeling arose. Not what you're thinking. It was more aesthetic, I guess. More mutually introspective."

"Ah ha."

"She was drawn to me," said Krell, though he pulled his hands apart, as if to illustrate a growing distance from her.

"Tell me her name."

"You know her. Dance class, back row. Dr. Zelen."

"What does she look like?"

"A handsome woman, like they used to say. Smudgy features, and a mane of gray hair. A lioness!"

So it was her, then. Should he mention the teeth?

"I do know the one you mean," said Knox, back inside himself, speaking slowly to adjust to the various shifts taking place inside him. "I never really learned the names, but I picture her. Sure."

"*Each of us is each other's neighbor, and every neighbor is a whole world,*" recited Krell.

"Now you're quoting the maxims."

"The good news for you is that you can have the suite to yourself."

"Oh, yes," replied Knox, shiftings at an end, whereas now he was losing energy in every cell, as if each cell were a battery that had to be thrown away. Shut up, shut up, shut up, he told himself. Too easy to go too far inside.

"I think the trustees, or I should say, the maxims, are encouraging that kind of thing," were the words he managed, later.

"Encouraging suites?"

"No, encouraging connections, marriages." Knox's stomach now felt reduced to the size of a drop of water, his arteries expanded to the width of canals. But still he could keep speaking.

"You might recall this maxim from a few weeks ago, Krell: *What a happy fashion it is… that those who love one another should rest their heads on the same pillow.*"

"Same pillow! Don't we each get one?"

"What I'm saying is that any marriage pleases the trustees. They arranged a gender balance, I think, just to embellish our world with love stories."

"I know you're being sarcastic. I can't do that. I'm all for the trustees."

Before he replied to this, Knox glanced out the window to see who could be watching.

"Well, there are trustees and then trustees, I guess," he acknowledged. "Good maxims, yes. But you know they're ancient ones, merely parroted for us."

"Maybe with the word *parroted* you mean selected in a very positive, guiding way, the way a parrot would select the most delicious cracker."

"What was your crime?" asked Knox, saying the four words in a rapid monotone, wanting it to sound a little like a robot voice, like a voice that it would feel illegal not to answer.

But Krell remained aloof, unable or unwilling to fall for it.

"Did you know?" asked Knox, changing the subject. "Did you know that the dome is actually thicker near the top than at the bottom?"

"Did you know," retaliated Krell, "that back home I was a contest-winning writer?"

"I think I did know that."

"A journalist. Articles and such. Championship writing festivals. The next one I hope to win involves writing an in-depth account of the weapons used in the recent war."

"Go on."

"The parts written so far? An unusual style. I write in the first-person voice of a gun passed from hand to hand, character to character, over continents. As the weapon is fired, over and over, it ends up telling the story of our war triumph, individual by individual."

That is not bad, Knox thought. But he didn't say so.

"It wasn't individuals who kept the war going," was what he said in the end. "It was groups, towns. Towns like this one."

"All right, but, if our town is part of a war, we'll win."

"How do you know?"

In answer, Krell, leaning forward in his chair, balancing on the two front legs, picked up and displayed the bottle of Victory Verymouth.

Knox mumbled something, not understanding the gesture.

"There's victory everywhere, even in the bottles," announced Krell, lifting his drink and making his jaw jut far forward, then decanting the liquid in there directly, careful not to spill.

The next evening Krell stepped forward shyly, holding something behind his back, then held up a bag of dessert chunks, and said he was sorry it was all they had for dinner, as that's what had been left on the doorstep, instead of the regular entrée chunks.

"Dessert for dinner is my idea of a perfect evening," exclaimed Knox, and it wasn't exactly a lie.

"You remind me of someone," mumbled Krell, mouth full again. It was late in the evening, and Krell seemed to be pouting and clowning at the same time, putting his tongue between his lips to make it look like he had three lips. His ponytail, even though it was behind him, was flecked with sweet crumbs, and Knox had to resist the urge to reach over and comb them out, guessing that if he did, his cellmate would be forever coming up to him to ask him to repeat the favor.

"Perhaps I remind you of yourself?" Knox, now drunk, suggested.

"No, of Zelen," Krell frowned. He then raised a quivering glass tosimilitude, or perhaps brotherhood. This time Knox pointedly avoided anyclink of their cups, and just took his own slow sip, while managing to spit a little on the table, where it sat in a trio of drops, rainbowed like gasoline. He got up to go to the bathroom. There, using the dim reflectiveness of the wall as a mirror, he checked for food in his hair, raking his fingers through it to give it an extra buoyancy, then spent a long time squinting at himself, opening his mouth in agony, not to express his own, but to try and recreate the agony of his victim, the dean he had chosen to choke, the roommates he might decide to choke in the future.

Posture perfectly straight in the mirror, thinking of Zelen and her hair and her teeth, Knox bared his own dentition, recently stained by some staining liquid. Then he clamped his mouth shut with the sound of a falling piano lid. In the ordinary passages of his own body, soul didn't matter, because soul, if nothing else, is compass. It tells where we are, where to be, and it had been determined by others that he belonged to such a world as ours, and then further determined that he would not belong to it.

The mind carves a closet-sized cave, and hangs inside it a suit of soulful intent. Not a maxim.

———

A year went by. Almost. Or more. We'd lost all track of time. Possibly it was ten months, possibly fourteen, but how to tell? Experiments on condemned men provide evidence of significant distortions of time. Asked to push a button when they think half an hour has gone by, they typically press it after ten minutes, five minutes, even a minute and a half in one famous case. For us it was a matter of waking up, and there it would be again, Blister Star, visible through the dome as a blinding smudge. But how long was it taking to cross the sky? Ten hours? Fourteen? Twenty? How to tell time, wearing a wrist watch manufactured in a different solar system? Knox's thoughts, unmoored from such orbits, kept turning, turning, spiraling inward, as if approaching a place where there was a crisis of time, an eternity of punishment that contained no hours, days or months. At such times he'd try desperately to count; to mark time, tapping his shoe on the floor, writing numbers on the blank pages in his mind, then accidentally knocking those pages to the floor of his mind, and mixing the order when he picked them up again.

Somewhere in a corner of this confusing temporality, he kept stumbling across her, the woman with the halo of gray, named Zelen, and partly he wanted to warn her against Krell, and partly he kept thinking, there is time, there is time.

Yet the next day the spiral reversed direction, and he couldn't help but think that, since this was a planet new to man, everything that occurred here defined its history. The marriage of Zelen and Krell would therefore define time, and he joyously looked forward to the moment when the wedding was concluded and he would be able to say, aloud, that it was the end of an era. A new maxim came to him during such meditations, a Knoxim. Write it down, write it down, with the pen of the mind:

Love is one of many forces that helps planets to rotate on their axes.

———

Nevertheless he continued wandering the streets, thinking that, with such a small population, he would sooner or later run into her, perhaps even smack into her physically as they both briskly turned a sharp corner—

and all during the time that he anticipated such a collision he convinced himself he wouldn't try to talk her out of anything, just breezily bow, renaissance-style, turn on his heels and walk away, thus making a spectacle of his insouciance.

Yet he didn't run into her, and so the wandering went on for days. There got to be more people on the street as several others, like him, got the urge to explore, but no, Dr. Zelen did not seem to be one of them.

Drowning, said the speakers, *doesn't quench a thirst.*

Then, a few days later, more opaquely:

Drowning doesn't wash away our sins.

———

The dome, when he bothered to look up at it, had the look of an unwashed goldfish globe. It was getting dirty, but from what? Presumably the stains were the result of the human vapors that each of us gave off in the course of being alive. So why not go ahead and kill us? Put a vent in the dome and suck in the toxins. The whole town looked speckled and unclean. It was already terribly old, terribly terrestrial.

———

Out of boredom, Knox started attending classes, thinking not so much that he could learn something but that, since his course was no longer offered, perhaps Zelen, whom he still wanted to talk to about Krell, would enroll in something else. First he tried the speech forensics class, and sat on the floor in a back corner listening as two students debated the advantages and disadvantages of space travel. How ridiculous they seemed to him, and also perhaps to the whole room, as there was a lot of snickering. But this is where I'm supposed to be, was all he could think. This is time I'm supposed to waste.

So he lingered, exhausted, and let the derision of his fellow convicts wash over him. Next night he tried the mental painting class, and because there was a shortage of chairs for such a popular offering, many students were lined up along the walls, each one with eyes tightly shut, eyeballs darting furiously underneath eyelids. Because there was an extra space along the back wall, Knox squeezed in and tried to conjure the still life that the teacher was describing, but ended up drifting, daydreaming, his sphere and cylinder and cone melting into a hopeless mess.

Zelen wasn't enrolled in that class either.

Finally, one night he tried a class that he hadn't heard of: a seminar on ethics. And sure enough, there she was, poised in the front row, her blurred aurora of hair making her unmistakable from behind, and although there were no empty spaces, and he had to stand like an auditor in the back of the room, he kept quiet, certain he'd be able to approach her and speak to her after class.

And ethics was a good sign of things. It struck him as exactly the kind of class that might lead her to reconsider any rash decisions. She was an attentive student too, taking notes furiously as he watched, and after a moment he forgot all about what he wanted to say to her and could only think how extraordinary it was that she should have a pen and tablet, the first he'd seen in the colony. He could crane his neck and see from where he stood that it appeared to be nice paper, square in format instead of rectangular, cream-colored instead of white. Fine stationery, and how could he procure some for his own use? Given that he had little to say on ethics himself, here was a possible point of conversation for them to pursue after class, and perhaps he could even convince her to share. "May I have a leaf of your paper?" he imagined himself asking. "You know, it's the same color as your retractable teeth."

The class ended, but he wasn't aware, in his revery, that it had. By the time Knox snapped back to attention, the seats were empty, several students had gathered at the front of the class, and Zelen was nowhere to be seen.

No, he was wrong, she was right next to the professor, laughing, and so he loitered just outside the door, waiting for an opportunity.

Yet, when at last she emerged, he lost his nerve, and ended up following her anonymously in the dark, like an undergraduate. Outside, in the main plaza, she paused, and he likewise paused, some ways back. Clearly she had stopped to hear the maxim that was coming on, and he turned his attention to it as well.

"Attention. Your attention please," came the throaty voice. "*Those who know their minds best, know their hearts best. Repeat: Those who know their minds best, know their hearts best.*"

Apropos, but perhaps not the exact advice he would have given her himself. Rather the opposite. Know your heart least, was his personal ethic. Was that even an example of an ethic? He wanted to shout something to her, anything, before she moved on, but then he was surprised to find that she stayed where she was. After four or five minutes of awkward waiting— he was sure that by now she must be aware that the two of them were the only people in the plaza—he realized that what she was doing was waiting, not for him, but for the next maxim, and a minute later, it arrived.

"Attention. Your attention please. *Old people like to give good advice, since they can no longer set bad examples.*"

Perhaps, he considered, they were both at an age that could be described as "not yet old" and so, if he were to give her advice, she might not perceive it as the overly cautious wisdom of the superannuated. But what was most striking to him at that moment was not the content of the maxim, but the fact that she had waited to hear it. In other words, she was as addicted to the maxims as he was, and now he couldn't resist an intrusion.

"Do you remember me at all?" he said, approaching slowly, clapping his hands for some reason, and immediately regretting both question and clapping. He had decided moments before not to bring up the stiltedness of their other encounters.

She had turned halfway toward him, and he tried and failed to take note of whether her teeth were visible. Still, she only appeared to be vaguely aware of his presence. Her attention, he perceived, was still fixed on the nearby loudspeaker.

"The best maxims are the minims," he said, trying to sound like an author of such sayings.

To his relief, he could see now that her teeth were white and visible between her slightly parted lips, and he considered again that, on that first day, he had most likely been hallucinating.

"The word *best* maybe isn't the right word," she said, sneering, apparently quite capable of being found in a sour mood.

Also, he had forgotten about her eyebrows, and now they added to her sullen demeanor. It wasn't so much their size that astonished him, he realized, as their texture. They weren't like hair, really, but like animal fur—a stroke of pure sable, or otter, above her eyes.

"What is the right word then?" he got around to asking.

"*Frightening*," she answered, softening. "Poetic, in a way. I like the style more than the content. More than anything, I love that avian voice."

She laughed then, and he was sure at that moment that someone like her would never marry someone like Krell under any circumstances.

He had placed both hands on top of his head, like someone who wants to show the police he has no weapons.

"I'd like to try writing some maxims myself someday," she added, turning away from him and peering into the depths of the loudspeaker again, as if it were the actual mouth of the broadcaster.

He might have said, oh, me too, but he didn't say that. This conversation has to end, he kept thinking, but didn't know how to end it.

"So everybody's a writer now," was all he came up with, and he knew it sounded arch.

"Guess so."

"One more thing. I wanted to ask you where you got your pen and tablet."

"Pen and tablet?"

She wheeled around to face him fully then, not visibly angry, maybe curious, just wheeling and shrugging at the same time.

"I noticed it in class a minute ago."

"You're in the ethics class? I haven't seen you there. Though I do know who you are."

"You do?"

"You're Dr. Knox of course. The dance instructor. You don't remember that I was in your class?"

She frowned, and then quickly tore off the top piece of paper from her writing pad.

"Yes, of course I do. It's just that you were always in the back of the room. I recall your name as well."

"You do?"

"Yes. It's Zelen."

"I hope you don't mind that Krell brought me into your room to meet you recently, and that you were asleep. So I saw you snoring for a second. I'd be embarrassed to say so, but of course here everybody sees everything, eventually."

"So you know Krell, then."

"Well, I'm hoping to know him better," she laughed. She turned toward him again and as she pushed her gray aurora off her face, he instinctively looked down, and took note of the fact that something was wrong with her uni. It was too large, and looked more like an old-fashioned jump suit. He thought immediately of offering her the second uniform, the one he had set aside, mentally, preposterously, for Mhurra, maybe, or someone. But then he remembered that he'd already given it to her, and that this was it. The extra-large! Had it already been a year? Was it meaningful that she preferred it over her first one, which had fit her fine?

He kept his mouth shut.

He had a strong desire to walk up to her and grab a handful of surplus fabric, like a tailor, measuring how much to take in.

"Well of course I know him already," she continued. "I said *better* because we're getting married pretty soon."

Knox imagined a drawer opening in his chest and conveniently sliding forward, so she could simply deposit some explanatory piece of paper there, and leave.

Then, in the silence, there came another maxim.

"Attention. Your attention please. *It takes a better man to bear good luck than bad.* Repeat. *It takes a better man to bear good luck than bad.*"

She was walking away then, waving at him casually, but turned back a second later, spread her arms wide, and if there had been even a trace of wind inside our insulated dome, our thermos, our pressure cooker, it would have ruffled the edges of her oversized uni, perhaps inflated it like a sail.

"I forgot to tell you about the pen and tablet," she shouted back at him, waving the torn-off sheet like a handkerchief at a train station. "You can get them at the store."

"There's a store?"

His feet were anvils.

"There is now. You don't know about it?"

"Where?" He looked around, as if the store in question might appear when spoken of. When it didn't, he took a painful clodhopper step in her direction. It seemed absurd that they were yelling to each other across the plaza.

"Right there," she laughed, pointing behind him, and because of the difficulty with his feet, he heaved his body around so he could see where she meant. Sure enough, though he hadn't noticed it before, one of the low, egg-shaped buildings that bordered the plaza had a small, hand-lettered sign over the door that read GRAND OPENING.

"Grand Opening," he said, very deliberately, like someone learning to read. "Is everything on sale?"

But when he turned around she was walking away, and too far off to have heard the question.

———

The next announcement that came on was not a maxim. While Knox stood alone in the plaza, hoping for one last piece of good advice before going to bed, something to set free his riveted feet and put them on a path toward home, a voice came on proclaiming that all prisoners, colonists, whatever we were, male and female, were invited to meet in the plaza for a gala event of music and dancing, in celebration of the creation of the canals. It was emphasized that the event was entirely voluntary, and that only if we really wanted to, we could show up for what promised to be a social ceremony of special fun and significance. The date and time to be determined, so listen to all broadcasts carefully.

———

When Knox finally made it home, at that hour when the city was beginning to fill with light from our fierce Blister Star, a square creamy piece of paper gleamed at him from the table top. Zelen's paper, no question. So she had been there before him! But, even from a distance, he could recognize Krell's handwriting, though he had never seen it before.

Dear Knox: As the maxim goes, something something about the pillow. Am I right? So off we go, Zelen and yours truly, to get married today, although who knows what time the ceremony is. We don't know what time anything is anymore, but they have promised us, as I told you, our own suite, one floor down, exactly below this one. So the place is all yours, and you can dance in it to your heart's content or play ping pong against yourself, and sincerely hope you will. See you in the plaza at the Grand Celebration of Mars' Canals or come by for dinner sometime. Actually Zelen instructs me to tell you to come to dinner lots of times, as she likes you so much.

p.s. My Earth crime was bigamy. Only kidding. Krell

p.p.s. Actually can we trade places, Zelen wants to know. Turns out she's crazy about ping-pong too, and the downstairs place doesn't have a table, and they're a nuisance to move. All the suites are identical so you'll hardly notice the difference except you won't have a ping-pong table in the way. Thanks!

He turned it over to the blank side, still anxious to try out the beautiful writing paper. However, no pen. So he used his forefinger and lightly, savoring the creamy texture, traced a new maxim: *If you do not ferociously twist your life for yourself, who will ferociously twist it for you?*

———

Generally, life under the dome began to take on a more entertaining quality. Maybe because of the intense illumination, it felt like we were all on television, all the time.

———

After a couple of hours of nervous and naked sleep that left him feeling heavier than before, Knox got up, slipped with some degree of pain into his uni, and considered the likelihood of an early death. Something might, it seemed, be the matter with his heart, and though it was beating blandly enough underneath the prison bars of his ribs, he could feel no movement at the wrist, as if again he'd been hung upside down and his heart, instead of pumping blood in a gracious and endless circle, was keeping it all inside the ventricles, hoarding it, as if afraid of never getting it back.

"Let go of it," he kept saying to his heart, forcing himself and blinking himself out into the world until he was able to collapse on a bench in the plaza.

The plaza was, in a way, a sentimental place for him now. The spaciousness of it opened the shoulder blades, made him less hunched. His blood flowed again, apparently. He liked to stand at times and stretch his fingers up toward the dome and shake them, as in primitive times, when people shouted prayers, and shook out hidden monsters.

Disappointingly, the store was still closed, as was evident from another little sign, this one hanging by the door, that stated as much, but he was ready to wait things out, thinking that if he simply lingered on his bench with a distracted air, someone would eventually arrive and turn the sign over to read "open." So he simply let the morning light penetrate him, let himself imagine that the dome of his skull was like the dome over the city, and that his brain was a translucent city full of weak, oleaginous light. He wasn't going to die after all. A thread of outer space lullaby, all microtones, drifted from somewhere. Soon he was stretched out on the bench, and soon he was nearly asleep.

When he woke up from next-to-sleep he thought it was the song of a bird that had jolted him. As if there were birds. But it was the voice of the maxim reader coming over the speaker in a more gravelly way than expected, like an owl that kept pebbles in its crop.

Merit may exist independently of youth, but youth does suggest at least some degree of merit.

Shouldn't they be trying to teach, he considered, totally awake and somewhat disoriented, that we all have exactly the same merit? Who would say such a thing?

And where, it occurred to him to wonder for the first time, where did these broadcasts originate? The voice was more alto and crow-like today, though definitely belonging to the same girl, and in the background one could almost hear a sound of flapping wings, as if she were aloft somewhere, flying near the apex of the dome.

But time to turn the insides inside out, because now here came Zelen and Krell, hand in hand, nearly leaping, and they were clearly the planet's first newlyweds, their names destined to go down in the planetary annals. Firstborn of Mars! That's what the earthly televisions might shriek, when and if they had children. First fruit of the Red Planet!

The couple, advancing a little skittishly, a little woozy, had spotted Knox on his bench, and so directed themselves straight toward him, too late for him to melt away. Softly, expertly, like a cloth napkin re-folding itself to sit upright, he arose and raised his hand in limp hello.

"Knox," laughed Krell, shaking his head as if doubting his own eyes.

"Krell."

"Meet my wife, I mean, see my wife. Look at her, Knox. You know this human, I think."

"Human?"

"Not a Yoohoo, I mean!"

Krell had turned unexpectedly clownish and musical.

"A beautiful day for anything human," grimaced Knox, shaking their hands in turn, forgetting most of the details of last night's meeting with Zelen in this very spot. And because she never mentioned it, such details were lost to him forever.

"Are the maxims on today?" he asked. He was still waking up.

"Of course," said Zelen. "And I'm surprised, since you're up and about, that you're not down at the little dome, listening."

"You call it what?"

"The Little Dome of the Maxim. Home of Dr. Maxim Illion," muttered Krell, never taking his eyes off his wife's uni, as if he too were put off by its puffiness.

Zelen laughed, in that fay, false way of the recently married, though Knox believed she was laughing both at him and at the little dome. But then Krell jumped in, very focussed, touching everyone on the elbows, and gave out painstakingly lengthy directions on how to find it.

———

On his way, Knox stopped and looked up at the grandly arching but yellowed ceiling overhead to see if there weren't some kinds of physical chips or flaws in it to help navigate, flaws that could be learned as stars, and so help to remember the series of turns needed to get to any destination. There were tints, shadows, alterations up in the roof of the heavens, but as he watched they shifted, and were an effect of the outside atmosphere. There were intrusions—lengths of wire, or hair, that would flash for a second, animated. But he lacked the will to step outside with a breath wand and evaluate. With a terrible coldness reaching deep within, he saw that he had come to find it commodious inside.

And something worse had happened, in that now he could only think in the language of maxims, though at least they were ones he'd make up himself.

Only criminals see the difference between what is and what is supposed to be.

A soul without kinks is as useless as a rope without knots.

Scratching a face on a rock doesn't turn it into a god.

Minutes later, turning a corner, crossing one little bridge he'd never noticed before, he found himself at his destination, identifiable from the little hand-carved letters above the entryway that read, in longhand, *Petite Dom*. But the light from above was still alive, and Knox leaned a shoulder very heavily against some plastic for a moment to try and clear his head and feet, thinking now that it must be his brain that was crackling, his sanity that was snapping.

The interior of the little dome was plain. There were a few rows of benches, a raised stage, with a young man on it. Knox had entered at the moment a maxim was being broadcast. The live performance today featured this young man, this little more than a boy, who inched in a wiry way across the stage, as if influenced by the light, or like the light influenced by the chaos in Knox's own brain, and would calm down if the latter would leave.

"Don't mind me," Knox shouted, inappropriately, and every face in the audience turned to examine him.

"Attention," said the boy, leaning at a bad angle, then reeling across the length of the stage. "Your attention please."

Then Knox realized that this was the regular maxim reader, one with an owlish voice, and though he had pictured no one, he hadn't pictured a boy.

The maximist stopped and took a quick look at the book in his hand.

A book! thought Knox. There was actually a book of maxims! Tear some pages out, he wanted to shout, and let me put in a few new ones for you.

But he didn't say a word, silenced by the surprise appearance of this one called Maxim Illion—a boldly scowling and even revolutionary-looking young man once you really took him in, with a juvenile delinquent's face, sharp and pock-marked, his eyes popping charismatically, speaking all the while in a voice sweet as syrup, the same voice that was heard every five minutes, every day. And here he was available for close-up viewing, and Knox couldn't help but feel that he was watching a celebrity. Twisting over his lectern, high-boned, Maxim Illion at length appeared to be praying. But no, just preparing something, getting ready for the next maxim, due in five minutes and counting. As Knox's eyes relaxed he looked around to view dozens sitting in the auditorium with him, some taking advantage of the break in the action to chat awhile with neighbors, some intently staring into their laps, as if memorizing what they had recently heard, and one gentleman, out of place, with his hands raised to the ceiling, as if expecting it to fall.

Finally, after the right amount of time had passed, Illion cleared his throat, took a long drink of water, and with an expression of fugitive skepticism, mixed with sheepishness, he straightened out his uni, ran a hand through his strings of black hair, and then looked hard at his hand as if something were also written there.

What on earth, Knox wondered, could have been the crime? Something brutal? Didn't he look like someone who should have been sent to the Yoohoo dome? We were supposed to be all academics in this group, but this one, unless he was a genius of some kind, was hardly old enough for that. Doctor Illion? Not likely. Someone of interest, someone to approach, to cater to, but at the same time to be a little wary of.

"I'm going to put the maxim broadcasts on replay again," the boy whispered into the microphone at the lectern, "and tell you people who have come here today a story based on one of the maxims. Will that be all right?"

There was a fierce murmur of approval, as if some in the audience knew this routine, and relished it.

So Illion told a story about how once an infant was born, healthy and normal, except for the fact that it was born skeptical, that it was nearly a philosophical baby. This was a child with a sense of the ridiculous, and it was always laughing—laughing at others, sometimes playfully, sometimes rudely.

So far, Knox didn't get the point of such a story. Maybe we all were babies, and we were supposed to grow up? It was hard to concentrate. This teenaged Maxim Illion looked familiar to Knox at this point, and perhaps had sat next to Knox for days during the voyage out, but he couldn't be sure. Taken the dancing class?

Meanwhile, the story about the baby dragged on. It was ridiculously long, interminable, not really about the colonists after all, and at one point Knox nearly dozed off again. He really hadn't had sufficient sleep the night before.

"You can't change anything," the kid was saying when Knox jerked back to full wakefulness. "So you needn't cultivate great powers."

Great powers, heard Knox.

"The baby wasn't really a baby. How could a baby be as skeptical as a heretic?"

Skeptical as a heretic.

"Self-absorb the love you keep sending out into space."

Self-absorb.

"Sometimes this all turns into a kind of useless escapism."

Useless escapism. Or wait. Still groggy. Had he said useful escape?

"The baby finally said, after losing his parents, that he liked it better that his heart should be broken."

Prefer that the heart be broken.

And that was it. The story ended. Was it certain that the story was over? There was light applause from the audience, and he found that someone had sat down next to him, and now the man's elbows were thudding against Knox's ribs, a result of overly enthusiastic clapping. One or two people started audibly crying. Had the skeptical baby died? It wasn't clear how much time had elapsed, how much he'd missed. Had it been a parable about how planetary prisoners might also die?

At that point Knox very pointedly imagined that he would love the chance to become the next Maxim Illion. Or perhaps he would take a different name—Mack Simulacrum, maybe? At any rate, his wisdom and his stories would be crystal clear, he thought, grinning into his hand, and how perfect also to work here, in the little dome, a sanctuary within a sanctuary, and share anecdotes, and give every prisoner some sense of something. A sense of escape? Really, the alternative idea, wasn't it, was to escape, if all other schemes failed, by burrowing into the planet as far as possible. To find the metaphorical if not the literal core. To be used rather than unused, to be used up finally, every drop of meaning wrung from him, and then to be sent home, in his old age, translucent and neutral as ointment.

Outside the hall he found the light from the dome still suffering from its recent jumpiness, but paid little attention this time, lost in his ever-growing list of possible customized maxims. Attention, your attention please.

And he would glance down at his own book, once he had a book of maxims, and begin:

It is always a mistake to despair, but remember it's only one of your thousands of mistakes.

Better to draw twelve numbers in a circle around yourself, and turn your body into clock hands.

You can lock a potted plant in a closet, but you can't expect it to make its own chlorophyll.

Sometimes the sky contains more than one sun.

Oh, that last one? Not really a maxim. Love and not love, advance and retreat, jump like a wire on a drum. Not maxims either. Zelen's body, he imagined, was frighteningly thin within that oversized uni, and at times it looked like her limbs were shrinking while her head got larger, and then vice versa. How could he know, as he felt he did know, that she was already regretting her marriage to Krell? Only because everything was regrettable? An hour before, in the plaza, her eyes had struck him as shifty, the eyes of a softened criminal (such as we all had sometimes), like a student cheating on a test, but in addition, and this was more disturbing, there was no reflectivity in them, matte instead of glossy, as if someone had taken a tiny cloth or Q-tip to them to blot any trace of moisture away.

If Mhurra were here, he thought, we could socialize with Krell and Zelen. Double date. Two happy couples!

Odd little brain. It wasn't working well at all. It wasn't awesome or brilliant enough to sort it all out. There followed the familiar weakening, the familiar strengthening. Of course there was Krell's position in all this. Krell! It sounded like the name of some useless grooming product. But the man wasn't so bad, simply tightened down a little, off-center. A man, you'd have to think, whom love would bounce off of like a ping-pong ball. Or whom desperation for affection would pump up like a balloon, until he burst, and the remaining shreds would settle to the floor like autumn leaves, souvenirs of both old and current affectations.

On the way home, Knox remembered about the pen and paper, and so, after sitting a while longer on a low and sagging wall, he directed his steps back toward the plaza, pretty sure that he now knew where he was, how to get where he was going. Turning a corner, whistling in a minor key, he found himself walking right behind Maxim Illion, instantly identifiable for his long raven hair and slight stature, and close enough to reach out a finger and actually tap twice on the shoulder.

"Oh, Dr. Knox," said the young man, wheeling around as if he knew who was accosting him before looking. "I saw you in the audience just now and wanted to wave to you. What a bum deal that they canceled your dance class."

It was of course the same owlish voice. Without that, it would have been hard to remember that this, out of context, was the maximist.

"You were in the class?" asked Knox. It seemed that everybody had been, and he hadn't known any of them.

"Oh sure. But don't worry, I know you had a lot of adoring students and I don't expect you to remember me."

Then they both seemed to have run out of words, and in the silence that followed, Knox noticed that there was still something going on in the air, and that now it was more a play of static electricity or something. In fact it seemed to center on the boy, in his eyeballs, in his hair, and it was tempting to run a hand through it to see if there'd be a shock. Or a magnet hidden in there, or a halo. Maybe it's the case, he thought, that youth, as it blooms, attracts a kind of indiscriminate wattage.

"Have you ever thought much about the canals?" Knox blurted out, imagining that the answer would have to be yes. Still he didn't wait for an answer, but kept talking. "You know what I'm saying? That they shouldn't be built? That the trustees don't have any idea what they're doing?"

Illion looked at him rather wildly. Then blandly. It was clear that this was not the best possible topic.

And Knox responded to the look by becoming wilder, and subsequently blander, himself.

"And then there's that baby of yours," he muttered. "The skeptical one. I'm sorry that I fell asleep."

The boy shrugged this time, yet he still seemed to glow, slightly. Was it electricity or a feeling of mutual understanding?

"Why don't you come with us?" he said at last, calming down, but returning to a twitchy and hopping metabolic style.

"You mean outside the dome?"

"Outside the dome? Wow. No. I meant come to the next live broadcast."

"I thought you meant something else," said Knox. Then, looking around, he whispered, "The two of us, I mean. Escaping together."

"A vacation?"

"No, not that. Running away. It qualifies as a thought."

"Trustees," mumbled Illion, fumbling his fingers near his stomach, or maybe checking a hidden wand that was recording the whole conversation.

Then he straightened. "I can't see losing my job over it. Can you?"

"I don't know!" hissed Knox.

Illion hissed back a little, and Knox went on, more comfortably. "My dear, I was writing a new maxim, and maybe you'll like it better than the running away idea."

"All right."

"The road leading away from pain is the one that loops back to it the quickest."

"All right."

This last, disappointingly flat response, Knox quickly decided, was a warning that a trustee was coming up from behind. He liked to think of himself as turning to confront the spy and strangle, as always, in a fake way. This time he would wrap more persuasively, press the thumbs down hard on the trachea, the carotids, watch Chemo's face, if that's who it was, blossom all over with blotches.

Illion could join in the effort. Together they'd lift Chemo off the ground by his armpits, and shake him in such a way that his feet would kick them both, without hurting them, in the legs.

But when Knox did turn around, someone was walking away from him, disappearing.

"Wait a minute," he said to the boy, not looking back. "I'm just going to check if there are more people around the corner."

Maxim Illion waved as if waving goodbye, and there was a long silence, as if the weather had cleared.

―――――

Also there was this, long ago: the two of them, Knox and Mhurra, seated, like upperclassmen, duke and duchess, at the crest of a long flight of stairs, steps that followed a slope in a park, switchbacking up past what once had been a waterfall, now a trickle of syrup, and reached the top of the hill, high above the rest of the neighborhood. There was nothing there, no apparent reason for the stairs, only a little nub of relative flatness, a cement foundation where a tiny house had once stood. A handful of bearded irises were in bloom, leftovers from the past, though Mhurra claimed that the stairs hadn't been built for the house, but only put there after it was gone, as an easy way to get up to the irises.

After some time spent circling the flowers—they were there to look for her lizards but also to be together in the last few days before his deportation—they sat on the concrete, on the next to topmost step, knee to knee, hand to hand, fingerpad to fingerpad, looking out over the endlessly sticky and dark city below. One brand new sign lit up the sky before all the million others, and it flashing only the word *Worldaway*. And though it was only the name of some corporation or other, the coincidence of it was cause for coughing, some internal drooping, and so in response they tried to draw closer, to draw strength from one another, neither knowing that the other had nothing left hidden in the soul to offer up. Still, Mhurra's hand went into Knox's opposite pocket, his into hers, their typical arrangement, and he found and fingered there a crumpled piece of paper. Without pulling it out, he knew what was written on it: *worse, worser, worst.* It was his note to himself, and he had put it in her pocket only the day before.

The best response to when and where they were seemed to be wordlessness, but in lieu of talk they clicked their teeth, fake nudging each other with bony shoulders, conveying without language the kind of motion it would take to launch themselves forward, tumble down the stairs, hurt themselves, hospitalize themselves, and end in that way all confusion. But Mhurra gathered herself a second later and explained what bad comic material it was, this tumbling. Not funny at all. Later she admitted that she liked how it had looked, in her mind's eyes, the picture of them rolling like a pair of tumbleweeds down the long steps.

"*Local couple tumble straight to salvation,*" said Knox, some snapping noise going on in the air, or so he thought, until he realized the sounds were coming from deep inside him, a cracking in his chest like hiccups centered on the bones.

"Couple tumble. I like that. Couple stumble, and rumple."

"Couplestiltskin."

In response to that she started flapping her arms rather beautifully, the opposite of tumbling, as if beginning to rise to heaven, and in such a convincing way that Knox knelt to awkwardly wrap his arms around both her knees to hold her steady.

"Don't worry," she said. "Neither of us is going anywhere. Right now, I mean."

He clung more fiercely to her knees.

"Above the city like this," he said, "you do think about the afterlife.

About degrees of punishment and reward."

"I think about before. The beforelife. Before I was born. Before things got messed. Before you dropped this mess on me."

"You know the note in your pocket? I want it back so I can write on the other side. I want to write *worst is worser than worse.*"

But then her knees wriggled out from his arms, backwards, up the last two steps, and when he looked she was already like an herbalist or witch among the irises, all of them different shades of yellow, her white pants stained with something red, a nice match, and as he watched she meticulously picked several flowers, threw them onto the concrete, then trampled them up there, lifting her foot like a hammer, bringing it down and rotating, until she had smeared every blossom into the cement.

"Flowers also have blood and bones," she sniffed.

"I'm the one being transported," he muttered to himself. He wanted the transports of love, but saw that there were none coming.

"Irises have the nicest anthers. Furry, like tiny mice."

"I want somebody to tell me something."

"When?"

"When I get back."

"Would you like me to call and get them to tell you something?"

She strolled back over to where he still sat and plopped down loudly beside him, as if she were as heavy inside her clothes as rocks in a bag.

"Did you want someone like me?" she asked. "Someone like me doesn't do that."

"Because."

"There are a lot of planets. A lot of humans. Anybody can be anywhere. It's a coincidence, Knox, that we're even on the same one. Do you know the words to any songs?"

"A few."

"In this world of people... staggering number of people...I'm sad there is you," she sang in something like the dove's deep hoo hoo voice, perhaps sarcastically, then pulling hair after hair from her head until she had a limp and tiny bouquet of them to offer.

Another time, another moment left to them in his few remaining hours of freedom, it was arranged to go out for dinner, but when he got home, there was a note on the door.

"Thinking less about dinner than about the whole inherently violent thing. What if I had strangled instead of you? Meet you at the restaurant."

But when he ran inside to change clothes, there she was watching television in the nervous, bug-eyed way she had when focusing on something below her level of intelligence.

"It's a show about the new worlds," she said, waving at him to keep quiet. "They're showing a lot of them, and I keep wondering if one of them is yours. What did you say it was called?"

"I didn't. It doesn't have a name. Let's call it Worldaway, okay? As in, I'll be just one world away from you."

"Okay," she said and got up and came over and squeezed his arm with one hand, as if judging its ripeness.

"Why aren't you at the restaurant?" he asked.

"Oh, the note! Sorry. Forgot I'd written that. I was remembering the stairs, remembering the flowers, how I stamped them down."

But Knox understood that Mhurra was not herself tonight, anymore than he could fix some identity of his own. She was much more physical than lately, kept both hands tight around his upper arm as they walked, as if she meant to drag him off at a right angle at any moment. Later, she gnawed a little on his shoulder, like a friendly dog, but bit so hard into him that they both felt a tug of teeth against cartilage.

At dinner they didn't do well. She swallowed her food with her mouth open, a display that was disgusting to him, not because of the sounds, but because it was all done to impress him with the fact that she was, like him, quite capable of antisocial behavior.

"Here's what I want us to do for each other while you're gone," she said, after taking one slug of wine, and he used one finger to precisely catch the drip down her chin.

"Anything."

"When I see something peculiar," she went on, "something staggering, or beautiful, I'll turn to point it out to you, even though you won't be there."

"Yes."

"And you'll do something similar, especially you, because where you're going, who knows what you'll find. Little green men. Lizards the size of houses. Houses the size of lizards."

"That's right."

"So my point is, don't point. Don't look around for me. Bottle it up."

"Bottle?"

"Like I told you before. Rope off one section of yourself and put up signs. Call it something else. Label that portion the Mhurra region. The Mhurramind."

"It's already there."

"Yeah, but make it permanent, and larger. And I'll rope one off too. A Knoxmind. That way this will all have much less useless tragedy in it."

———

Maxim Illion was walking away. There was a sound of nervous cursing or tongue clicking somewhere down the street. Drumming, it might have been, actual drums, with drumsticks involved, or someone making a rattatat-tat in their throat, and Knox wondered if he ran to find the source he might find people dancing to the rhythm he believed he heard. Dancing? He could picture former students moving around somewhere, maybe in the plaza, like the lonely savages they were, leaping from one spot to another, as if on stage, baring their canines, and bouncing their palms off their stomachs. And then their faces—full of crime, and not full of crime.

But here, now, walking toward him, as bright as if lit from within by the plasticky light, was a fellow prisoner. As he came up closer Knox saw it was someone who did not look like a criminal at all: an elderly and multi-complexioned fellow, with a goatee as white as lamb's wool, tan cheeks, but with blood boils encircling his neck that gave him the unsettling appearance of having maybe survived a strangulation.

"You're probably another student I don't recognize," was all Knox could think to say.

The man stopped only a foot away, uncomfortably close, and stood there staring, until Knox put out his hand and set him back a few inches. The sound of drumming had abated a little, and the man knitted his brows in a show of concern, as if Knox were the sick one. Next he put out his hand to display something. Knox at first thought it was a lemon, a glowing and impossible piece of fruit, but instead, when he looked more closely, it turned out to be a ball of yellow-orange dirt that glittered on the man's palm rather like a mud pie flecked with gold.

The only possible explanation, at the moment, was that this was an elderly prospector, arrived from a mine.

Knox made no comment, merely squinted.

"Don't you see?" the old and piebald fellow finally asked. "It's wet. Dirty wet. It's raining outside and the magazine said it would never rain."

"Raining?"

"It sure is. Didn't you see all those sparks in the dome a while back? That was lightning or something close to lightning."

Raining. That was what had been making the drumming sound, and it was still going on, but not as loud.

"Where did you get the mud?"

"Some people went outside for a second, and they brought some of it back in. When I saw you I thought I'd give it to you."

"Why?"

"Oh, only because I enjoyed your class so much. I wasn't in it, but I watched from outside. That's all."

So Knox reached out and took the proffered item, the magic rain ball, though when he pocketed it, it lost its form, and became a damp pile of dirt in his pocket.

"Go see the rain!" shouted the fellow as he hurried away.

So Knox did go take a look, out at the very edge of town, where the dome came arching down like a plastic rainbow to meet the planet's surface. His hands pressed against the inner curve, and as trickles of water meandered down, he traced their paths with a finger tip.

Knox thought he understood what was happening—that it was Mhurra, precisely, passing this knowledge on to him, this joy, because it must be raining and drumming at that very moment on Earth, and she was mutely pointing to it. But no, in fact she had said that she would send him nothing, absolutely nothing. So he knew it was just the wanting of things, the dying for things, and yes, now he did see her actually, out there, outside the dome, walking straight toward him in the downpour, her clothes soaking wet, her hair hanging straight down and transparent, as if it were part of the rain, part of the flowing. He watched, utterly relaxed, as she came right up to him and leaned forward to apply her tongue to the outside of the dome, as if to swallow some of the rain that poured down in rivulets there. Then it looked as if she wanted to kiss him through the dome, and he went so far as to close his eyes and put his own lips and tongue against his own side. Then recoiled at the bad taste.

———

In the plaza, people were pushing, swearing at one another. One woman rode on the shoulders of an especially tall man, holding her palms up, smiling a moist smile.

Through the walls it was possible to glimpse any number of prisoners doing push-ups, maybe inspired by rain to build strength. But strength for what?

Things were a little out of whack.

Knox ducked into the store, entering with his hands deep in his uni pockets, as if about to pull out a gun and stage a hold up.

And there, walking forward from the back of the store, was the same fellow he had seen only a few moments before, the old man who had stepped forward to present him with the ball of dirt. Unquestionably, it was the same person, though here he was now standing behind a counter, next to an old fashioned cash register, as if this were a store where one would pay money for things, like a living museum, a recreation of some cash-based era of the past, and to top it off they had hired an elderly cashier to add to the period atmosphere.

"So today is your grand opening?" asked Knox.

"It's not like that," answered the cashier. "Everyone is confused. The name of the store is Grand Opening."

"Oh."

"Did you go take a look at the rain?"

"Not really. I came in here, actually, to get away from the rain. And to buy a pen and a pad of paper."

"Sorry you missed it."

"No, I saw it, I saw it."

"Pleased to know you. I go by the name of Dr. Waugh. And of course I don't sell things. I distribute."

"You mean we simply take what we need?"

"Within reason, yes."

"What brands do you carry?"

Waugh stroked the soft surface of his goatee, and frowned. "I'm excited to tell you that we carry only those items deserving of the Victory label. Would you care to take a look at the Victory line of fine products?"

"No. But who gave you the idea for that name?"

Knox was already making his way toward a shelf he'd spied immediately, one that held dozens of roller-ball pens, and next to them, exactly as he'd pictured it, one thin lovely tablet of cream-white paper, an antique perhaps, bound on the left, like Zelen's, with a spiral of thick, brassy wire.

But that was it. The rest of the store seemed more or less dedicated to liquor, every one of the bottles displaying the "Victory Verymouth" label.

So this had to be where Krell shopped too. Had the store really been here that long, and he'd overlooked it?

"Victory over who, or what?" asked Knox, posing one of the surprisingly slender and ink-fragrant pens beneath his nose like a mustache.

"Ourselves."

"You mean we haven't achieved that yet?"

"No, dear fellow."

"All right. Maybe you carry gin? The thing is, I have verymouth at home. Also, do you have a martini glass. I mean a real glass, made of glass?"

"Do you mean a Victory Glass?"

"If that's what they're called, then yes."

"Afraid not," said Waugh, collecting the few items that Knox had picked out—namely, the tablet, several pens, and one of the bottles. He coughed as he did so, coughed again, but with greater noise. Putting the bag down abruptly, the clerk collapsed down to rest his head on the counter, sucked air deep into his lungs, and subsequently moved his head and mouth around in a circle, like a vacuum hose trying to pick up all the dust, or in this case, oxygen, in the vicinity.

Then stood up, recovered.

"I wish I could stock more stuff," he breathed. "But as far as I can tell, there are no glasses of any kind on..."

"On what?"

"On Mars."

"You were about to call it something else," Knox shot back, improving his posture.

Waugh tilted his head to look at Knox with an expression of sharply honed sadness.

"Did you just call it Mars?" Waugh asked.

"That was you."

"Well, all right," Waugh whispered, leaning slightly forward over the counter. "Sometimes I *don't* call it Mars. You'll excuse me for telling you that sometimes I don't call it that at all."

The victory over ourselves, Knox maximed to himself, *can only come when we say the right words.* Here was someone else, he thought, maybe, maybe, who could use the language properly. Who could whisper secrets, articulately. One strand of Waugh's long white hair had fallen from behind his ear and swayed there like the snapped filament of a violin bow. Everything inside Grand Opening struck him as somehow out of whack with the blandness of the dome. It had an indefinable atmosphere of Earth. There were dangers. Out in the street Waugh's eyes had appeared to have the same waxiness as the town, but now Knox sensed there was a transparency to them, a transformation to another kind of substance, solid and gleaming as ice. But then Waugh closed his eyes, and seemed like one of those fragile seniors who can topple over at the slightest touch.

"What's the matter?" asked Knox.

"Oh," said Waugh at last, opening his eyes, straightening further, smiling without showing teeth, acting as if nothing had happened. "I guess I'm out of sorts with the sheer pleasure of it."

"Of what?"

"That someone would ask me that."

"You mean about victory?"

"Oh, everybody comes in here to pick up liquor, though they rarely ask for a glass. I guess you're the first one to want paper. Wait, no, not the first. At least it's a rare thing. And you wanted a pen too. Interesting! I was wondering if anybody else besides someone else who shops here would ever pick one up, or if they were here for no reason. But no, I meant that you asked me what was the matter with me. No one ever asked that before."

Knox remained silent for a while, and then went ahead and asked the question not allowed to be asked.

"What was your crime, then, Dr. Waugh?"

"Excuse me?"

"The reason you're here. What you did. Maybe you don't like my asking."

"Oh," brightened the old man, holding his hand in front of his eye, and moving it, as if to practice focusing. "Asking is all right."

"So what was it?"

Waugh slapped his hand down on the counter and leaned forward again." Take a good look. I mean at my face. They say our crimes are written all over our faces. See if you can tell me mine."

"I can't," said Knox, frankly.

"Really? Because I've been told it's easy to read, that I'm a walking billboard for what I did. And yours, now that I look at you, is certainly written all over you. Headline style."

Knox was trying to imagine such facial messages when he heard a word, or exclamation of some kind, in a voice that seemed to emanate from the back of the store. He peered in that direction, into darkness, and saw no one. Maybe it was a bird. An owl.

"There's someone else in the store?" he asked.

"Quiet," said Waugh, holding up his hands, breathing hard again. "Listen for a second."

But there was nothing, though it could have been that the old man's harsh breathing, rough as sandpaper, was drowning out something important.

"Come here and I'll show you," said Waugh, recovering. "But don't make too much noise, as I don't want us to come off as voyeurs."

"What do you mean?"

"Customers. You customers see this as a store. But my job is service, providing favors. The trustees instructed me to make things happier here."

"Okay."

"Now turn and look straight ahead. Look at the door with the plasticky screen. Don't go any closer. And see how you can't see through the wall? It's my storage room, and I wallpapered it on the inside with labels."

"Labels?"

"Labels off of filthy old Victory Verymouth bottles. I mean fifty. Ha. I said filthy."

"Why?"

"Because we *are* filthy. You and me. The criminal breed I mean."

"I mean, why put up the labels."

"To screen. You know. First, it was for me. To sit alone in there and shed tears. I mean it. What did they call it? When you are put by yourself?"

"Solitary. Shoe."

"That's it. Though in my case, solitary refinement."

Then there came, clearly from behind the curtain, another vocalization, a human hoot, as if asking *who goes who goes*. Knox came close enough, and now he saw that the door screen, woven from rainbow plastic streamers, had draped itself over a pair of twisty legs, as if to say the show is over. Knox felt slightly ashamed at the crassness of it. Two bodies rotated inside the little room, partly outside it, but the self-absorption of it was interesting to him. The only conclusion was that the one with the hooting voice was Maxim Illion.

"Customers of mine," whispered Waugh. "The two of them were in here one day, and found out about my... refinement. Then asked if they could use the place for a while, and I said sure, sure, sure. Put on a show for each other."

"And they did."

"And they did and they do. And so do others. At times like this, I wish there weren't quite so many labels. Have you got someone you'd like to bring by?"

But all Knox was tempted to do was to march right in and put a stop to it. Not out of prudishness. Not out of morals. It's just that he knew an angry lesson he could teach them—that sex is distance, sex is lack. Don't bother with it when it's here, the object within reach. Give them a maxim or two. Lay it on thick. *Don't bother reaching for what you already have.* Or how about this one? *Just don't bother.*

Knox took his purchases and started to leave, only to find Zelen on her way in. He already knew, of course, that she shopped here, but still, as they came up against each other in the doorway, neither able to pass, smiling with the strain of multiple uncertainties and unable to speak a single inane pleasantry, Knox found his face mere inches from hers, and her features—

smooth, rufous, dark, pinched—struck him for the first time as neurotic, even juvenile, and for the first time he saw how to read someone's face, like Waugh, and spell out the crime. Reading hers on the spot, perceiving now that she, like him, was guilty of precisely the thing he was guilty of, he saw a strangulation. She'd had her hands around somebody's neck, and, for a moment, loved the sensation.

As satisfactory as embracing a marble column.

And she would have to be admired, loved openly, for the crime. How not to, because they were kith and kin, and could talk, and share the recollection of the marble coldness and texture of necks they'd known, the girth, how older people—had she noticed this too?—are intricately folded, and raw, almost rooster combs.

Zelen passed brusquely by him and entered the store. Almost immediately she was in conversation with Waugh, but they whispered beyond earshot, possibly gossiping. Put a small town under a dome on a small world and everybody knows everything in time. Small enough town, and it's also easy to fall in love, not with a single fellow inmate, but with the several that stand out, with the few in front of the all. Knox held his breath and leaned closer, listening for any faint words to reach his ready ears. Maybe they were discussing the blue chamber. Maybe Zelen—oh?— was booking the room. Sexcapade for her and Krell. Or her and Knox. Or five or six of us standouts at a time, maybe. Knox filled a space in society that seemed scissored out of cream paper, paper the same color as the dome. With that kind of invisibility, anything was possible: comedy, inversion, abjection, humbug, blissfulness. Revolution! He was sure Zelen, like him, would be the type to overuse the exclamation point. After revolution, what do revolutionaries have? Exclamation-point sex. Then, rekindling of rebellion.

Unable to hear a word of what she said, Knox could only watch how Zelen's hands moved when speaking, how they spiraled down constantly, perhaps even shrinking in size a little. But that, after all, was familiar. Most of us felt most of the time that everything kept reducing. The planet under our feet kept curving down to a degree that felt smaller and harder. The effect, one that we talked about often, was that of standing on the crown of a bald head.

"But why is it all shrinking?" some asked.

"Everything is recoiling from us," came the reply

It wasn't a maxim, but someone said that they overheard a trustee speaking on the same subject.

Control, he was reported to have whispered, *recoils upon the controller.* Or something to that effect.

———

Maybe another year went by.

———

A true friend is the greatest of all blessings, and that which we take the least care of all to acquire. But most of us, maybe in a desultory way, were finding friends, and did not need to be instructed by loudspeakers on how to get or to value one. Many went beyond friendship, and there were a handful of marriages. Rehabilitation implied eroticism to some. *A new mentality will make you more attractive, more popular among peers.* Others went reclusive. Self-absorption was a condition not exactly approved, but it received no censure, only an encouraging counter maxim or two. Knox wasn't one of those who, despite having never influenced a single person, see themselves as leaders. However, because the weight of approval fell on the side of fellowship, there was pleasure taken in the illusion, common among us, that Knox and Krell were close friends. After all, they had been suitemates for a while, and after Krell's marriage to Zelen, after the swapping of suites, Knox was often observed (everything so easily observed) climbing one floor up to join the newlyweds for meals, Zelen needing only to stomp her foot twice on the floor to issue her blunt invitation.

Knox responded to thuds, but didn't know his own motives for dining there as often as he did. The three of them, drinking, sitting in silence, eating, slouching, were a picture of dome cordiality that might easily have been held up as a source of more maxims. They turned into a kind of television show, with some of us lingering in the street late in the afternoon to watch the three of them sit together.

A true friend, etc.

One day Knox lay on the floor of his cell watching, overhead, the

upstairs couple play ping-pong. Although he could only see the soles
of their unis with any clarity, it was obvious which one was Krell and
which one Zelen, even possible to roughly follow the progress of the game
by listening to how the ball hit or did not hit the table, or noting how
someone's feet would go up on tiptoe for a moment to grab back a ball that
had died right at the net.

Lulled by the rhythm of the game, and bored by the fact that Krell was
repeatedly the winner (evidenced whenever he hopped up and down in
glee), Knox fell asleep. Minutes later, he was awoken by the two familiar
foot thumps from overhead, and was astonished, glancing up, to see that
this time Zelen had gotten down on her hands and knees and was pressing
her face into the floor to make a comic distortion of her features. Lips
were flattened, nose bent to the side like a snail. After a second she pressed
her whole body against the translucent floor and kicked her feet and fists
against it, in imitation of a child's tantrum—a mockery, Knox suspected,
of her husband's immaturities. So, of course, he ascended.

Taking the stairs two at a time.

The dinner itself was silent and forgettable.

"How have you been?" asked Krell.

"Pretty much the same," answered Knox, and the three of them went on
to focus on the chewing and ingestion of tasteless prison fare.

A true friend, etc.

After dinner, Zelen dashed off, without apology, to another one of her
classes, and that was that.

Sitting with his former suitemate, sometimes peering at him
peripherally and slyly, sipping at the mouth of the bottle, Knox grew more
and more agitated, more restless with the other man's persistence and
pathos, and made an effort, with one hand over his eyes, to imagine how
it might come about that they could trade suites again and Krell be sent
downstairs, alone, where he belonged.

"I challenge you," said Krell at some point.

"I know."

"You do?"

"Yes, you're challenging me to ping-pong, which I said I'd never play
with you. But okay."

Krell won the rally for serve, and was about to begin the game, squinting, balancing the ball pretentiously in the middle of one hand, pretending it was tricky to balance it like that, preparing to toss it up, when there was a knock at the door, or door frame.

It was Chemo knocking, but the next moment he was stepping without fanfare or greeting into the living room, twisting and untwisting his mouth, his tie. Peering rudely into every corner. No one had really seen much of him since the day of the canals, but here he was, plopping into one of the empty chairs, and as the other two stood in silence for a long minute, paddles still in hand, game only halfway finished, Knox couldn't help but notice certain changes. Chemo had entered the room without that tiptoe affectation that was traditional for the trustees. Too tired for it, probably. His hair was notably thinner, and the sebaceous scalp glistened with an artificial but quite pretty diamond pattern that hadn't been there before. Deep and almost alarming furrows above the ears gave his whole head a squareness, a vitality. When he spoke his voice was more gracious than ever, rather whispery, free of saliva strings, and it turned out that his reason for dropping by was to give Knox what he'd been dreading for so long: a new job.

But he also had a new job for Krell, and what he wanted was to give both of them the same assignment. A brief outline followed. The job had elements of passion in it, science. Chemo wanted the two of them to prepare, that night, for departure on a journey of importance: an expedition to the highest latitudes, to the top of the world, to the icy northern pole.

"The trek, by foot, will take a certain number of days, but not too many," he explained, still smiling to himself. "The length of your trip is determined by the relatively small and maybe even shrinking circumference of the planet. However, that's something you know as well I do. I don't mean to say you don't know it. I hope you perceive me as affable, a friend at home in your home, Dr. Knox."

"It's not my home."

This fact, of local importance to Knox, went unremarked.

"And the thing is," continued Chemo, "you don't have to get specifically to the pole, just most of the way into the interior of the ice field. And there we need you to melt all the ice in question."

Chemo paused there, and looked at the ceiling, counting something on his fingers.

———

The dome served as panopticon, also as echo chamber. Every utterance had its eavesdropper. In no time word of the polar job got out. Knox and Krell, Knox and Krell, was the phrase on everyone's lips.

A belief in heroes obliges us to constantly construct new ones.

During the time of their excursion, they'd be exposed to the toxic air, but provided with plenty of breath wands. There would be the chance of a confrontation with Yoohoos, but they had slim ray wands, meant for melting ice, but useful as weapons too. The ice field was cold, but our unis adjusted to every climate, every temperature. Also there was the prospect of canals filled with water, crystalline and new, all across our little planet. The maxim about heroism could have applied to everyone, for a while, if by heroism includes enthusiasm. Even Knox was momentarily proud to be Knox, and touched, as he and Krell strolled for a while together through the streets, by the gestures of love and gratitude that we others, the less adventurous, offered at every turn. As for any actual improvement in our lives brought on by water coursing through the canals, that was unclear. Water for water's sake, maybe. For the moment life pumped more clearly and lightly, and try as we could to resist a little boost to our morale, we found we couldn't.

It is difficult to disabuse ourselves of the abstractions we revere.

Next morning, Knox heard some thumping from above while lying flat on his back in bed. Zelen wanting to seem him again so soon? But this time it was Krell kneeling on the floor, thrusting his palms downward in a way that clearly conveyed the idea that they should postpone their departure till the next day. After all, as some additional gestures seemed to ask: how urgent could it be? And Knox, happy at the delay, held his hand up as close to the ceiling as he could reach, and signaled with a cockeyed thumb that postponement was a good idea, though his arm ached as he held it steady there and considered the surprise that came with agreeing so readily to any idea put forth by Krell.

———

That evening no dinner invitation arrived, and anyway Knox preferred sitting in the evening gloom, trying to see through the buildings and the dome and out into the natural planetary landscape beyond. Was there a sunset? It seemed like there had to be, but then the outer world went abruptly dark. So then he wondered about stars, but the dome was like a perpetual cloud and there was no trace of the Horsehead Nebula, if that's what was out there, or any stars at all. If there were stars, they were distorted into smears the size of paint drips, and he spent hours staring at the smears, trying to make sense of them. Meanwhile he could see that many apartment lights were on, softly glowing, all around the city. The insomniacs among us had the habit of puttering around their cells, or friends' cells, in the small hours, pouring themselves generous drinks, talking to themselves, asking very loudly what time it was, what year it was, sometimes slipping outside to sit on a bench in the plaza and absorb the uplifting but banal entertainment of the maxims. There they'd fall asleep, but then awaken into sleepwalk mode. Standing up, arms held out straight, they'd head right back to apartment and to bed, only to suffer there from more half-awakeness.

Early the next morning, with no hangover, wands dangling from the corners of their mouths, daypacks cinched lightly but so tight against their backs as to impose a ramrod posture, a yogi's discipline, they set out. Brittle Star hadn't come up yet and there was little to plot a course by except for a horizon that merged dark gray into pearl gray into white, a strata of bland non-colors. There were no bird calls to greet the dawn, no rumblings of garbage trucks, no squeaks of cats or growls of dogs. In this gloomy hour they could see in the distance the outline of the ship, the old *Antibody*, and as they came up close to it, it was possible to tell, if anything, that it was more ruined than before, more collapsed, little more nor than a rust bucket, not rusty per se, but a heap of twisted metal and exposed wire. There were noises coming from inside, multiple clanks and clicks, as if someone were pulling it apart from inside. But the two explorers chose not to investigate, and in fact chose not to say anything at all to each other about the ship.

Finally the sun rose and, instead of blasting them with white-hot beams, it barely altered the temperature. Something had happened since the last time either of them had been outside the dome. It was a different sun.

Sun number two. They hadn't known, or been told, that the two stars shining on this world had finally traded places, though it might have been possible to guess from the recent rain that something unusual was going on. What had happened was that Blister Star had at last slipped behind its companion like a shy child behind its mother's skirts, and now here was the dim one, the subordinate one, and what a difference it made. For one thing, they could look at it directly, like a moon or a planet, and not be blinded by its light. As a matter of fact, it was difficult for them not to stare at the thing for long intervals, because the surface of this sun was in some mysterious fashion very fractured, and marked by strange divisions. All across its surface there were narrow areas of intense blackness, cracks perhaps, but these lines were surrounded by areas of bright light, so that it seemed like a sun where dark archipelagoes floated on a sea of white lava. Or like a pomegranate, split open along its seams, revealing a nuclear and kaleidoscopic interior. All together the impression was one of frailty, of fractiousness. It seemed like a sun that had nothing to do with its companion, Blister, but contended only with itself, to keep from entirely falling apart and raining down its melted substance on the surface of its planet.

"I want to be the one to name it," announced Krell, mesmerized.

"Go ahead."

"Then I name it Brittle Star," smiled Krell, shyly, waxing unexpectedly poetic, and Knox for once could do nothing but nod in strict, surprised agreement.

And as Brittle Star—as that was from then on what we all called it— rose in the sky, and gave a hint of its projected arc, they understood where to direct their steps to advance north, toward the pole. It was bitterly cold, at least in comparison to what had gone before, and they were grateful for the fact that their unis were equally as warming in the cold as they had been cooling in the heat. Still, just as in the heat of Blister Star, their hands and heads were vulnerable to the cold, and after a few hours of trudging along, Knox noticed that Krell's ponytail had developed a thin dusting of frost, and he reached out to brush some of it off onto his palm and show it to his comrade.

"I don't get it," said Krell, rubbing the coolness into his skin. "I didn't think this world was supposed to have any moisture."

"Any moisture? Didn't you see that rain the other day?"

But it turned out that Krell had had no idea of the storm, and was surprised to hear about it.

"Everything's fishy here lately," said Knox. "The rain tells us that there's water on this planet somewhere. All right, but big deal, it doesn't matter, because we can fabricate water in the dome, and not really care whether it rains or not. But if we melt the ice cap, that might make a huge difference in the climate here. With all that water spread around, we could be in for rain all the time."

"I welcome rain," answered Krell, in an imperious, off-handed tone. "If you live in a dome, you get to laugh at the rain. Ha ha ha."

"That's not my point," frowned Knox. "It's that this planet wasn't designed for that. Oh forget it, Krell. The way I see it, and I know you don't, is that everything the trustees do here is a violation, a crime, a strangulation. A crime much worse than anything any of *us* committed."

"I do understand you," answered Krell, testily. "Some of us welcome change and some of us are enemies to it."

"So you like all kinds of changes."

"What's not to like?"

"The whole place, the whole thing. Don't you see how they've designed this world for ninnies? Or worse, for tourists, the most passive ninnies of all. They've actually admitted that now, and of course the whole idea makes sense. They're engineering things for those who only want to see what they've already seen in their heads. The planet they wished for, rather than the one that is. There's a maxim in there somewhere."

When Krell made no reply to this outburst other than a low growl, and left the conversation hanging, Knox felt supremely satisfied. Maybe it was the end of cosmic time, so none of this mattered. Say that the planet, just by the act of liquefying one polar ice cap, would be severely disoriented and even made to wobble into disorientation and destruction. Say that melting the ice would, in a way, melt the world. But the cosmos, and all the people in it, are just that: moments in an endless series of meltings and freezings. So just keep walking toward the pole.

———

After a time they moved, as if by agreement, toward the nearest canal, and because it pointed directly north, they followed it, walking near the edge, tiptoeing dangerously sometimes, and glancing down when possible into its gleaming interior.

"Remember the idea that the canals would be turned into highways, and that we would all be given a high speed car?" reminisced Krell, dreamily.

"Actually I don't."

"Of course I wish we had a car like that," Krell sniffed, never far removed from some fit of petulance. "I don't think any human, low gravity or not, is capable of walking all the way to any north pole."

"Not much further to go," observed Krell, not thinking of their trip, but thinking of end times.

"What do you mean? Dr. Chemo said it would take a week of walking to get there."

"Listen, if you wanted, you could try walking in the canal," suggested Knox, feeling that it would be good for the two of them to separate. "Look how glossy it is. Maybe you could sort of slide or skate along, use less energy."

Krell laughed. "Oh, how did you know?"

"Know what?"

"How I hate to walk, but how I love to skate," he said, readjusting his daypack, sticking his breath wand in his mouth a little deeper, and walking faster than before. By nightfall they had advanced, in Knox's opinion, a very impressive distance.

———

That night, their first outside the dome, they were cheered and psychologically warmed by the pencil of crystal light put out by a ray wand set at its lowest output, and sufficiently comfortable in their fabulous unis, sitting cross-legged on the ground, negotiating the delicate act of tube-breathing and eating at the same time. Stars were out, and naturally they stared up at them, particularly at one strange rounded mass in the sky, a ragged bird's nest of stars, surrounded on the edges by empty space turned black by its own bottomlessness. Or toplessness.

"Horsehead?" asked Krell.

"I'm curious to know something," said Knox, not paying attention.

"What crime did you commit, Dr. Krell? I'm not saying that it matters."

"What crime, what crime, you say."

"That's right. Your crime. Your atrocity. I've been trying to read it in your face."

"That's supposed to be taboo."

"The crime, or talking about the crime, or reading faces? You don't have to say a word about anything if you don't feel like it."

After a while, Knox re-introduced the topic. "It's just that out here there's a feeling of freedom. Don't you think? I thought for once two people could speak freely to one another."

"Let me think about it. Maybe I'll tell you later," said Krell, wiping his mouth with his ponytail.

"What about *your* crime, Knox?" he said at last.

"That's a question you don't need to ask, because you know very well what happened. You pretend not to, but you do know, and I know that you know because on the journey, on the *Antibody*, you told everybody about it. You broadcast it, you even turned it into a maxim. I didn't care that you did. You know that too."

"Have you ever considered repeating?" asked Krell, his eyes shining buttery yellow in the glare of the single light. "I mean another strangulation."

"Another?"

"Sure. Say, of me. Or Zelen."

"I am as harmless to you as a little baby boy," laughed Knox, stepping around the topic lightly, but self-consciously. "Soft as Chemo's naked body. While I do feel as if I could murder someone every now and again, it certainly couldn't be you."

"Do you mean to say that you killed the person you strangulated?"

"The correct term is *strangled*."

"Did you?"

Knox decided to lie.

"Yes," he said, shifting his lips to convey something like the hardness of a killer.

"And you feel proud about that now?"

"I feel all right," laughed Knox. "Filled with remorse, if you like. Here is what I like to say about my crime, about my punishment, since you ask.

That all men should die a violent death, in order to taste, for once, their own brutality. After that, everything will come up roses."

"Roses. Roses come up?"

"Never mind. The roses are on their way. They'll be here soon enough, even on this planet. Don't you feel that there's always something on the way? If there are no gods, then, once humanity is extinct, the gods will probably have a chance to be born."

"Oh!" blurted Krell. "You remind me of a joke I heard, Knox. How do you stop a trustee from walking that stupid walk of theirs?"

"I don't know."

"Shoot. Shoot him. Or her."

"What?"

"Listen. You fire at them. Then there they are, dead in their tracks. No more walking like that, and no more walking at all."

Was it being issued a ray wand, wondered Knox, that made Krell think of shooting people? At any rate, while this was a side of Krell never revealed before, all he could think at the moment was, why not just strangle, or even strangulate, which now seemed like the better word? And if it came to that, he wondered if he could manage to leap and throttle before Krell had a chance to aim his wand.

But he said nothing, rattled by all the complexities in his partner, and in himself. Exile changed everything, and that much more when you were free to wander through the landscape of exile.

A certain number of days later, they reached the region of the polar ice cap.

————

From a great distance, when it appeared as a straight white stroke across the whole horizon, icing on the cake of the world, there was no reason to think it was not made of pure H20. But now, closer up, it began to look mottled and impure, more curdled perhaps, a dirty cheese topping to the yellowish dirt found everywhere else. The two colors juxtaposing like that, the urine yellow and the cheesy whiteness, gave the impression of a nasty wound, that the planet was oozing pus at its crown, and Knox felt a touch of fear to think that here was evidence that the planet was alive, in the way that animals or at least other unknown phyla are alive. Not an intelligent planet maybe, but it could be breathing underneath them, feeling the tread of their feet. It could be waiting, like a sunbathing tortoise mistaken for an island, to flip its intruders off, in this case into outer space. After all, it had suffered more than simply being walked on, with numerous wounds now criss-crossing its skin since our arrival. It would come as no surprise to find that here, at its crown, it had squeezed out a planetary discharge, if that's what it was, since that was sometimes a way organisms had of purging themselves of foreign bodies.

Such as ourselves.

But still the two prisoners had to walk and walk, much farther than it appeared, in order to get right up to the cap and find out what it really was, and even then, like a mirage, the whiteness at times seemed only to move backwards from them, like a rapidly receding hairline.

"Don't look at it," Knox warned, suddenly a seasoned polar explorer. "It's playing with us. Keep your eyes on your feet. The cap doesn't want us to know what it looks like up close."

He followed his own advice and watched his uni-footed steps for awhile. Then when he did raise his eyes, it was to discover that the cap was right there, a few steps away, a wall of ice about the same height as themselves, the surface of it, at eye level, stretching to the horizon. Rush up to the wall and touch it, something inside him demanded, but he felt shy, deferential. The problem now was that the substance, ice or not, glinted so brightly that he had to cover his eyes and squint at everything through the cracks between his fingers.

"Oh Lord!" moaned Krell, dropping to his knees, then to his hands, as if shot by a distant sniper. But it was only to pray. However, it soon became clear from his mutterings that it wasn't a prayer to any spirit being at all, but merely to the trustees, thanking them for sending him safely all this way, but also damning them for not providing some goggles to shield against the strong white glare.

"Otherwise I'm blind," he wailed, sitting up and pulling the skin below his eyes downward with his hands, as if to make his expression more vulnerable, more puppy-dog.

"Do this trick with your fingers over your eyes," advised Knox. "See what I'm doing? Like making slits? It helps. Meanwhile, let's check if the holy trustees answered your prayer before you uttered it. I bet they did put goggles in our packs."

It turned out they had. So the two of them continued walking along the periphery, two men with goggles on. What to do, what to do, was the only prayer that Knox could repeat and revolve in his mind, and because there was no destination for his prayers, there were no immediate answers. His daypack, as he had already verified, contained a number of little thermal wands, supposedly to be dropped into holes drilled by the ray wands, but what *really* was to be done with them, or what was to be done with Krell, were mysteries yet unsolved. So he centered his mind, why not, it always helped, on Mhurra, pointing to things on the ground that he thought she would want him to point to if she were there walking with him, or better, point out things not to her but to that portion of himself that could be labeled Mhurramind, Mhurra portion, just as she had instructed. So, look, dear portion: a stone more white than dun, curved and slightly pointed at one end like a dinosaur's egg; a boulder shaped like an easy chair, and a spire of rock next to it shaped like a lamp; a dust devil shaped like a dog chasing its tail. Like a dog, it veered toward them for a moment and then veered away, as if asking to be chased, then dissolved into the shape of a planet, and vanished.

Naturally, the Mhurra portion was delighted with all of these things, and the remainder of him, by way of the interweaving of souls, was delighted as well.

And what, at that very moment, might Mhurra be pointing out to that portion of herself she called Knox? Her Knoxmind? Maybe, in some garden on Earth, an iris with furry anthers. Maybe, perched on some ruined wall, a decrepit fellow ripping off a grasshopper's wings before scarfing down the thorax. Maybe, in her kitchen, a calendar on the wall with a date circled in red, showing he'd been gone two years, perhaps two years to the day.

"Be patient with me," he said out loud, both to Mhurra and to the poor guy eating the grasshopper.

"Why?" scowled Krell.

"Oh, not you. I was talking to someone else."

"Oh yeah? You know what they say. Even minor criminals are famous for eventually going mad."

"If you want to know, it was a goddess that I was talking to. Understand? Praying to her to get me off this rock."

And though he meant it as a joke, it sounded, as the words came out, intelligent and true. After all, what if his extraordinary Dr. Mhurra were exactly that, goddess-y, and had the power to reach out toward the Horsehead Nebula, and swoop down her hand from space and grab him up in one cupped hand, as if he were a misplaced figurine, then set him down gently on the planet where he belonged?

Krell went on to say something about his atheism, but Knox didn't listen, as he was suddenly recalling a time when the two of them, Mhurra and he, were out for a walk, and she had suddenly bent down and snatched up a lizard for study. However, its skin completely sloughed off in her hand, and she held up the ghostly lizard shell for Knox to admire, while the reptile scurried away, freshly scoured and reborn.

———————

Their eyes protected by their high density sun goggles, they could reach out and touch the low glistening wall that stood before them. They could absorb, palms to oily surface, its shocking and then very satisfying cold.

"It's ice," observed Knox. "It's discolored, but it's ice."

"Don't you think there's other stuff in there too besides ice?"

It was true. What Knox discovered, when he looked more closely, was agglutination. Some other parts, relatively opaque patches that gave off trails of vapor when touched, were carbon dioxide in its frozen state, and the whole endless mass of it was marbled with dirt and other items and splotches of darkness, dryness, oiliness, cheesiness. But the top of the cap, which was low enough that they could reach up and rub their palms on it, seemed mostly pure and glassy and smooth, like the top of a white piano.

Knox remembered then an old story, about a flesh-and-blood man, and a woman formed entirely of fog, who met and fell in love. Ecstatic love! Oh, but so what. In time the fog woman dissolved, and then, in time, he of course dissolved as well, just more slowly, dust-to-dust style. Whatever force it was that shaped her out of mist had lost its power, and years later the force that shaped him out of flesh and blood lost its power as well. So even if one learned to emit affection, like a bulb emitting light, and find that one could love even such a planet as this, and regret its transformation, its tarting up—still, the planet was no more immortal than he was, just longer lived. In this case he was the fog, and the planet was the flesh and blood. Wherever Knox went when he died, the planet was sure to follow. But was that a reason to like it here?

"Shall we proceed now or later?"

Krell was already on his knees, opening his daypack, and these words and movements startled Knox out of his thoughts.

But he said nothing.

"Um, what day would this be?" asked Krell, pausing to squint up at the sky.

"What day is it? You mean day of the week? How can you ask that?"

"I ask because there must be days here, just like back home."

"Then name the day. It's your opportunity to name one."

"All right. Then today is Krellsday."

"No. It's Knoxday."

But now they sounded like an unfunny comedy team, and they shut up.

"Even if there were days with names," Knox said after a while, "we're at the north pole, the one place where there aren't ever any days. It's just one long day here. Or one night."

And saying this, Knox felt as if he had failed, once again, to match up with the moment, with the general time known to everyone else. Here, at the ice, the past and the present and the future were all ironed out, flat as a frozen sea, and so he was not surprised by the sound of birds chirping, rocks splitting, rockets flying low overhead. These must all be things that had happened, or would happen.

"Knox, are you listening? Should we climb up there and insert the melting devices? Now or later? What do you think?"

"When we reached the ice we touched it," murmured Knox, still fingering it, sneezing, thinking of extinct birds, reunions with lovers, about how remarkably wintry it would probably be if they didn't have their unis. "We made a connection with it. The ice, I mean. What I say is that we don't melt it at all."

"All right."

"All right?"

"Sure. I don't care."

"You surprise me."

"I surprise myself sometimes."

But what if it was a trap? What if Krell had been instructed to provoke Knox into some act of disobedience?

"Listen," said the latter. "It's a couple of meters high, or less, so I say we hoist ourselves up on it, and keep exploring."

Krell smiled, and seemed pleased with the plan, like one who had no particular one of his own, and, after helping each other, slipping backward, mewling like kittens as their feet fought for purchase, eventually standing up triumphant on the great surface, Knox felt himself on stage, like Maxim Illion, ready to declaim, to change his life, or at least make life-changing remarks.

"Ice skating!" shouted Krell then, and Knox couldn't help but laugh at the reasonability of the idea, because the surface itself, they discovered now, was indeed as hard as a rink, and one could even imagine that the line of low, egg-shell hills, just off to their left, formed a kind of natural stadium.

"Or ice dancing," smirked Knox, calmly, "with me as the instructor."

"I picture this," said Krell, wheeling around to his partner and grabbing him by the wrist. "I picture turning this into the colony's skating arena. Think of the tons of enjoyment!"

"And I'd like it to be the planet's hat. Its thinking cap. Every being needs beautiful headwear."

"If it's a thinking cap, can we skate on top of it? Will we hurt our little planet?"

"I don't suppose so."

"That's fine, then."

"OK, that's fine."

"That's fine that it's fine."

"Then we're fine."

And thus they agreed to proceed in whatever way seemed fit, sliding on their uni footies in as close an approximation to ice skating as was possible, stopping at one point to proceed cautiously around tiny craters they found in the otherwise perfect surface, depressions that Knox said were likely punched by meteorites and Krell said were likely scooped out by the sampling spoons of previous visitors. It was curious to note how the surface had a way of losing its shimmer all at once, would shift from alive to dead, as if a deep nuclear fire or other source of energy had been breathing out from below and then, maybe taking a dislike to its visitors, turning dull as dishwater. Though they didn't dare throw away their breath wands, there was the question of whether or not the air there might be free of contaminants, given how the ice itself seemed very cleansing. They looked at each other with longing eyes, understanding each other, taking their wands out of their mouths for longer and longer intervals. Knox, spinning in a circle, crouching, running in place, thought far ahead and was especially anxious to know if the pole might be, once they strangled or at least fake strangled all the trustees and escaped from the dome, a place to build a new city without a dome, a city to be called, by its founders, Airville. It may well be, he thought, coming to a halt because he was running out of breath, a place to breathe without thinking about breathing, a place to feel alive at least in a pulmonary way, at a level of molecular purity that might in some ways mimic a purity of spirit, a purity of exile.

For anyone who has never peered inside a vertebrate's body, it is always a nice surprise to see how alike we all are. There is the heart, the liver, the stomach, the kidneys, the lungs, all nested in more or less the same pattern in all the higher animals.

Inside any lizard, for example, the heart has that familiar heart shape, only in miniature, and, as in us, appears to have grown like a bean on the stalk of the esophagus. Also, as in us, as Mhurra explained, creamy white is the wrong color for lizard hearts. That means it's artificial, that someone has been tampering in there, extracting the real heart for its modest value and swapping in a tiny heart wand in its place—usually, unfortunately, a nearly expired wand. When the lizard dies a few days later it looks like a natural death, giving the thief time to move on to some other region and perform a quick surgical transaction on more lizards.

Knox came to know about and see a number of these fake hearts, learning how they worked, and because there were always rumors of organ harvesting among convicts, it occurred to him at those times when he became quickly exhausted that he might have a human-scale version in his own chest, replaced during secret penal surgery. Better not to strain then, and now, better not to overdo the polar movements. So he planted his feet far apart, took some long inhalations on his breath wand, and settled every limb and organ down. Now what? Quivering Krell was heading on without him, no need to object. Stay close to the edge, he decided, ready to leap off the ice at a moment's notice. What is the opposite of claustrophobia? For a moment he thought of yelling something to Krell. Are you joyful and sickened too?

But his partner was sliding back in his direction.

"What do we do now?" asked Krell, his arms wide open, launching himself into short little sideways slides, dancing, in fact, and appearing transformed, in his dancing, into something more than what he had been, or what Knox had allowed him to be.

"Get to work!" yelled out Knox. "Get out those drilling ray wands, now!" He was kidding, really, testing, and he wanted to put on an extra gruff and stentorian voice, but it came out squeaky.

"I think you mean I should get out the party wands," trilled Krell, and merely to show off, he jumped and came down in a kind of half-split, sliding several centimeters on his uni footies, but then sticking, and badly stumbling.

"A pair of skates would fix that," he observed, massaging his belly.

Meanwhile, overhead, Brittle Star hesitated, shone down on them in fits and starts, like a bad light bulb, but when it was steady it was beautiful to see how its cracks, or whatever they were, reflected everywhere in the ice that spread out before them, so that the whole of the north pole appeared to be crazed and crevassed, though it was not.

"Oh, for a maxim right now!" proclaimed Knox. But, more to his joy than his annoyance, he couldn't think of a single one.

There came a sweet faint screeching from somewhere far off and irrational. On any silent and extremely distant planet, noises of any sort are naturally horrifying. This one started out that way, raising the hair on their arms, but then, after a second, it sweetened, turning into something more pastoral. As in the bleating of a sheep. Or a shepherd unsure of how to play his flute. But all this was happening on an observably dead planet, and therefore not happening, unless our explorers had crossed the border into some inside-out zone. Both of them heard the screech, distinctly, but both felt immediately safe and cheerful in believing that it was made by the other, like some bestial clearing of the throat, or a shepherd-like passing of gas. And neither said a word.

Instead they lay on their backs on the ice, determined to be ecstatic, trusting their unis to retain body warmth, staring straight up into the blue. Knox thought about the screeching some more, and realized that, like other examples of his imaginings, it could come from the future, or the past. Half an hour slipped by, a time of subtle levitation but also stagnation. Impulsively, perhaps suicidally, he set his breath wand down on the ice, and left it there for the longest time, betting at last that the air held no danger.

As far as he could tell, it didn't.

"I have a new maxim," he said at last, speaking more freely and with more enunciation.

"Okay," whispered Krell, reverentially.

"*Of all our faults, the one hardest to forgive is our inability to see our faults.*"

"Heard it before."

"You did?"

"In the dome?"

"Yup."

So Knox furrowed his brow, as if that would help him to come up with something more original, but at that moment the shrieking recurred. And then repeated itself.

"You hear that?"

"I did."

"Me too."

"It's human," said Krell, whispering, drooling a little on himself as he uttered the words.

"Maybe not. Maybe animal," whispered Knox.

But they could just as reasonably have said it was a wraith, or a power tool, or the sound of some prisoner in surgery without anesthesia.

"There it is again," Krell said, but coinciding with it and speaking so loudly that he almost drowned it out.

"Again."

The next shriek, minutes later, felt so expressive of pain that it might have broken harder hearts than theirs.

"It's coming from over there," said Krell, gesturing toward the low bare line of hills. "It's coming from that canyon, the one that's closest to us. The one that looks so cold inside."

Knox peered into the gap that Krell meant, a dark comma between two hills, but saw nothing.

"Oh, come on," frowned Knox at last. "There's probably some sheet of ice in that canyon, like a glacier. I remember hearing that, for a fact, glaciers tend to groan."

"Hey, you lost your breath wand."

"No I didn't. It's right here. I wanted to try breathing without it."

"Okay, me too, then," said Krell, taking his out and casting it carelessly aside.

"So what about my groaning glacier theory?"

"I don't think so, Knox. There's someone in there. Someone followed us from town and now they're up in the canyon, in some kind of trouble, and we've got to go check for ourselves."

"You make it all sound very routine."

But Knox had to admit that there was a human note of pleading, as if someone was tied up, and someone else had a knife, or a ray wand, or a heavy and abrasive rock, and whatever it was was being applied very slowly, as in the ancient days of human torture.

So Knox lumbered up to his feet, expecting Krell to follow, but when he looked back, there was his companion, still flat on his back, and holding his hands to his ears.

Their eyes met. Krell put his hands down, and at that moment the ghostly cry came again. Knox winked, and Krell laughed. In a way, the two of them were friends.

———

Shift forward a few weeks, though, and things became more difficult between them.

Knox fell in love with Zelen. Not really. Not like that. But in a way.

All of us, at least all who were still paying attention to each other, knew something was going on between the two.

If the alpha of love is foolish obsession, and the omega is devastation, Knox stalled in a series of letters somewhere in between.

"Sorry, sorry, sorry," he often mumbled, in that period, to no one in particular. He didn't really know the woman very well, and was always about to ask the questions that would lead to understanding her better, but in the end he realized he would never be comfortable with such depths of understanding.

There is such a thing as falling in love with someone you're not in love with.

Most times he let her go on speaking, squinting at her, neutral toward her, neutral as the planet. Sometimes as he spoke, she was, he understood, squinting at him for the same reason.

And why shouldn't they be alike, two criminals? We were all rather similar. Her demeanor fell somewhere between attraction and distraction, as did almost everyone's.

"Don't call me Zelen, call me Zelly," she said once, speaking very hastily, smiling more than usual, fiercely twisting a floppy handful of her uni in her fist, as she often did recently.

For Knox, that was exactly what he could not call her. He couldn't see how he could get casual and animated about anyone, and this invitation from her, as he saw it, to be less isolated, now that a couple of years had gone by—hadn't they?—turned him slightly inside out. One hand in the air, one hand on his heart. Binary starry-eyed. Everything preposterous. So he often sulked in his cell, lying face up on the floor so he could keep an eye on the couples' footsteps through the ceiling, their heels and soles patterning overhead in circles and lines, like vintage dance instruction diagrams.

One day it felt that a less criminal thing to do would be to walk upstairs and present himself forcefully. He got part of the way, and gave up.

Once he turned over to lie on his stomach, and there, directly below him, was his downstairs neighbor, prostrate in the same spot, looking straight up, and though the material wasn't transparent enough to make eye contact, still it was unnerving to be nearly staring into someone's eyes, and he quickly flipped onto his back.

He hadn't thought much about it before, but of course she, Zelen, must be able to see him sometimes in that same way, and look down on him, if she chose, like a guardian angel, or a judge for an underwater swimming competition. And this degree of interaction might, he thought, be exactly right.

If there can be platonic couples, there can also be platonic voyeurs.

Meanwhile, it was a very slow, very punishing time. It felt as if we were all swimming underwater. It was the effect of living in a goldfish bowl that was more like a silverfish bowl, with all of us somewhat liking each other more and more, but also with a sense of not wanting to, of the grieving that sometimes comes, like a premonition, after the loss of a loved one, or friend, that more bad news is on the way.

Also, the official maxims had gradually grown more ugly and dispiriting. *Indolence is the laboratory of moral experimentation,* for example. But please, that was the last thing we needed to hear. You could say we were becoming more affectionate with one another. Some even intimate. But what if we were to admit to ourselves that certain desires came from something as simple as a sense of uselessness? Of primitiveness? *Even savages can seduce,* the speakers may as well have proclaimed.

As for Knox, he slipped into the persona of one who intensely dislikes all people, not just convicts, but innocent men, women, children, and mental cases in particular, and even allowed himself to make fun of Zelen in front of her husband, as if the two men could or ought to share some crude perspective.

"My God, how abrasive she can be sometimes," he once said to Krell, though out of earshot of the wife. Or other things, such as how he didn't like her sentimental side, or how he couldn't stand her fragile, gray, nearly overacted beauty.

Inexcusable, earshot or no. But he said such things anyway, more to himself, and repeating himself unnecessarily.

And Krell had no visible reaction.

He lay in bed one morning, in a stage between waking and sleeping, one hand rubbing purposelessly against his penis. In this vague state he inhabited a different portion of the area between alpha and omega, and dreamt that Zelen was walking across the room toward him. When he reached the halfway point between waking and sleeping he dimly perceived that she really was in his room, and that she was asking something about borrowing a glass.

"There aren't any drinking glasses on Mars, you dope," he muttered, dopey himself with sleep, then sitting up straight, aware of where his hand had just been, wondering if it was her plan to zip off her uni and slip into bed beside him, naked as plastic. But she was frozen, staring at him, loftily, with the expression of a prejudiced juror. Then she wheeled and walked briskly out of the room.

Later, Krell was so cold to him that he knew she must have related the rudeness of his comment to her. For her part, she actually seemed friendlier than ever.

———

When Knox and Krell, breath wands firm in their mouths again, reached the mouth of Cold Canyon, as they started calling it, they had a hard time maneuvering in the gravel, which seemed to Knox to show evidence of some ancient stream cutting through. But now all was dry, all of the rocks sharp-edged, nearly crystalline, pale as yellowish-brown gypsum. Sometimes they'd come across an especially perfect rock, the same size and shape as a birthday present box, with red striations very much like ribbon, and Knox would point to it, describing it to Mhurra or to the Mhurra portion, under his breath, until Krell started emulating him, but pointing to rocks that were not nearly so perfect.

The shrieking continued, as if routine, and they varied their speed, sometimes with and sometimes without the belief that they were on their way to rescue someone, or something.

Once in the canyon, they meandered as the canyon meandered, sometimes walking nearly shoulder to shoulder, sometimes in single file, avoiding contact with each other and with the nearly perpendicular walls of rock. Knox tried to pay attention, despite his lack of knowledge, to the strata divisions, the intrusions of blue and black rock here and there, the traces of history, some sort of history, in these rocks. There was geology to read here, if he knew the language. But why bother, he started to wonder, when the next corner might reveal the source of the sound, something that, likely enough, would kill the two of them, and leave all questions moot, and mute.

But, a quarter of a mile in, there was still no sign of anything out of the ordinary. It seemed they had made a mistake, imagined things, but the shrieks kept repeating, not often, somewhere further ahead.

Then, turning another corner, they found what they were not expecting.

Perfectly parked, brilliant and erectile, bullet-like and appalling where it reared itself between the narrow rock walls:

A stainless and needle-nosed rocket ship.

It came from another time, but not from an unknown place. There could be no question that it had launched, ages ago, from Earth. Some Earthlings or other had evidently beaten us to this planet, journeying here all the way from home, taking much longer, pioneers or maybe exiles who floated through interstellar space at the speed of everyday life, flames flaring out of the tail end of their ship with all the energy of a family campfire.

Of course we had seen such vessels illustrated in our childhood history texts, ships built by the so-called precursors, so Knox and Krell knew immediately what it was, and where it came from, but coming upon the real thing had to feel the same as rounding a corner on the street and bumping into someone recognizable only from historical portraits. This was fine for Knox, he could take it in, but he also had the sense that they had stumbled on a kind of failed venture, something embarrassing to those involved, and that really they ought to apologize, and slink away.

Both men realized at the same moment, pivoting toward each other, their eyes full of wild surmises, that they were both wheezing very hard through their wands, and that they were holding each other's hand.

"Do you think there's someone inside?" whispered Krell, between exhalations.

"Do you mean making the noise? No, look."

And Knox, regulating his own breath, let go of Krell's hand in order to point to an open door, or hatch, more than halfway up the body of the rocket, that was swinging on its hinges at the touch of some light breeze. As they watched, it blew closed almost all the way, then blew open again, and it was a little strain of steel at the end of that opening arc, they understood now, that gave the hatch an operatic voice, like the glissando of a heroine, or a mental patient.

———

So that was one mystery solved, and now there were a thousand others. Such as how to get Krell to calm down. To stop breathing in such a ragged way, as if he were about to clutch at his heart and levitate.

"It's all right, Krell. Try to think about Zelen."

"But do you think there's anyone inside?"

"After this much time? That's ridiculous. You're not thinking of Zelen."

"Yes I am. But what exactly is it?" asked Krell.

"You know what it is."

"I just can't understand why it's here."

"Let's see. Can you understand why the *Antibody* is here?"

"Not really."

"So there you go."

Compared to the *Antibody*, this ship was of course very primitive in construction and style, except that it was still possible to appreciate the way it perched very elegantly on its own nearly paper-thin fins, how its surface, a chrome and convex mirror, reflected the rocky surfaces around it, like a trophy mounted in a grotto. Then there were the scads of tiny rivets that appeared to fasten the craft together, like precious nails, thickly spaced at the bottom, where the rocket engines must have spewed fire, and thin at the top, bubbles rising in a glass.

Knox could hardly bear, after a long time of staring, to use his eyes in that way any more, and so he tightly covered them. Immediately he could see, in his fancy, the rocket at its moment of launch, blasting off in slow motion from where it stood. A narrator's voice came on then, saying, *This is what must inevitably transpire,* and then, more disturbingly, *You must remove knowledge in order to make room for belief.* Therefore, believe! After all, engines, no matter how primitive, fire. Rockets, even in the ancient world, take off, and this one, a remnant of a mighty past, might be ready to go, needing only someone inside to charge of the controls. Knox, with his eyes closed, could picture an antique knob engraved with an arrow, and in his mind's eye he turned that arrow to the mark on the dial labeled *Earth,* then used both feet to push a great accelerator pedal to the floor.

The next morning, Knox opened his eyes to find Krell already up and about, using a ray wand to warm food chunks, filling the air with a rusty, bready aroma. The day was clear and marbled, as was always the case under Brittle Star. Meanwhile, Knox's eyes felt all wrong. He had pressed so hard on them the day before, blocking out the present world and time with his thumbs in order to see the future, that when he stood up they felt loose in his skull. He went blind for a moment, lay back down again, and let the blue of the sky seep back into his vision.

"I have a little surprise," Krell sang out, turning it into a funny melody, his ruddy and toothy face suddenly blocking the sky.

Knox was reluctant to learn of any surprises. "No thanks," he muttered.

"No. Come on. Take a look."

It was impossible not to obey, as Krell was holding out both hands to show off four long and identical steel knives, handle-less, unpointed, and sharp only on the sides, as if designed for shaving, or cutting throats.

"Murder weapons?" asked Knox.

"Ice skates," frowned Krell. "Skates for the ice."

Knox felt his stomach shrink. "Where did you find them?"

"Made them, you mean. While you were still asleep, I cut these beauties out of the edge of those rocket fins, one from each fin. Flimsy steel from dark times, but good enough for us. So now we can race, if you like."

"You did that," pronounced Knox, giving a verdict, though his voice was gravelly and weak. "You did do that. Cut the ship, I mean. Ruin my plan."

"Oh, don't," said Krell, angrily grabbing his ponytail and squeezing it, milking it.

"I didn't hurt it," he continued in the voice of a child, squeezing continually. "Please don't make me your next strangling victim. I don't have the throat for it."

"Don't yourself."

"Just keep your hands to yourself, please," pouted Krell, as if putting off a boyfriend.

"But look how you've imprisoned me. Imprisoned everybody."

Krell stared, then cracked up, finding something funny in the situation, but soon moved a few steps away, and set himself to further work on the blades, carefully drilling out various holes in them with his ray wand, then proceeding to grind the four knies to greater sharpness against the surface of a nearby rock.

"We'll lash them to our feet with some rope," he explained as he worked. "I'll do yours for you. *Convicts Show Off Skating Skills on Distant Planet,* we'll call the newsreel. It will show on multiple screens back home, show us skating the figure eights that we are about to execute. That's how to go about feeling better about me cutting up the ship's fins, which I'm sure did them no harm at all."

"If you say so," Knox muttered, lying back, unable to bring himself up to any describable condition.

But he had the same condition as the rest of us. Here we are where we are, where we don't belong, but where we can be found. Life intruders. Employees. The rocket will be great for the coming tourists! They will want to have us lead them through the canyon to the site of the antique craft, an unexpected feature of the planet and part of the romance of a bygone age. Then thoughtlessly but rather sweetly forgetting our criminal pasts, they'll hand us their cameras and ask us to snap them posing in front of the spaceship. Even then, though, mused Knox, someone will ask about the fins, and why someone has cut little pieces out of them.

———

Krell ended up displaying some wonderful craftsmanship in marrying the blades to the shoes, and the skates looked fantastic. Once on the ice, once balanced, pushing off with help from one another and sliding forward across the horizon, the highly sharpened edges lightly scored the white surface like pairs of delicate scissors, and what resulted from that was an urge to go all out, to ignore the fact that they didn't know the geography, to ignore Knox's misgivings, and find out what lay at the true pole, somewhere out there in the creamy center of the cap. It seemed best at such times, given the stretchy flex of his dancer's body, to clench both hands into fists, tighten the thighs, lower the shoulders, turn the hands into a double pendulum, and just skate hard, and straight. Straight ahead there was nothing, because there had never been and never would be a larger frame of mind, Knox decided, than the frame he had then and there.

Krell, who in some circumstances favored victory and in others fake victory, was all about speed, and was already a little ahead, if in some way this skating could be regarded as a race, and Knox was happy for the moment with not catching up, let alone taking the lead.

So they continuously fell without falling, gliding and pulsing like meteors down the slick surface, perpendicular, as they scooted north, with the revolving of the world underneath them, so that instead of a straight line they traced a very elongated spiral.

Knox knew how to skate, had skated as a child on a frozen pond that formed annually in an otherwise weedy parking lot, and the giddy, seesaw, crazy-legs motion he'd mastered there came back to him easily, abruptly, with a kind of seizure. It was clear within five minutes though that Krell was the one with the more powerful muscles, and that he was going to cut a figure in this world as one of those overweight men who surprise us with thunderous speed. Knox saw right away that he wouldn't be able to keep up, and sent up a shower of ice with his abrupt stop. For a moment he rested, breathing hard, then roused himself to skate just a tiny bit more, and did a figure eight or two, watching how little wisps of gas would float up from his loops, his lovingly drawn infinity signs.

Some daytime stars were out, visible in the deep blue sky of Brittle Star season, and it was a strange joy for Knox that those same stars could be seen reflected in a dim furry way in the ice, clearly enough that he could steer a course by them as the urge arose, and aim the point of a skate directly over each reflection in turn, slicing it in half as he glided. Connect the dots, and find a way home for Knox.

His eyes turned sometimes toward the nearby low hills, the low canyons, and he believed that once or twice he could hear the squeaking door of the ship again, and that it spoke to him in a new and different voice, and asked who are we, who are the precursors?

Our ancestors, is the correct answer. Men from Earth from long ago, space colonizers, madmen, maybe criminals. Or so the stories went. Everyone knew that much history. The tyrannical and brilliant precursors, or preekers, as they came to be called. Certainly they were mad and savvy enough to come this far, that long ago, thought Knox. And at that moment he became determined to board the ship.

Krell, by then a small figure on the horizon, a point on a line, was fading from view, and then was lost entirely to sight. Perfect. Knox hurried to the edge of the ice, undid the skates, found his breath wand, and sprinted back toward the canyon, knowing that Krell might come streaking back any minute across the ice and catch up with him.

It was simple enough to climb the rickety ladder, with only a tight squeeze at the end to get his body through the hatch and into the intimidating darkness, there to get such a blast of some foul odor that he

131

nearly fell, nearly tumbled backwards out of the ship. But no, he could hold his nose, no time to worry about such things now. Maybe it was the smell of the past, as well as the smell of his own ecstatic future.

The first chamber he found himself in was tight, oppressive, with curving walls that were thick with old tech: needles, levers, calibrators, thermostats, meteor coils, broken suspension springs that drooped out and down from the ceiling. Immediately there came to him a heart-sinking impression of impossible age, of inoperability. Dozens of dials, but what might they measure? Dozens of flip-switches. For what? To make matters worse, one wall of the room had been severely damaged by something, perhaps an explosion, as there was a jagged rent there, steel ripped open and out like cloth, and on the floor were piles of broken glass and a few tiny meter needles as fine and black as brush bristles. No convenient dial that one could point toward Earth. In the middle of the room stood a table, presumably some kind of navigational area, as it was covered with old charts, dotted with stars, printed on paper that cracked and crumbled at his touch. Had they really needed paper maps to know where they were going? Flying such a craft, he could see, was a forgotten art, like sewing a button hole, or playing a card trick, or remodeling a house. Meanwhile, he flipped a few switches, pushed a few preposterously large red buttons here and there, panic buttons perhaps, trembling at the possibility that the thing might instantly shoot up into space. So long, Krell! Meet you back home! However, after all, there was no way of knowing how long such an antique craft would take, and just imagine the joke of getting all the way back to Earth and cracking open the hatch to find Krell and Zelen waiting at the bottom of the ladder, grinning, ready to embrace him, having served out their sentences on the penal planet, gone home on a speedy new kidney craft, and now were pushing their grandchildren forward for introductions.

In any event, it was the case that no matter how many combinations of buttons and switches he tried, the ship didn't make a sound, or tremble, or lift off, or explode in a ball of flame.

———

As his eyes grew used to the dark, Knox made out the entrance to a spiral staircase, with dark wooden handrails, steps leading down to some lower level. So down he climbed. There was hardly any light to see by as he descended, but in fact, as he kept going, the foul smell diminished, so much so that it felt like a great relief to go that way, despite the dread that always comes to any of us when lowering oneself into a pit of darkness.

For some reason one always imagines snakes, or worse, snake's eggs.

As his eyes adjusted, what emerged was another circular room, one level below and something like the first, but there were shreds and rags and strings hanging all around, as in a haunted house, draping nastily across his face if he took a wrong turn. After an initial reaction of disgust, he understood that these were only the remains of some fabric or tapestry that had once covered the ceiling, but now hung in wretched tatters everywhere. Here there were no dials, no switches. Just an atmosphere of abandoned domesticity and a circle of lounge chairs, outdoor furniture really, with aluminum frames and weavings of blue vinyl.

Tense and weary at the same time, Knox sat down in one. But then immediately jumped up, because in the middle of this circle he now saw something fascinating: an upright and tightly oval container, something like an old-timey pickle barrel, definitely made of wood, like so many things from the past. And of course he wasted no time in prying up the simple wooden lid, feeling that great secrets or objects must be stored in such a container, and by the little light that was there he saw inside a layer of lumpy objects the approximate size and color of footballs.

Vintage food chunks, perhaps? A way of sustaining himself away from the dome?

Sticking his head in, peering closer, he was disappointed to discover that said objects were nothing more than elaborately fashioned figurines, maybe half a meter in length, each one different. Pupils dilating, Knox began to make out a surprising level of detail. Clearly these were sculptures of particular individuals, with perfect hair and perfect flaws, eyes depicted as shut, as if modeled in a moment of sleep, or trance.

Pieces for an oversized chess board? Statuettes to decorate a terrestrial recreation room? Carvings for religious rites? Maybe the precursors, he speculated, had the habit of sitting in the chaises longues and watching as a priest performed some kind of service, a worshipping of the ancestors, or a simple tribute to loved ones left behind on Earth. Afterwards, it seemed, they stored these statuettes of loved ones in the barrel, and went back to piloting the ship.

It was another lost art. Who could craft such things today? Of course Knox felt compelled to look more closely, to understand, and so he picked one out, gently scooped it up, and held it nearer the light, as if he had turned connoisseur, and in fact he had had a class or two, long ago, in art history. To inspect with patience and passion, he recalled from those days, is to learn a little more of the human story, a little of the visions and triumphs of the past. As he turned the object gently in his hands, he could see it wasn't made of ceramic, as he'd first guessed, but of something denser, yet more vegetable, more brittle, like shale, but definitely baked, like a very heavy and stale cookie. Maybe it had been cooked in a mold, like a gingerbread house? In texture it was very smooth to the touch, polished, as if cooked with infinitely fine-grained flour, and it made Knox think of images he'd seen of artifacts from paleolithic times, over-endowed fertility figures, though the one he'd selected seemed meant to represent a man, a remarkable man at that, with a high forehead, expressive mouth, bony shoulders, arms crossed on the chest like an Egyptian, and even, at the center, the tiniest of penises, visible above a scrotum worked by the artist into very delicate wrinkles.

Knox awoke from his meditation on the advanced aesthetics of earlier times, and tried to connect further with the object by stroking the pair of curvaceous, pudgy feet solely for the sensual effect of it, then tickling the delicate and perfect toes. Finally there were the long, very claw-like toenails, which, when he drew them across the top of his hand, scratched five perfectly parallel fine lines.

Then what? It might not have been wise to touch the thing at all, especially if, as it seemed, it might be a sacred component of some powerful old ritual. It felt like sneaking into a church late at night, breaking the reliquaries, fondling the bones. But it gave a puffed-up sense of belonging, of lighter-than-air communion. As he stood there, featherweight, lightly puffing on his breath wand, his eyes adjusting better to the dim light, he considered for a moment the possibility of staying put. Of moving in. It was a shabby but homey interior—how odd but how perfect to hang wallpaper inside a space ship! And then there was the problem, unless he could find and revive the oxygen supply, of hoarding enough breath wands to stay here for any length of time. Best of all, there would be Krell—that is, no Krell.

Or even better, there would be no Zelen. Well, Zelen on the brain, maybe, but only for a while, and while he didn't yet dare pull out a second figurine, he had glimpsed, and knew he had glimpsed, and for some reason avoided, some that were obviously female and equally represented as nudes.

In the end, he wrapped up his masculine *objet* in a scrap of stellar-patterned wallpaper. Wrapped it to go. A souvenir. Certainly no one now could be said to be the proper owner of these things, as the preekers were long dead. He was tempted to rummage through the pile of statuettes in the bin to see if there might be a female version, one vaguely similar in appearance to Mhurra, but the desire struck him as excessively crass, and in the end he carefully descended the outer ladder with the wrapped figurine clasped tight to his chest, already falling in love with it, despite its sex, as if it were a cunning substitute for something missing in his life.

Back at the ice there was still no sign of his partner, and Knox instantly slipped the statuette into his pack, just in time, for here was Krell a moment later, braking to a halt with a great shower of ice, panting as if he'd skated the entire pole, which maybe he had.

"How did you do that?" asked the skater, putting his hands on his knees.
"Do what?"
"Beat me back here. You don't even have your skates on."
"I'm fast, but I know I didn't go as far as you. You were always ahead of me. I took a detour."
"Then you would have to say I'm the champion, wouldn't you."
"I would, and I do say so. Krell is indisputably the champion."

———

It is true that the year before, shortly after his initial arrest, Earth authorities introduced Knox to certain examination techniques, though nothing particularly painful. At first they tried, through an ineffectual use of his food allergies, to get him to confess to a worse crime, a robbery of millions from some treasury or other, but the result was merely some mild vomiting. Then they switched to reason and persuasion, but instead of pushing him toward admitting to any personal crime, tried to get him to denounce his wife. He was surprised that they would know so much about her—that she was a biology researcher, specializing in lizards, that they had been married six years, that it was a third marriage for him, fourth for her, that they went on long walks in the more squalid zones of the city, that her recent readings focused not on lizards but on teaching techniques, though she was not a teacher. In the stated opinion of his interrogators, such facts gave evidence of a bad character, and suggested that maybe she was the one performing the illegal heart transplants on the lizards. Could he enlighten them on that? Knox, instead of going silent, spoke up, and told them that everything they knew about her was correct, except for the transplants, which was ridiculous, and that the only possible complaint he had, speaking frankly, was that whenever he told her he loved her she responded in a subtly comic way, as if her love for him could only be expressed with a degree of satire.

It was not what investigators were interested in, but it was what he had been wanting to tell someone.

Later they switched to a different form of persuasion, this time obligating him to watch an endless stream of footage taken from a time when the Earth was covered in verdure and crystalline waters, all the while assuring him that they would untie him if he would just agree to sign a document that would detail other of Mhurra's crime that it was absurd to believe she had committed. His own crime, his degenerate act of strangulation, would still be punished, only lightly, and henceforth referred to in all reports as an example of human and generally forgivable neurosis.

You can go back and strangle anyone you like, was what he thought he'd heard them say, though of course it couldn't have been that. In the end, brought to tears by the endlessly heartbreaking images, he gave in, and with one curt nod, signaled his agreement.

The screen went dark. A moment later, the document was produced, his signature called for, and then, thinking better of things, he refused to make the deal. Still, they released him, and later he had great stretches of exile time to understand why. Even though he hadn't signed, he had agreed to, and that was a second crime that weighed far more heavily on his conscience than the first.

Since then, and he hoped this was a kind of revenge against them, against himself, he adored her, without her, with a brilliance that ignored her satires. A brittle star formed inside him, and why not admit that the paper and pens were partly about writing new documents for the courts, later to present them, crawling, when he got back. Dear Mhurra, he wrote, this time with paper and pen: You don't remember me, but I remember you. Your wit may be dry, but mine is sopping wet, not with tears, but with whatever fluid it is that surrounds the wit. Picture two brains, one labeled innocent, the other labeled guilty, floating in bright liquid in two laboratory beakers. The words are all around me all the time, like the liquid. Pain from another planet is already a book title. But the one I'll write is called two brains from another time.

———

Far back, far away, when Knox and Mhurra were first spending time with each other, she invited him to join her on herpetological jobs.

The job description that season was to get a count, within a predetermined zone, of frickling flies, the favorite prey of certain lizards. Mhurra had a research permit just for that year, and had to use it while she could to increase her salary. She spent time in a relatively unbuilt area, a gray zone between two cities, to sift through vacant lots, awkward ruins, tunnels, and count how many flies occupied an area that, before counting started, had to be measured and meshed off, to keep the flies inside. There was a keen public esteem for lizards, and a special affection for one species, the so-called cement lizard, with lavishly fringed toes and its ability to chew and digest cement scraps, a habit that let it adapt quickly to ruins. The task for Mhurra was not just to count the flies but to catch at minimum one lizard per day and deftly insert a needle camera into its head, so its movements could be watched on remote screens for the rest of its life (made only a little briefer by the camera), and maybe even broadcast to billions if the needle were inserted perfectly and the supervisors could craft an entertainment program out of it.

Much of this daily work of hers coincided with Knox's sabbatical, and, though he hadn't known her long, he accepted her invitation, and went out on the lizard quest every day.

One afternoon they found themselves further from tall buildings than usual, in a wide vacant lot. It was a vacant landscape, almost enough to give them horizontal vertigo. Obscured by weeds in the center of all this was the foundation of a ruined ranch house, maybe the first one ever built.

Most important, there were one or two acres of weeds behind it and a chance of finding what they were looking for.

"Can I be the one who puts the needle in the frickling skulls?" asked Knox.

"The fricklings are the flies. Flies don't have skulls."

"I meant the lizard skulls."

"Don't worry about that," said Mhurra. "We'd be lucky to see one, let alone catch one. Just help me with the flies."

Yet after a while he realized he didn't have to scan too diligently, because it became clear that there were no fricklings in the area at all. House flies were common enough, swarming around fresh piles of human feces, but the fly they wanted was absent, and soon they gave up the search. Also, Mhurra, stomping as she talked, constantly tucking her mass of curls into her hat, revealed something she hadn't mentioned before: she would get paid whether they found any flies or not. In the end, they turned the afternoon into something more carnival, or awkward lark. Once they decided at the same time to clutch each other's arm, as if grabbing at an offered cane or support wand. The clutch upset equilibrium, and they fell forward into dirt. Standing up, smacking their lips at the taste of the oily dirt, they took turns with their tongues to clean each other's mouth out.

Later, after a walk down a faint dirt road, with pauses for a few more and forever clumsy tonguings—it was as if each was trying to be the other's toothbrush—Mhurra, on a sudden impulse, broke away from him and jumped atop a fence. She seemed to have the idea of putting aside cleaning and putting on an impromptu high-wire act, throwing her arms out to the side for balance, laughing, falling off the fence, then hopping back on top of it to try again. Knox reached up to hold her hand for a second, but she was so well balanced, so good at it, that she threw away his hand like a cane a second after taking hold of it.

Later she pirouetted on a cement-anchored post.

They weren't right at the coast, but a smell of seaweed came up strongly on a puffy wind from the west. Mhurra called out to Knox to breathe it in, that it was a rare treat, but a second later she had forgotten all about him, and lurched around faster and faster, performing her pirouette, dashing to the next post, repeating.

And this went on until they came to a more mysterious fence, attached but perpendicular to the old one, and a bit higher. There were no posts or rails, just a ribbon of white, spongy plastic, or hardening wax, a seamless and brand new construction flowing away toward the ocean-scented horizon.

"Extruded from the soil," said Knox, aloud. He'd recently read of such processes.

"As long as it bears my weight."

"Don't get on top of that monstrosity," yelped Knox, suddenly male and peremptory.

"Why not?"

"Too narrow," he answered, putting in a fake laugh to make up for his outburst. "And too ready-made. What happened to craftsmanship?"

"What would be great," mused Mhurra, bouncing straight up and down, sure of her skills, childish but with the seriousness of one about to compete for a cheap prize, "would be to ice skate along it, exactly on the top edge. You think I don't have good balance, but I do."

With a note of grandeur she lifted her palms toward the wind, in a gesture of egomania, as if about to complain about Knox's odd sternness to a classroom of sea creatures. But then she dropped her hand and leapt up, frickling-like perhaps, to the top of the newer and taller fence, and here, holding her arms out straight again, she began to rotate them for balance, backwards, more frantically than before, unsteady looking and afraid looking.

"So toss me an umbrella!" she said, not looking down at him, inching forward.

"Say it again?"

"Didn't they have umbrellas in the old days? What did they do in the circus when they walked the tight rope?"

"I know it wasn't umbrellas," muttered Knox, holding up a hand to help balance her, though he could only reach as high as her feet, and knew better than to touch her.

"What did they carry with them?" she insisted.

"I think they held a bouquet of hair."

"Hair? Are you sure?"

"No, it was flowers. Daisies, I think. A bicycle?"

"I know. It was poles."

"Poles?" He could only think she meant north and south poles.

"For the really high wires. For balance. But I think a lovely lady on a low wire..." She nearly lost her balance here, but regained it. "I think a lovely lady on a wire, say about this high off the ground, would have an umbrella—I should say she would *sport* or *spurt* an umbrella."

"Spurt."

"Yes it's spurt," she replied, with an air of intense concentration, this time not on the fence, but on him. "Knox hates to be wrong, doesn't he?"

He hated in a way to watch her, but kept looking. In fact she put on a high-class act, ready for the stage, ready for the audience to love whimsy and grace. She was ready for the audience to love her.

"Oh and what if I do fall?" she said after a while. "Is that what..." Again she faltered, again windmilled her arms. "Is that what bothers you?"

"Nothing bothers me. You're a sensation. The instant success. It's just that if you lose your balance, and, imagine, fall away from me, I'm not sure you'd be able to get back."

It was a fact that the fence was high, two meters or so, though when he looked into the far distance, where it curved through a neighborhood of chocolatey brown structures, it only looked an inch high, like something from the perspective of a child.

"What's on the other side?" Knox asked. "What do you see when you look down?"

"Did you really think that flies have skulls?"

He didn't answer, lost in a kind of fizzy panic, and Mhurra's voice got smaller, more tightened.

"Okay, I'll *check*," she said, speaking with exaggerated annoyance. "Let's *see*. There's some kind of half tube running along forever. A plastic ditch, I suppose. And another wall just like this one on the other side of the ditch."

"Oh, jeez. Get down, get down."

And again he reached for her closer foot, determined this time to grab hold of it and snatch her down, like a statue off its plinth. Knox knew what she was describing, as he had read about the new drip trains, flowing like liquid in broad pipes, confined by walls to keep people out of danger, but it hadn't occurred that this endless fence, vomited out of the ground to grow up among weeds and broken cement, would be part of the route.

But Mhurra froze, as did Knox, because at that moment they could both easily hear the sound of something approaching. It wasn't loud, but obviously a train, a drip train, was not far away, growing not louder but lower in tone, as if supersonic, not hurtling but advancing, in the way that an overhead jet, if high enough, hardly seems to move. Seconds later there it was, horrible, bearing down, part of it visible above the fence, but only as a line of semi-liquid projectile. Under different circumstances, it might have been thrilling to see it streak by, to grab one's cap and wave it in the air at a new wonder of the world.

"Jump," he commented, icily, hardly able to get the word out, as he had already given her up for dead, already puckered his lips in kissing, mourning.

But instead of jumping away, because she didn't have time to jump away, Mhurra crouched down, compacting into the shape of an oyster. Gripping the top of the plastic with her hands to steady herself, it looked like she might be ready to jump. But the train at that moment streaked past, almost silently, with just a soft gurgle, the sound of a baby nursing on a bottle, moving with such speed that a significant vacuum formed, so much so that while Mhurra could hang on to the fence by her hands, her feet flew backwards, parallel, sucked in by the vacuum of speed, her body stringy and taut, and in that position she fought for herself, eyes shut, gripping tight. Knox's fingers could reach high enough to rub her furthest knuckles, and maybe that helped a little, though all he could feel there was how the knuckle bones kept inching up the wall as her body, on the other side, inched backward.

And the train was endless. It seemed to carry thousands of passengers, but then there were thousands more cars. But after an interval the butt end of it came into view and, with an electric beep, stopped where Mhurra now draped vertically on the wrong side of the fence. In spite of Knox's efforts to jump and grab at her wrists, or find some way to scrape her over onto his side, she let go, and disappeared behind the fence completely.

"Is everything in order?" he shouted, banging on the wall as if it were a door that she could open to let him in.

And then, surprisingly, not right where he was banging but a few meters to his left, there came a breath of warm air, and the wall did in fact open, the hard creamy material quietly softening and parting itself like a skin around a deep wound. A moment later about twenty workers filed out, marching off to somewhere with their workers' hats pulled low over their eyes, daypacks hanging over one shoulder. Probably government clerks.

They dressed alike, and none of them took the slightest notice of Knox as he tried to thread his way through them in search of love.

And there she was, red-eyed and wild-haired, at the end of the line, the last passenger, stumbling through the opening just as the drip train, its surface eddying and flowing, slid away again, slowly this time, then gathering speed, then vanishing.

"Mhurra."

Her mouth had an expression of intoxication, or religion. There was a tender wooziness to her movements, like someone stepping from boat to pier, and finally she let herself plop down heavily, cross-legged, on the ground, where she gained balance, then extended her hands back to rest, palms down, behind her.

"It was like a bird," she croaked, shivering, craning her neck wildly, as if wanting to escape from her own body. "I mean, I was like a bird."

"Stop dwelling on it. Think of something else."

"I won't. There was, I was, wonderful. A medieval romance. Though I was worried that I wouldn't see again. I mean see you again."

Knox looked at her everywhere, thinking there could be some hidden injury, but she was in a state of goofy transcendence and success. It had all been an accident, a foregrounding of tragedy, but now she glowed there, triangulating backwards with her locked arms, like one of those that spend millions to sit on the ground somewhere. It seemed to him, actually, when she walked through the wall, returning to him with her hair electrified and straight out all around her skull, that she had just then arrived from another world, an alien sent to repair planet damages.

"Not see you *exclusively*," she continued, talking out of the side of her mouth. "Worried that I wouldn't see anyone. You know. As a result of my braggadocio. For a woman it's braggadocia."

"You were like a rag," he said, sitting down to face her, holding his face in his hands, leaning forward to gently gently touch his forehead hair to hers. "Raggadocia, let's call it."

"No. That's where you're wrong. More like a bird." And inching back with hiccup-like spasms in her shoulders, she gave him a look of bewilderment.

"See everything my way for a minute," she continued. "I say like a bird because at that moment I felt like I had the gift of feathers, but all were slowly being plucked, sucked off, like I was being prepared. Like I was to be served."

Knox and Krell, Krell. Krell and Knox, Knox.

Mhurra and Zelen, Zelen. Zelen and Mhurra, Mhurra.

Knox continually rearranged these names around in his brain like food pushed to different sides of a plate, food that had lost its color and only appeared in varying shades of gray, none of it presentable, none of it alive.

As the two men shuffled away from the ice cap, missionless, dumbfounded, following the empty canal in order to trace their way back toward the dome, the less camaraderie they were able to generate. Or manufacture. An old distaste returned, and, taking the form of a third explorer, bedraggled and heavily bearded, only ever seen in peripheral vision, it walked sullenly between them, nudging them apart. Both of them, or perhaps all three of them, dreaded the dome. They sucked all the harder on their breath wands, the better to mask the dread with heavy breathing sounds. So it was, in the noise, that they missed the whisperings and other peculiar sounds that had begun to emanate from the bottom of the canal they paralleled.

Later, these noises—persistent snaps, birdlike chirps, pops and high-pitched murmurs—grew loud enough that the two of them, without speaking, started to pay heed, and so drifted slowly toward the edge, slanting their steps in order to see what was going on. At the edge, expecting to find fellow prisoners working on some maintenance job or other, Knox was surprised to note that the canal was as empty as ever, but that the glazed bottom was rent by cracks, some of them profound, some still forming.

"Oh God, it's the Yoohoos," hissed Krell, wheeling around to see if a gang was sneaking up behind them with palms outstretched, meaning to push them over the edge.

"What do you mean?" sighed Knox.

"Hammers. Somewhere they're hammering, wrecking the material. Jesus, they're more angry and powerful than gods."

"No, you're wrong. I think it's the planet that's angry. It's rebelling against us. Breaking itself to pieces in the process."

"No, you're wrong."

"Not this time, Krell. Believe me. I had the feeling that detonating those thermal wands would make the whole planet fall apart. Turns out it's falling apart anyway."

———

There was nothing to do but tiptoe further along the edge, agitated, finally unsure what more to say about the deterioration of the material that made up the canal. Later, with the dome coruscating like a pearl on the horizon, welcome and unwelcome sight, home and anti-home, the two men began to hear yet stranger noises emanating from the canal, and peering in again were astonished to see a clear fluid bubbling up from the cracks, whispering, rising, as far as they could see in either direction.

"There's a lake of stew," recited Knox, "and of whiskey too. You can paddle all around it in a big canoe."

"Oh, nothing," mumbled Knox. "An old song. A new maxim."

"Maybe it's rocket fuel, perfect for our getaway ship back there," suggested Krell.

"It's water, and it must be that there always was and has been water. In the clouds, in the water table. So excavating the canals was like digging a well— making a place for water to break through, now that the canal lining is cracking."

"But who would have thought there would be so much of it?"

"And if it fills one canal, it must be filling all of them. But the main thing is, it lets us off the hook."

"What?"

"Think about it," said Knox. "We failed in our mission. We decided not to melt the ice. But we don't have to tell anybody that. When we get back, we take credit for this water. We say we set off the heat wands, watched them go to work melting the cap, and here's the water you wanted."

"Okay."

"Okay."

"But what should we do with the thermal wands? They might notice that we still have them. Didn't detonate them."

Knox stopped walking and put a hand on Krell's shoulder in a show not of warmth, but authority. Warm authority. Krell was showing promise, getting into the habit of deferring to decisions made by someone other than himself.

"What we'll do," said Knox, "is bury the wands right here, and forget about them."

So they rummaged through their packs for something to dig a hole with, Knox careful not to let Krell catch a glimpse of the figurine. First they tried their beam wands, but those just heated the soil, even melted it, which made things worse. Then Krell, with an expression of someone who is about to play a practical joke, pulled out an empty verymouth bottle, and of course it became clear then that he'd had it from day one, and had been sneaking hits from it when opportunities arose.

"Sorry, Knox. It wasn't full when I packed it. I just had one or two sips this whole time, and that was enough to empty it."

"It's all right. I have no complaints."

"Anyway, I'm thinking we could use a heat wand to slice it on the diagonal. That way it turns into a kind of trowel. Two trowels, really, if you count both halves of the bottle."

Knox nodded, and with a flash of light, it was done.

"Krell! Good work. You're very handy to have around. Now dig the hole."

"But I just made the trowels."

"Then start out by testing which one of them works better."

"All right."

And before long Krell had dug the hole, not without grunting, heavy breathing, and flipping his ponytail out of his face a dozen times. But the cavity he dug was soon deep enough for the devices, as well as the two halves of the bottle tossed in for good measure, and a minute later they had stomped down hard on the loose dirt, and were heading south again, sticking close to the edge of the canal and in that way keeping an eye on the slowly elevating water level.

The moment Knox re-entered the dome, paused, and tossed away his breath wand, he felt a little sick for some reason, even began staggering down the street a little, as if the air inside had become silently poisonous. He couldn't get over the feeling that invisible fingers were wrapping and squeezing around his neck. On his hands and knees in the street, he couldn't remember how he'd collapsed. He wasn't vomiting but he was heaving a little. It was clear that whatever acclimation he'd once had to life inside the dome was lost, and now it felt like a suffocation, a confinement with a wasp-like stink of human secretions, a premature burial in a sarcophagus carved from white meat.

"I think I'm dying," said Krell from somewhere nearby, slurring his words, and Knox managed to stand up, only to see that Krell was sick too, kneeling on the ground, the same slick threads of digested material swinging from his lips.

"We're not so sick as all that are we?" wondered Knox, brightly.

"I don't know," said Krell. "But I have to stand up straight. Did you see that they're coming to greet us? I guess to acclaim?"

Knox looked up to see a group of colonists advancing toward them from down the street. A hero's welcome, he had to agree. A delegation charged with pinning medals.

But when the crowd got closer Knox saw that it had nothing to do with them.

It was a funeral procession.

The bereaved, heads bowed, were crowned with improvised mourners' hats, flimsy things made of feathery black plastic, an inappropriate substitute for the rich stuffs of more traditional funerals.

"Come on, everybody," said Krell, weakly. "Cut the clowning, now."

It wasn't said loud enough for anyone to hear. In the compacted air inside the dome, voices didn't carry.

Ashamed that waves of weakness and illness were washing over him just as a puzzle was presented, Knox had the urge to run forward, stop the procession, and announce the success of the canals, as if that would somehow reveal the general lie. Best to let everyone know that no one was going to die.

It was near the end of the day and the odd, mottled light of Brittle Star, distorted by the dome, had turned as dark as chocolate light on Earth, and the loudspeakers were broadcasting old style music, a classic piece from some historical era that gave Knox, in addition to his dizziness, an airy, hollow-in-the-head ache. Krell, next to him, put his face down toward his outspread hands, and began carefully crying into them, as if hoping to collect and save a pool of tears.

"You don't even know who it is," snapped Knox, raising his fist as if to knock some sense into the man.

But Krell seemed too upset either to imitate or flinch from the fist, and Knox let it drop, turning heartsick too, though angry about feeling that way. In the end he succumbed to tears himself over the fact that he was about to succumb to tears. The music was tragic too, and he had to wonder where they found such a piece, so appassionata and minor-key that it could bring anyone, convicted felons, to tears.

So Knox and Krell wilted a little more, then recovered their equilibrium, dusted off their unis, raised their hands in greeting to the passing mourners. Leading the way was Chemo, not dead, his tie limp as string, walking with the formulaic step peculiar to old-fashioned rituals, legs locked straight as a robot's, eyes rolled up to heaven at times in imitation of the dying. Butler-like, he carried a silver tray before him, in this case the tray for honoring the dead, and Knox was at that moment struck by the fact that the tray held not one name card, as was normally the case. Instead there were a dozen or more cards, all handwritten on creamy paper, all jumbled together, some of them overlapping precariously at the edge, as if Chemo had either been mixing them up on purpose or walking carelessly.

"Why the long faces?" blurted Knox. The comment seemed inappropriate. Someone way in the back was singing in a strident way, but the melody went at odds, like a siren, with the sad music of the broadcast. One name card fell off the edge of the tray and into the street, drifting to the gutter, and someone in a tattered uni, someone Knox didn't know, ran up and grabbed it. There, within arm's length of Knox, the fellow paused to scrape the scrap of paper along his cheek, like a razor blade. Others in the procession, who saw this gesture, echoed it, scraping their cheeks with an imaginary card, caressing themselves as if this were a rehearsed and conventional part of all funerals.

Knox glanced over, and saw that Krell was making the gesture too.

All right, said Knox to himself, not daring to speak out loud. This is the nadir. This is the worse way this could have gone. Imagine we all die here. Imagine we live here eternally.

"Funerals for the living!" he shouted at the mourners, because it was all he could think of to say, but his principal obsession was to single out Zelen in the crowd and place her in the category of the living.

He looked at his hands and saw that they were red and dirty, either from burying the wands or from the many times he had quietly stuck his hands inside his daypack to fondle the figurine.

The procession, made up of only twenty or thirty of us, did not take long to file past.

And there she was, near the end, almost unrecognizable. Her gray hair was much shorter than when he had seen Zelen last, buzzed down to pretty much nothing, and her skull had a prisoner look to it now, a bony and bumpy case for the kind of brain sketched out in rough pencil, drawn to crime. But at least he could proceed. At least that. And in her case, she didn't look terribly grieved, simply curious to see what would happen next, and while he was anxious to catch her eye, to grab her out of the procession to explain what had happened, he was too slow, because there was Krell approaching her, gathering her into his arms, then moving away with her, their unis unusually bright, two day-glo-green figures hand in hand, turning down a side street, but still visible for a while, refracted through translucent walls.

So Knox squeezed himself into a doorway, a spot to stand and watch, free of any urge to join the cortege, or enfold in his arms.

Now everything is possible, he thought, because everything is impossible. Vice versa. Every step in the wrong direction looks the same as every step in the right direction. First allot, second exhaust.

His throat felt colder and stiffer than he remembered it feeling, and he wrapped his dirty hands around it to bring some warmth there. Tightening his grip, Knox realized one could never strangle oneself because one's fingers would run out of strength at the same time one struggled for air. The worst damage that could be would be unconsciousness. Should he try it anyway? Then wake up, and repeat, and so on? Always, allot and exhaust.

"Tell me what happened," he demanded at last, speaking in a constricted voice to no one in particular, finally stepping into the street again, approaching the last man in the procession. It turned out to be Fermat, tieless, as he often was for the dance class.

"Twelve dead," Fermat declared, stopping in his tracks. "Not twenty-nine. Not three hundred."

To Knox it seemed as if the trustee were talking to the backs of the mourners.

"Fermat, it's all right. It's me, Knox."

"I know you." He seemed rational. "You're Dr. Knox."

"How is it possible? How could anybody die?"

"What do you mean, how? Where were you?"

"Krell and I were out on that job for a few days. The ice cap job."

"Don't know about it. I'm not in on things. I'm not trusted anymore."

"Are you sure it's twelve? Could it be more?"

"Not twenty-nine," grimaced Fermat, placing a hand heavily on the back of Knox's neck, like father to son, then putting that hand atop his own baldness. "There was an accident. Terrible accident. I didn't know people could die here, either. I mean I know they do on Earth, but for some reason I didn't think that happened on other planets. Well, now I know. They were trying to escape, but escape from where? We're supposed to refer to them as truants, but I guess they were just bored or something, and tried to go out and make it on their own."

"At the ice cap?" interrupted Knox, but focussing hard on his determination to say nothing about their discoveries there.

"No, no. Maybe. I don't know where. Anyway, they stole dozens of breath wands from somewhere, but didn't know they were used ones, duds. So they didn't get far, and when they realized the problem, tried to get back here. But their bodies were found just a little ways from the entrance to the dome."

"That's it?"

Knox kept worrying about his hands, how horribly dirty and dry they were. Evidence of digging, as if he had been the one assigned to bury his fellow prisoners. He wanted to ask Fermat for some more details, some names, but he just kept studying the red skin on the back of his hands, the veins that protruded there like surface roots.

"What do you mean?" he asked at last, "when you say you're not trusted anymore?"

"Just not. Not for a while now. They blame me for the escape, because I was director of inmate security. I didn't even know that's what I was. So I'm one of you now. See? No tie, brother."

They walked a while, Knox elbow to elbow with Fermat, both in meditation, keeping their heads down, but shifting eyes back and forth, toward one another, away. More than anything he wanted to show Fermat the figurine, but hesitated. People were perched above them, looking down from balconies. Visible in one of the lower cells was an older couple, perhaps husband and wife, both wearing the awful black crowns, except they had both pulled them down to circle their necks, like spiky dog collars.

"Fermat, how long have we been here?"

"I don't know. Do you have an answer? Why are you asking me?"

"I just want to be sure I've got a rough idea," mumbled Knox.

"I've got it calculated at something like—I'm really not sure—a year and a half? That about the same as you?"

"I guess so. I don't know. I thought maybe two. And I guess you know about the whole tourist plan."

"I've heard about it."

"And when will the exile—our exile, now that you're one of us—when is it supposed to end? It was supposed to be one year. Right? But now it just seems to me like we're waiting for the tourists, so that there's a new ship to take us back. In the meantime, we're effectively slaves."

"Slaves?"

"Aren't we?"

"Maybe, but guilty slaves. Don't forget our crimes."

Knox was surprised. "You mean how you let people leave the dome?"

"Well there's that, but I mean what we did back on Earth. Those crimes."

"But you were a trustee, not a prisoner."

"What do you think the word means? A trustee is a prisoner who's sufficiently cool to be in charge of other prisoners. My crime could be uglier than yours, for all you know. Now I let people die. Mostly the younger people."

Again Knox thought of taking Fermat aside into some alley to reveal the contents of his daypack, and tell him the whole story of the rocket, the preekers, everything. Maybe it was a story to inspire hope, though that was hardly clear. But not yet, not yet. Instead he merely slipped his arm through Fermat's, and they trailed the others in silence for a while. The music had ended, and it wasn't clear where the cortege was going, or why.

"Wait a minute," said Knox, after a while. "What's going on with the maxims? Wouldn't this be a perfect time for some observations on, I don't know, the shores of eternity or something?"

"No," said Fermat. "No maxims today, and none anytime soon."

"Why not?"

"Maxim Illion."

"What about him?"

"One of the truants. One of the deceased."

———

Later that afternoon, in his cell, lying flat on the floor, warding off what felt like a cold, or death, Knox tried to remember details of the deceased— at least some specifics of that afternoon in the street, the moment when he met Maxim Illion face to face, and thought he could love him. But lately he had a hard time thinking, as if something were whittling away at his brain, and all that was left there were random fragments of Earth, such as winter trees, misty street corners, blurred ballerinas, alarmingly close faces. Why so much blindness and deterioration, he wanted to know. That should be one thing that a new world teaches: seed new pearls, tap deeper veins, extrude out from the soil, dance like never before possible. But the breezelessness inside the dome had a flattening quality. After a while Knox got up, opened his daypack, peered inside at the peculiar figurine, whose features now reminded him of Illion, and at last extracted it, cautiously, only to grow nervous and put it back, afraid of accidentally damaging the thing, or of someone seeing him with it, or worse, finding himself entering into some kind of labored or embarrassingly needy relationship with it. Then he sat down at the table and wrote a few maxims about youth, about death, then crumpled those up, then uncrumpled them, as it seemed so wasteful not to use the other side of the paper.

In further honor of Illion, in further contempt of others, Knox turned to the page containing the phrases that had struck him at church that day:

Great powers.

Skeptical as a heretic.

Self absorb.

Useless escape.

Prefer the heart to be broken.

After a moment he drew a jagged circle around each one. His beloved pen was scratchy, spitting out droplets of ink as it scraped across the paper like a feral tooth, so the circles were really messy clouds, inky thunderstorms confining each phrase, except for the last on the list, where he crossed out *heart* and above it wrote the word *dome*.

Then directly over his head came the sound of shuffling feet. It was Krell and Zelen, apparently unfazed by the catastrophe, beginning a lively round of ping-pong.

Things changed. For one thing, those of us who still living had to be assigned to new positions, or even double positions. Krell, immediately understanding the implications, began putting on trustee airs, including a pasty smile and even the vaguest hint of a mincing gait. To underline his ambitions, he seldom removed his belatedly donned mourning crown, even contriving to pass his ponytail through a hole in the back of it so that it hung neatly behind, scrupulously free of crumbs. It must have been the right strategy, because Krell almost immediately began to be seen more often in the company of Chemo, who replaced Knox as the upstairs couple's most regular dinner guest.

One evening, though, Knox heard the familiar old invitational thump on his ceiling, and ran upstairs, pleased to get back to the prior eating arrangements—only to find Chemo already seated at the table, and Krell already well into his performance of what had become, since their expedition, a torrent of jingoism.

"Our attachment to the planet," he was intoning, as he handed Chemo the bottle, "must always be growing in both height and depth, *as well as width and breadth.*" Krell was undoubtedly getting better at it, and even claimed to have composed, without assistance, several maxims in the same vein. For the last couple of days the width and breadth adage could even be heard on the broadcasts—not surprising, now that Zelen had been given Maxim Illion's old job.

"What is good," he went on, obviously in top form, making the barest wink at Knox as he sat down, "is the progress the colony has made, thanks to both trustees and prisoners. What is better is to stay here for the long term, not as prisoners, of course, but in service to the crowds of tourists, thousands in time, that will be on their way to share with us the beauties of Mars."

"I don't think you understand the character of the modern-day tourist," observed Knox drily, at the same time thinking he should be as nice as possible toward Krell, out of gratitude for his never having mentioned a word to anyone about the skating, or the ancient rocket ship, or the buried thermal devices.

"The way I see it," continued Krell, not appearing to hear this, "we'll be the elite among the tourists, the ones they look up to, simply because we've been here the longest."

"Oh yes," put in Knox. "Krell's right. He always sees the beauty in everything, and now I see a wonderful future too. What a privilege it will be to work as tour guides here! As interstellar docents! Wait, I know—as canal gondoliers! Excuse me for asking, Dr. Chemo, but when that happens can we get new uniforms, with our names embroidered in big letters on the back?"

No one seemed to catch the sarcasm, with the exception of Zelen, who kicked him under the table, for reasons he thought he understood, but wasn't sure.

Chemo looked up balefully from his meal as if he were only then beginning to bother to listen.

"All I know," he sighed, peering at each of them in turn, "is that nothing is certain here. Everything's in flux. We're all undergoing a transformation. We're all evolving."

"Did you hear that, darling?" Krell said, beaming, teeth white as candles, turning to his wife with his mouth at a skewed and possibly ribald angle. "We're all *evolving.*"

"I heard it," she answered, neutrally, bringing a finger to Knox's arm again, as if every one of her remarks were made with him in mind, though she never directed so much as a glance his way. "I heard it and I don't believe it for a minute."

"But your disbelief *is* a transformation," observed Knox, staring at her, speaking only to her. "Ever since Brittle Star season began, I think we've all turned into skeptics in one way or another. We're cracked, we're uncertain. Everything has a thousand explanations."

"Like what?"

He didn't really have an answer to that, as his observation wasn't quite accurate. So he invented a few facts.

"In the streets I hear questions like, is there really any such thing as a Yoohoo? Maybe some trustee concocted that as a lie to keep us confined. Not you, Dr. Chemo. Why are we still here after two years? Or is it three? Maybe our new jobs as canal gondoliers, or whatever, won't be optional. Maybe it all amounts to a form of slavery."

"But it hasn't even been one year!" blustered Krell. "Our sentence isn't up yet, and you can measure it by the suns. When Blister Star comes back to the foreground, then you'll know it's been one year, because that's the way our orbit works."

"Any comment on that, Dr. Chemo?" asked Knox.

But the trustee had been intent on his food chunk and his drink, and only now, when Knox laid a hand on his shoulder, did he swallow and rejoin the conversation.

"Speaking of canals," he said.

"But we weren't," interrupted Knox.

"In that case we'll speak of them now," Chemo answered, in a slow and, even for the trustees, highly professorial manner, staring down his nose at the others, placing one finger on his forehead. "May I say that you two gentleman did a marvelous job melting the ice cap, and we all regret how, in all the turmoil and mourning you came home to, your achievement was barely acknowledged, let alone celebrated."

"Oh, that's all right," said Krell, fiddling with the angle of his crown. "We understand, don't we, Knox? Anyway, whatever reward the trustees have in mind for us, I'm sure what little we did doesn't deserve any special consideration."

"Oh, no, there's no special reward, besides a long rest anyway," said the trustee, opening his eyes so wide that it seemed like he was about to pounce on someone. "But there is a new position that's kind of interesting. Good for someone who hasn't much to do. Not that I'm suggesting it for either of you."

"Go on."

"It's funny. You alluded to it already, though in light-hearted fashion. You referred to yourselves as gondoliers."

Now Zelen's hand fell onto Knox's arm again, and remained there, warm and prickly even through the layer of uni fabric.

"It's not a gondolier job, of course, but you weren't completely off. Now that the canals are full of water—again, thanks to you—we'll need somebody to go out in a boat every day and conduct tests for a good while. You know, check the water for unacceptable chemicals, minerals, etc. If it stays as clear as it is now, and continually passes inspection for a few months, you know what? We could start using it as drinking water for the penal colony, and devote our fabricators to a more interesting liquid. What do you say to the idea, for example, of a locally made gin? Hmm?"

"Yeesh," grinned Krell, stroking his ponytail too rapidly, with alternating hands. "I'd say, I'll take a Mars-tini, barkeep."

But Knox wasn't listening. He kept going back to the word *evolving*, and, for a few dreamy moments, envisioned all of us morphing over time into new species, ones perfectly suited to circumstances, just the way certain cement lizards back home had evolved to survive their lung transplants. He had no interest in working as a hydrologist, or a ginologist, whatever the case may be—it was a position that struck him as demeaning—but the idea of a species that adapted to life in the canals was seductive, and he pictured himself then as a kind of sturgeon with a humanoid head, arms and legs evolved into fins, gills pulsing along the neck. He would spend all day undulating slowly and deliberately underwater, sometimes shooting forward in a surprising burst of speed, and devoting the remainder of his life to exploring, hunting, dreaming, flirting, mating.

—————

One day it felt like the town under the dome had died—or maybe had been put under a dome because it died, a specimen to save and display. In that case we residents, then, were preserved for all time, with the air removed and formaldehyde pumped in. On that particular day, there was the impression that everyone was mummified, if only for a while, in their individual cells, bubbles within one much larger bubble. No one moved a muscle, except to turn over in our sleep. There was nothing to do anymore but sleep. Then, without warning, the loudspeakers emitted a feedback screech, loud enough to shock us straight upright in our beds, rubbing our eyes to discover that a strange darkness had descended everywhere.

Someone, far away, screamed. Someone else could be heard loudly theorizing that an enormous bird, mythical size, had landed on the dome, mistaking it for an egg, and was trying to hatch it. So some of us made our way out into the main plaza and looked up, only to discover that the sky was only a little darker than usual, and that, as was often the case now, it was raining.

"I love the rain, and that's my maxim," someone shouted.

"Trying to sleep here, and that's mine," came a voice from a high window.

The next voice we heard was Zelen's, delivering nothing more unusual than an actual maxim. There were more yelps of feedback from the speakers as she spoke, but lately, since Krell's wife had taken over the job, there had been a lot of technical difficulties. Also her voice, though pleasant enough in real life, came over the airwaves as harsh and unmusically corvine.

"Um, your attention please. Here we go with the maxim thing today. OK? Here it is. *No one would wallow in the mud if it were poison mud.* Wait. I'm not sure that's right. Maybe it's no one would *swallow* mud. Or no one can *follow* mud. Oh, but that's revolutionary, isn't it? I don't know."

Knox was prostrate on the floor but not quite sleeping. His limbs were splayed out almost at right angles, with an emtpy bottle just out of reach on his right, and his tablet and pen just out of reach on his left. It wasn't so much that they seemed familiar, like he had written them, but that he would have written them, if he'd been that clever. A moment before he had been thinking about one of the older maxims: *I prefer my life to be shattered, in order to examine each piece more minutely.* Yet, in a way, depending on the version, here was the opposite concept.

"Do you want a picture of the future?" the voice continued after a while, more pleasant and warbly now, more songbird-like. "Do you want a new kind of maxim?"

Several people were heard to shout out yes. Knox peered up through his ceiling and could see that Krell was standing facing his window and perhaps listening intently too.

"Then pay attention," she continued, with an odd touch of warmth to her voice, and Knox had the impression—as we all did—that she was speaking exclusively to him over the telephone, like a sex worker.

"All we can do is do what we do and do it well." she said. "I mean, do that, or do as well as you can, whatever that is. A new assignment. Does that make sense? I'm not sure these qualify at all as maxims.

What if I were to say, *Do whatever pleases you, because you're way past the stage of caring*? Did I get that right? Come by the little dome and let me know if that makes sense to you. Or not. Over and out. Putting this thing on autoplay."

Knox sprang up, and, not many minutes later, stepped through the door of the little dome. The light, like the light everywhere those days, was shadowy, unsettling, but he immediately saw Zelen, pacing back and forth on stage, her posture strangely bent, her hair even shorter than the last time he'd seen it.

She wasn't paying attention to the handful of people in the audience, but was thumbing through Illion's old book of maxims, sometimes pausing to run the same hand rather quickly over her hair, the back of her neck, her forehead, as if thumbing through her brain as well.

"How do you know," she finally read out loud, having found what she was looking for in a piece of paper inserted in the book. *"How do you know but that every world that cuts the airy way...is an immense...bird of delight?* Wait. Can that be right?"

Too many immense birds today, thought Knox. But change *world* to *rocket ship,* he mused, and you might have a maxim. Change *bird* to *world,* et cetera. Or start from scratch with ship, bird, world, girl, lip, word, curled, delight.

"Want any help?" he asked softly, standing at the foot of the stage.

"Knox!" she laughed, then covered her mouth, then remembered she wasn't on the air at that moment. "Yes, of course. Help! I seem to have forgotten how to do maxims."

"Maybe so."

She was taking shallow, neurotic-sounding breaths and stepping sideways, crabbily, exasperatedly, as if not sure what part of her job was next or, more broadly, what part of her imprisonment was next. She gulped hard, blew out her cheeks, made a kind of lady-like burp, and the microphone, abruptly on again, picked up the eruption and amplified it to sound like someone opening a bottle of champagne.

For his part, Knox thought only of jumping up to the stage, perhaps with the kind of romantic leap that only a practiced dancer can pull off, and monopolizing her, passing on to her all the new maxims that were stuffing his head, ones hardly different than the ones she had come up with. But when he prepared to jump he found himself jammed in, cheek by jowl, even arm in arm, with other men, most notably with Krell, who must have come in a moment after him, all of them scrambling to hoist themselves on stage with their own monopolies and questions. With the result that in this way they immobilized one another, and Zelen took the opportunity, as they only discovered much later, to slip away.

Meanwhile the press of male bodies had become unbearably hot, and a moment later Knox was relieved to find himself pushed in the opposite direction, and finally out into the street, where he felt a jolt of elation, as he had ended up there by himself, free from all jostling. He was still shaking slightly, but shaking alone. Some of the men had filed politely back inside, while others had dispersed into the emptiness of the town. When he listened, yes, he could hear not only the patter of rain on the dome, but the diminishing patter of footsteps on nearby streets. He had to admit to himself that, just weeks before, he might have enjoyed the mob mentality, because it would have inspired him to imagine the possibility of us all getting together and clamoring for change, then using our ferocity to achieve it. Now, since the death of the escapees, he hadn't the strength for any visions at all, whether of uproar or hibernation. Instead he focused all his energy and attention on the little figurine stolen from the rocket ship, in a mad belief that it would somehow speak to him, or carefully listen to him, or both, and in this manner reveal the deepest secrets of all time, or at least other times. So he rushed back to his cell to continue the consultation.

Once there, he had the urge, for one frightening moment, to smash the statuette with a hammer and open it up to see what might be hidden inside. Or, if nothing, to see if he could then spend the next several months gluing it back together. After all, the new reigning philosophy under the dome seemed to have become nothing more complex than *Do what you please, as long as you do it under the dome.* Did that mean smashing not just figurines, but everything? Did it mean surrendering to every darkly human desire? Attacking and killing the tourists when they arrived, as long as such murders were committed under the dome? But no, he had to admit to himself, after an hour of fruitlessly staring at it, that, in the end, all he really wanted to do was to make a formal gift of the figurine to Zelen, and from then on just let the planet and its two stars spin out their own private narrative.

Knox got up, went out to the plaza, and strolled aimlessly for a while. The rain stopped, Brittle Star emerged from behind the clouds, and everything under the dome was bright but freckled and stippled and creamy blue, like a wild bird's egg. Because there were no maxims on the speakers, he knew exactly where he would find Zelen, and so made his way over to the Grand Opening store.

His instincts were correct: there she was at the counter, chatting with Dr. Waugh. On seeing him burst in, she smiled, her mouth full of broad white teeth, and he felt that it was a secret and special smile, teeth extra-extended, one that she had never revealed to anyone before, much less to him, and that it answered all of his questions about the future with a definitive yes. Including the killing? Yes. It was a killer's grin, a lover's grin, a polar grin. He tried to answer it with one of his own, but then, his mouth was full of some bad taste, and all he could do was swallow and hold his hand over his mouth as if to hide any feelings, positive or negative, he might be keeping from her.

"There aren't any left," she said as he came up to the counter.

"Any what?" he asked, finally smiling , lopsidedly, with his mouth closed.

"Any tablets. I've got the last one."

"What made you think that's what I wanted?"

"Dr. Waugh here told me."

The old man was beaming upon them in an oddly fixed way, tilting his head in the style of an automaton, a robot fortune teller, ready to spit out a love horoscope with the push of a button.

"I wasn't actually thinking about paper today," said Knox. "I only came by to see if the back room is empty." And he continued on boldly through the store, and shouldered his way through the lacy curtain, not concerned whether there was anyone he might step on. But no, it was empty, and he stood in the dark by himself, realizing what a small room it was, barely large enough to lie down in. His eyes adjusted to the darkness, enough to make out the word *Victory* spelled out dozens of times on the labels that Waugh had used as wallpaper.

Zelen came and stood on the other side of the lace, and peered in at him.

"Why do you care if it's empty?" she asked, wide-eyed, and Knox wondered if Waugh had ever shared the secret of the storeroom with her.

"Because it's dark and private," he answered. "You see how Waugh has made it a privacy space?"

"Yes, of course."

"He did it to get out of earshot. Out of eyeshot. Doesn't it ever feel funny to you to live in a city of peeping toms?"

"Let's see. I think I have a maxim for that. We do need to look at each other. Right? I remember it now. *We must not act as voyeurs, or as judges, but as guardians.*"

"Did you learn that one in ethics class?"

"Actually no. I wrote it myself."

"No you didn't," countered Knox. "I heard that one broadcast months ago."

"Really?"

"Believe me, it's easy to get the feeling that you wrote them yourself. Remember *Do as you please,* etc.?"

"I was just reading that one an hour ago," nodded Zelen.

"That's one that I wrote. Approximately. Or should I say, I thought it a thousand times before you said it."

"Ah."

"Why don't you come inside here with me?"

"Why don't you come out?"

But she moved through the curtain and there she was, an inch away. They were shielded from human view, and of course he could hear Waugh sliding his feet along the floor, coming closer to see what the two of them might end up doing in there.

"Maybe *you* don't crave privacy," whispered Knox, sitting down on the floor in one corner and inviting her with a gesture to do the same in the opposite corner. "But I do. Waugh calls it solitary confinement, and I think it was arrogant of me not to condemn myself to that here once in a while. Also, there's such a thing as dual confinement. Today, for example, I wanted to meet you here, where no one could see the two of us for a few minutes."

"Why?"

In the dim light he could see that she was definitely not grinning as she had a few minutes before, but looking at him sideways, suspiciously, even though, because the room was so small, their legs had to tangle together in the middle, and the fabric of their unis made the familiar crackling sound as they squirmed very lightly against each other.

"I remember that it was you who first pointed out to me how our unis work. That they have stripes, and they crinkle."

"I don't remember that."

"It was the first day. You sat next to me. I was amazed by your teeth."

"Oh, those," she laughed. "You haven't seen this kind before?"

She opened her mouth wide, and to his surprise, her teeth, bright as bathroom tiles when she grinned at him a minute earlier, were gone.

"Now, watch this," she said, and her upper teeth came down, lower teeth came up, as if, like a shark, she had an extra set ready to extrude at any time.

"Okay," he gulped, running his tongue around his own teeth. "That's kind of how I pictured it."

"I was in...an accident," she explained, "and all my real teeth got knocked out. Long story. The teeth got lost, so they couldn't just put them back in. Anyway, as long as they were going to give me artificial ones, I asked if they could be retractable."

"But what's the advantage?"

"Advantage? Oh, I don't know. I just thought it would be interesting. After all, when you're not eating, what do you need teeth for?"

"I have something strange too!" he laughed. "Something rather unusual to show you."

"What is it?" she laughed back. "You have something retractable too?"

"Maybe retractable. Because after I give it to you, I might want it back."

"Okay."

"And you don't mind meeting in here? In the dark?"

"Not if you don't."

"All right, then, we'll arrange something sometime and I'll bring you your present."

She was fingering the brightly colored, tightly knotted plastic strands of the lace curtain doorway.

"Did you know," she said, "that I made this?"

"You did? How?"

"It's wiring from the *Antibody*. Somebody pulled it out—pulled all the poor thing's intestines out and brought them in, in steaming piles, inside the dome. You can get some too if you want. It's free. Not steaming anymore.

Anyway, I wove this curtain out of the stuff, because I liked the way it looked. I ended up giving it to Waugh, because I knew he wanted a little more privacy here. That was before he thought of plastering it with labels."

"You do understand solitary confinement then."

"Oh sure," she said, shrugging, getting up to go. "Also, it turns out to be nice for any couples who want a little bit of privacy."

———

At some point we changed the name of the dilapidated old *Antibody*, and called it the *Antigrave*, meaning that it had served its only purpose, and that was this: to deny us the privilege, at the end of our lives, of being buried on our homeworld. Death, it was said, would never come to us here, because here we were already "in the heavens," in some heaven, a kingdom only the chosen could rise to, and that was us, the elect.

Another way of looking at it was that maybe this world was another planet's hell. But of course that's what they used to say on Earth all the time, and it wasn't at all clear which would be which.

That's not a maxim either.

But consider our dead comrades. It seemed possible that they weren't dead, so perhaps not buried. The rumor got started that they had succeeded in escaping, and had made it to the other side of the world to join the Yoohoos, and although brutality and ignorance were said to be the reigning themes of daily life there, at least it was a change, perhaps a desirable one, a welcome contrast to the numbingly utopian charms of our own side.

Where it constantly rained. Where Zelen's voice came over the loudspeakers with so much static it often could not be clearly understood. Where there were no more writing tablets at Grand Opening, and Knox's was nearly filled. Where he kept thinking he ought to go upstairs to talk to Zelen, and arrange their meeting in the store room, but couldn't find sufficient vigor to get up off the floor.

Still, somebody, somewhere, had some life left in them, and one day Chemo showed up at Knox's rooms with another announcement. Fermat happened to be over, just hanging out, and the two of them didn't even bother to get up. They lay on the floor and listened to Chemo explain, in his apathetic way, that the nearest canal, just outside the dome, was to serve as the venue of a canoe race, open to anyone who might wish to compete for first prize.

"What's the prize?" groaned Knox, putting his hands over his face. His uni was covered with food chunk crumbs.

"The prize," said Chemo, "has not yet been determined. But it will be generous. Also, not everyone is encouraged to enter. Because the race takes place outside the dome, the most likely winners are those who have spent a long time out there breathing through wands."

"Do you hear what he's saying?" Knox asked Fermat, gripped with a sudden enthusiasm for the event.

"Yes," answered Fermat, lazily. "I heard, and I'm already training for it."

"Training? How?"

"Like this," said Fermat, and without getting up, he moved his arms in a vague paddling motion on the floor.

———

News of the competition filtered through town over the next few days. When the specifics could finally be sorted out, it was clear that although the race would be long and strenuous, and not recommended for most, everybody not racing was encouraged to line the edge of the canal and watch, taking on the role of fans, but only if we understood that it was a serious occasion, and bored or sarcastic remarks were not to be tolerated.

First, they said, there would be a qualifying time trial, just to see who was up to the challenge of actually rowing a canoe the distance of one hundred meters. The next stage would consist of a real race among three qualifiers, until, by the end of the day, some number of eliminations later, a particular champion would emerge, and be awarded the still unspecified prize.

In the end, only a few dozen people showed up. Yet another rumor was spreading, this one claiming that stepping outside during Brittle Star season was especially dangerous. That although it was the cooler of the two suns, it was mysteriously more malevolent than Blister Star, and sent down a flood of spasm-inducing magnetic energies, enough to bring you to your knees, people said, especially if you were foolish enough to stare up at it and observe its vast fiery islands scraping and grinding, manufacturing negative electrons, or negative demons. Or mood-enhancing sprites, as others had it.

But those of us who did go out to act as spectators and supporters were glad of our own rationalism, or bravura, because it was one of the most glorious days anyone had seen on that world. True enough, Brittle Star was still our champion star, casting its shifty, wiry light everywhere, creating a dance-floor effect of light and shadow, figure and ground. And, once we were all lined up on the edge of the canal, we could just stand, our heads in an exalted position, basking in Brittle's fitful effulgence, our heart beats maybe synchronizing with its eccentricities. What's more, when we looked back toward town, it was interesting to see how a number of the orb clouds had gravitated to the top of the dome, each little puff of whiteness gently attaching itself to the outside, like cotton balls stuck to the surface of a static balloon.

And then there was the canal, with its water, which most of us had not yet seen. It made for a striking spectacle, this precisely crafted river filled nearly to the brim. A few sighs were heard as some hearts melted, as some always do, at the juxtaposition of desert and water. Whether it was a premeditated outcome or not, a few of us felt a tiny bit more at home in the world that day.

The water was so high in the canals that it was possible to lean over the edge and actually touch the limpid liquid, splash one's fingertips in it, like children, until we were yelled at, and told in no uncertain terms that the water might someday be used as drinking water, and we were not to even think of going in it, for fear of contamination. Well, we were a little skeptical of that pronouncement. Were our bodies so terribly filthy? Was it a subtle bigotry against convict? But why rock the boat, as it were, and so we took one step backwards, kept our hands behind our backs, rolled our eyes, whistled.

Then a signal was given, and Knox and Krell and Fermat, the only ones who had signed up for the competition, emerged from the dome and approached, raising their hands in salute, like gladiators, or magicians. When at last they stepped up to that point of the canal where three streamlined and translucent canoes were moored, Dr. Chemo handed them new, shrink-wrapped unis to put on, together with a shrink-wrapped paddle, and from this it became clear that the idea of avoiding any contamination of the water was taken very seriously. So we moved back a few more steps at that point.

"Courage is inconsistent with caution," someone said, and it appeared to be a maxim, but in fact it was somebody just making a wise remark, and then it seemed rather sad that one couldn't say something smart anymore without everyone first assuming that it was a maxim.

A preliminary bell was rung, and it was announced that because there were only three athletes, the time trials had been eliminated, and now there were to be just two races, with one man being eliminated after the first, and one more after the second, leaving a champion.

The three competitors, once they were all suited up, took their positions in their respective canoes. Dr. Chemo stepped forward to give each of them a special breath wand, larger in circumference and dark brown, designed for heavier breathing. With these planted firmly between their lips, the three of them raised their paddles high overhead, and then, at the sound of another bell, threw themselves into the contest. Or had they? Were they indeed starting now? Yes, but not impressively. The three boats moved forward, not at all in an expert way. As a matter of fact, all three were rocking dangerously from side to side, no one quite sure of the proper technique. However, two of the canoes soon straightened, found an equilibrium, and moved forward with appreciable swiftness.

The third canoe, the sometimes drifting and sometimes misdirected one, belonged to Knox.

———

He had been so surprised at first by the lightness of his canoe that he over-paddled significantly, and put his craft into a bad wobble, splashing water pointlessly, speeding off at entirely the wrong angle, more a demonstration of slapstick than athleticism. Some spectators laughed outright. Even hooted. Meanwhile Knox was quite bitterly aware that his opponents were already ahead of him, gaining speed.

"Why," we heard him mutter, "did I bother?"

The length of the race was one hundred meters, and, at the end, it was Krell who first crossed the finish line, winning by several lengths, making it look easy, with his left ear cocked higher than the right, as if listening to instructions from the trembling demons or sprites of Brittle Star.

Fermat crossed second, and Knox, despite finally straightening his craft and getting into a good, rhythmic stroke, never exactly finished, bringing his boat to an abrupt halt when he realized that the race was over, and that he had come in third.

"My congratulations!" he cried out in his comrades' direction, sportsmanlike, professorial, in defeat.

However, after a moment, it became evident that something was not quite right. Instead of pulling up to Krell's canoe beyond the finish line, Fermat simply kept paddling, even notably faster than he had paddled during the race. Soon all that could be seen of him was his back, far down the length of the canal. There was a momentary glare of sun on his baldness, and then none of us could make him out at all.

No matter. It seemed plausible that he'd simply misunderstood the length of the race, or that he was so pleased with the joy of paddling that he wanted more. Or maybe he had decided that, as runner-up, he had to prove some kind of machismo. Or was drunk. Or was on his way across the planet to a secret destination, thinking that his fat breath wand would last a good long time. The stories multiplied, becoming more fantastic the longer he was gone. After several days went by, someone suggested that Fermat was intent on circumnavigating the globe, and that we'd soon see him approaching from the other direction.

But for the purposes of the race, forget him. He had forfeited his participation in the contest. It was time to stage the champion-of-the-world finale: one race between the two remaining competitors, Knox and Krell.

As he returned to the starting line, Knox strategized. Krell, with his round and heavy arms, his ruby-red jowls, and droopy ponytail, not to mention a pair of rounded shoulders, plus neck folds that appeared all soft and sticky above his collar, never had the appearance of a serious athlete. But Knox understood that the man was mysteriously gifted with inner mechanisms, the kind he had displayed skating on the polar ice, and had to be taken very seriously at all times. It was a good idea to take notice of, for example, the fact that his arms, though thick, were exceptionally long, distinctly simian, with strangely defined muscles popping up in unexpected places, like tumors, but hard as pistons. Also, Knox had noted in the first race how Krell had stroked long and low, as if he didn't want the paddle ever to emerge from the water, dipping his hands under the surface, something that Knox, despite the gloves, had felt a little reticent about, given all the warnings about contamination.

An opposite approach, Knox considered, could lead to the prize. He felt sure he now knew how to proceed—yank the paddle out cleanly with every stroke and reinsert it, like sticking a sharp knife into a distant cake, then cutting himself a huge slice, all the while taking advantage of his own thinness and lightness to turn the canoe into a dry leaf or eggshell skimming like wind at the very surface-tension boundary of the water.

But, at the starting bell, things again began to go badly for him. Again, he couldn't establish a rhythm, and a theory he had about making two strokes per side instead of one was a disaster, upsetting the symmetry rather than establishing it, veering him at first off the straight line, so that he had to revert to traditional technique—the previously losing technique.

What's more, some of the old skepticism crept in. Where and when would it not? He was needled by little doubts, and hated himself for being distracted by nothing more than a lousy attitude, a useless sense of the essential uselessness of all physical exertion. But he paddled on, gaining speed, not sure whether to puff harder and harder through his fat wand or spit it out. He gained on Krell, at least a little bit, but was tempted any number of times to quit, to give the whole thing up as a bad job. What kept him stroking, and striving for that remarkable, leafy lightness he had imagined for himself, was the possibility, outside our city of eyes, of one particular set of eyes remaining more fixed on him than on his opponent. Once or twice his gaze wandered from the absurd competition to take in the edge of the canal, the line of people visible there, as he couldn't help but wonder if there were one in the crowd who might have come outside to watch him, and only him, though there could be no chance, with such quick sidelong glances as he was making, of picking this certain someone out of the crowd. And even if he did recognize her, and even discovered that she was waving her arm in greeting and encouragement, how would he know which canoeist she was rooting for?

His thoughts alternating between earnestness and irony, Knox steadily made up distance, but as the finish line approached he could only hope that Krell might succumb even more to the temptation to turn his eyes and mind to the spectators. Was he the sort? Probably not. Still, Knox kept a close watch, not so much on Krell's paddle as on Krell's ponytail, in order to catch some craning of the neck, some hesitant twitch upward, a twitch that might give a loser a chance to squirt forward and take the lead.

But Krell made no such motion, and all Knox could do as he pulled closer was observe how frantically the man paddled with his equine arms, each stroke a shudder of dewlapped flesh. In contrast, his own arms felt avian and hollow. Flesh versus bone, and maybe it would be better to toss the paddle away, skip all the nonsense. All savages paddle, so just lean back, puff as leisurely as possible on his fat wand, and let the canoe slip forward, sun-propelled, like an emperor's barge.

But he was catching up, until, look, there they were, neck and neck, sometimes even grazing each other's paddles, just as they had once, in another race, grazed ears. Sharp glances were exchanged; they monitored each other for weaknesses. Most significant was that it had become more and more difficult to suck sufficient air in through the wands, and Knox could glance over to see, as we all could by then, that Krell wasn't using his anymore, had accidentally dropped it or thrown it away in frustration, and now as he paddled he began to cough, then went into a fit of bad hacking, failing in his stroke, mouth open, a stricken look, his lips rubbery and slack, hard to look at, so just don't look.

"Look at Krell!" someone called out. Knox glanced over again to see that Krell appeared paralyzed, his paddle frozen in mid air. Of course his canoe didn't just shudder to a halt, and what momentum it had carried Krell to and across the finish line. But that's where Knox already was, already the victor, enjoying the applause, already offering to share his breath wand to the loser, already checking the crowd for a glimpse of Zelen.

But she wasn't visible, at least to Knox's eyes. Chemo stood nearby, wearing a neutral expression, and there was Dr. Waugh, dancing the saltarello, waving his hands in celebration of Knox, and for some reason it seemed wonderful to have someone like that on one's side.

———

And though it was a victory, he reflected, as he crawled out of his canoe onto the landing, feeling empty headed, it was incomplete, having come down to being able to keep his breath wand clenched between his teeth, no evidence of innate advantages. The problem was that by winning he'd made things worse. He could see Zelen now, helping Krell limp back toward the dome. But what did he care about either of them? What he had wanted was a mystique, an enchantment that could drip inwards to the deepest corners of exile, and somehow shatter it. But, truthfully, he hadn't thought the whole thing through. He'd won, but he didn't understand from the start that the qualities he would accrue from the act of losing, namely, submission, and self-reflection, were the qualities he needed now, not boasting and eclipsing. Any star could achieve brilliance, and then be eclipsed in its turn. By letting himself become obsessed with Zelen and her esteem, or whatever it was he wanted from her, he'd neglected to turn his exile into an act of reconstitution. He'd written useful maxims, and neglected to follow them. *Let all emotions dim, and soon true feeling will emerge.* Or, perhaps better: *No two windows ever let in the same breeze.*

And still, and still. Dr. Zelen hung before his eyes, gray, like an intricate lace curtain, bound with secret knots, a furry, retractable labyrinth. There was a squeaky sound in his lungs, or his brain, and he felt so sick that he guessed he might have ended up sipping in a dose of atmosphere. Or maybe, more likely, great swallows of disappointment.

You have armored your soul incompletely for this world, or any other, he may have mumbled, and then passed out.

———

The effect of lying down and staring up, especially upon awakening, is to become aware of the directionless nature of direction. The sun had set and there he lay, sprawled beside the canal, just as he often lay on the floor of his cell, with now the bowl of stars sometimes above him, sometimes below, feeling that any minute some mechanism that held him to the planet's surface would release, and he would fall face first, loins second, arms and legs spread out to slow his fall, into one abyss or another. Could there be clouds in outer space? There could. He still had the fat breath wand jammed between his teeth and his cheek, and he was breathing more lightly. After a while he knew where he was, and thought he should just go home. Still, there was a strong sense that he couldn't really get up on his own, and, though there was no danger of freezing, it was with a wash of relief that he realized, a minute later, that someone was leaning over him, then grabbing his jaw and turning his head this way and that, switching out his breath wand for a new and slender one, and sighing a warm, root-beer-candy-scented exhalation into his face.

"Come inside, you big dope," this someone was saying, and he realized only then that it was Krell, and that he had left the dome to come look for him and save him.

He was pulled up, dusted off, given an arm of support around the ribs, and marched back inside, then taken directly not to his own suite, but to the one right above, where Krell lay him on the marriage bed, brought him a glass of water, and sat holding his hand for a while, like a crusty, long-haired nurse in an old novel. In time Zelen came into the bedroom as well and fussed over him, even held his other hand, though that was awkward. They were both so sweet to him, so reassuring! Zelen unzipped his uni halfway in order to sponge some dirt off his neck, and in his thick-headed state he was under the impression that they were going to unzip him all the way, and crawl into the bed, each one determined to warm up one half of his body.

Hours later, the next night in fact, dinner was served. They all ate noisily and excessively, especially Knox, who hadn't had such an appetite since the first day on the planet. What was it about the food chunks? They struck him as significantly better than usual.

"So it turns out," said Krell, finishing up, "that I won the race after all."

"How do you figure?" asked Knox, too warm and happy to care.

"Check the suit."

Knox did check and only then noticed that Krell had added something to his clothes in the last few minutes. He was now wearing one of the famous trustee ties. Also, instead of his familiar squint, his eyes were very open, as if he were balancing a heavy brick on top of his head, and needed constant, wide-eyed concentration.

"Oh. So you're a trustee. Wow. That's a nice promotion."

"Correct."

"Did I ever ask you what your crime was?"

"Question not allowed."

"Is that why the food tastes better tonight? You guys get better stuff than we do?"

"Jeez, I think you're right. I hadn't thought of that until just now."

"Congratulations."

"Thank you."

"Have I been promoted too?"

"To trustee status? Dear me, no."

Krell, as he spoke, was sitting up straighter and straighter in his chair, as if to carefully match his posture to his new position. But he wasn't wearing his mourning crown anymore, and once again his ponytail was full of crumbs.

"Watch this," he said after a while. "We trustees have bigger brains too, once we inflate them."

And saying so, he stuck one finger in one ear, got Zelen to stick a finger in his other, and used his free hand to hold shut his nose and blow.

"Is it bigger now?" asked Knox, astonished.

"Yes. Yes, it is."

As for Zelen, she pretty much kept her mouth shut during the meal. Never leaned over to touch Knox. Finally, the two men ran out of things to say, and when the silence became unbearable, she spoke up.

"It looks like there is something going on tonight at the canal," she said, looking out into the distance.

The others looked where she was pointing, and yes, through the transparent crystal of the building, out on the other side of the dome, you could see that some great light was shining.

"Maybe they're still looking for Fermat," joked Knox, rubbing both sides of his nose, because his sinuses still felt leaden, still throbbed.

"I hope what they found was his corpse," said Krell, excusing himself from the table, and disappearing.

Knox and Zelen, then, were left alone, but he found he couldn't look directly at her.

"Are you feeling better?" she asked.

"Much, much, much. I'm grateful, you know."

"You mean grateful to Krell, because he went out there and got you, and brought you in."

"Of course."

"So you know, I've been waiting."

"Waiting for what?"

She looked around to make sure Krell had left and, leaning in closer, whispered near his ear.

"You were going to show me, or give me, your, um, possession."

"Right, right. I'm sorry. I guess all the business with the canoes put my mind off that. Are you sure you want to see it?"

"I have no idea! You won't tell me what it is! You just make it sound so mysterious."

"What about tomorrow? Shall we meet at the store tomorrow?"

"Tomorrow. Yes!"

And, instead of putting her hand on his arm, as he thought she might, she put it on top of her head.

"I was thinking," she said, "of cutting off all my hair. No hair at all. Like Fermat. What do you think?"

"I don't know," he answered, cautiously. "I only know that I like Fermat."

"So do I," she smiled. "Especially after today. On this world I like everybody better when I can't see them."

———

In what century will people stop behaving like spiders, or poisonous mushrooms, or wolves? Not this one, evidently, though there may have been a time in the past—some people insist—when there was a degree of humanity, an era of justice and elegance and even wit. Others mention the precursors, and speak of a time marked by endless war, endless decline. One story has it that these fanatics of olden times would put on endless parties where they danced in special shoes that allowed them to levitate a few millimeters off the ground, achieving something akin to beautiful ice skating on any given surface, even the rough ground outside. However, the manufacture of these marvelous shoes involved a type of toxic mineral, and the young boys who were hired to insert the mineral into the shoes were poisoned by it, even to the point where their arms and hands would take on the hovering quality, so that they were no longer able to perform the insertion task, and had to spend the rest of their lives with their hands above their heads.

The greatest lie about history, Knox maximized in his head, *is that knowing it will make a difference.*

The unspecified prize for winning the canoe race, finally announced by Dr. Krell, when he returned to the dinner table, was Knox's appointment to the position of senior and official canoeist.

The real reason for the race, it could now be revealed, had been to draw out members of the community who might show an interest in canoeing, and subsequently to find out who had the greatest talent for it. Not a contest, then, but an aptitude test. Not an entertainment, but a deception. When he was told of this promotion, Knox understood the thinking behind it immediately. While it was hardly a prestigious position, neither was it the bottom of the hierarchy. Really, he was all right with it, and received the news calmly. The very next morning he was provided with a text wand with language that explained each procedure involved in monitoring the quality of the water and determining over time if it could provide not only some glistening canal-ish scenery for tourists and inhabitants, but also fill their drinking glasses.

"There has to be a greater effort to maintain standards," said Krell, handing him the text, then going back to fingering his new tie.

"There can be no repetition of the mistakes of the past," Krell added.

"What mistakes?"

"You know," answered the new trustee, staring bleakly across the table with the smirk of someone talking while simultaneously having his feet massaged. "What if that's how your comrades died? By drinking the water?"

"I thought the idea was that they died because they were out in the air without wands."

"Maybe they drank the water, and it was contaminated."

"There wasn't any water in the canals when they left. Come on, Krell. You know that as well as I do. You, who claim to have inflated your brain! And they're not *your* comrades anymore?"

"There might have been a trickle of water by then."

"Krell, have you told the other trustees about the rocket?"

"I have not."

But it was a topic that Krell found uncomfortable, as was apparent in the way he inserted a finger between his uni collar and his neck and pulled the collar away, as if trying to let out some troublesome gas.

"And you won't tell them?"

"Stop it. No. What would be the point? It's just some crummy old relic.

This world is the way we like it now. No reason to worry about what's out there on the edge. Don't you tell anyone either. Maybe when the tourists show up, we'll see. We could take a group out there, maybe. They'd probably enjoy a view of antiquity. Maybe you'd be the man for the job. You should go up there again someday and go inside, see if it might be possible to take people through it."

———

On the way across the plaza to Grand Opening, there was rain. Yellow light shifted to gray, and there was the sweet sound of the world respirating, a living world, as Knox always thought of it now, exhaling rain on the dome the same way you might fog up a mirror with your breath. So why not give back, fog back? The only way to move forward sometimes is to breathe forward, and when he entered the store he was distracted by his own respiration. He had both hands underneath the straps of his daypack, a palm on each lung, leading with his lungs, as if they were the engine that had just pulled him through a year, or two, or more, on planet X.

The place was empty, except for Waugh, who stood behind the counter eating lunch. Food chunks in those days came in different shapes to indicate flavor: square for meat, round for fruit, triangle for vegetable, and Knox saw now that Waugh had the knack, possibly a leftover trace of some fad in his childhood, of shaping his mouth to anticipate the food, so that when he put any given chunk in his mouth, he was ready for it, and appeared to be fitting a puzzle piece into its pattern. Catching sight of Knox, he nodded, took a drink straight from the bottle to wash everything down, and wagged his finger at length before he spoke.

"The paper has arrived!" he announced. "Plenty to go around."

And Knox saw that there were stacks of creamy writing tablets everywhere.

"Can't get rid of them, though. No pens!"

"No?"

"There doesn't seem to be much coordination in the central office, or whatever they want to call it. I guess they devote the fabricators to one kind of merchandise at a time, and the result is a crazy shortage, and then a crazy surplus."

"I'll take one," said Knox.

"You got it, Doc. But I take it you're staying a while longer."

"Staying where?"

"Here. You're sticking around to meet someone, and I just wanted to let you know that the storeroom is free."

Embarrassed, Knox walked away, and pretended to browse the merchandise. Outside in the street he could hear Zelen's loudspeaker voice stumbling over maxims, and could only hope that it was a recording and that at that moment she was rushing to meet him.

But time wore on. Eventually he parted the curtain of the storeroom and went in, where he sat cross-legged on the floor, took off his daypack, crammed it into a corner, lay down, and ended up asleep.

And dreamed that she came to him. Oh, but which she? A kind of hybrid creature, horrible to see, a pastiche of mottled skin and breasts and pubic hair. Not just two women, but he himself was in there as well, part of this torrent of genes, and as the creature neared him, slipping like gas through the lace curtain, and standing triumphantly over him, the victor in some bewildering contest, he could now make out its antlers, its hooves, its phallus, its ribcage.

"Wake up," the monster said, in a cartoon voice. "And submit to the evil of the precursors."

But, and such is so often the way of dreams, he could not find an answer, and though he wanted to shout so loud as to split the creature, and create many out of one, an army of preekers, he lay as crumpled and lifeless on the floor as the *Antibody*, his intestines ripped out for use in arts and crafts.

"Wake up," said Zelen, because of course it was her, and she resolved into a dim but focused version of herself as the dream faded.

"I brought it," he murmured, rubbing his eyes. "I brought you your present."

"Let's see, let's see," she breathed, and they sat cross-legged on the floor in opposite corners while he fumbled in the sack, and, after checking through the curtain to be sure no one else was in the store, brought out the thing, the sacred statuette, the ritual simulacrum, the thing that had no purpose or name.

In his hands it seemed to him subtly larger than before, and now felt almost dirty and antiquarian to the touch, but so detailed, rather porous in its surface texture, like volcanic rock, but with the surprising weight of something cast in pure steel. He set it down on the floor between them, more intrigued by it than ever, and sorry to have thought of giving up such a delicious antique, one that he felt almost compelled to take a bite out of.

"What is it?" she asked. "Is it an entertainment device?"

"Maybe a sculpture," he murmured, taking it back in his hands for a moment, disappointed in her.

"Wow."

"It's a gift, Zelen," he repeated, more to himself than to her. "I'm giving it to you. You don't know what it is, do you."

"No."

"That's all right."

"Oh, but wait a minute. I do know what it is now. It's a sculpture, and I like sculptures all the time. I mean always have. I was just thinking the other day how nice something like this, something arty, would look in our apartment.Thank you, Knox. Truly."

So there on the floor of the storeroom, the two of them crammed into corners, making themselves almost as small as the figurine, their eyes getting used to the light that filtered in through the plastic curtain and slowly brought out the details of the thing, Knox told the story of the trip to the ice—how the two of them, her husband and himself, had followed the strange screech into the canyon, where they found the needle-nosed ship, and how they recalled their history classes and the frightening stories of the preekers, and how Krell had recklessly cut ice skates out of its fins, and, finally, how once Krell had skated out of sight, Knox sneaked back and climbed right up into the ship and found the miraculous statuettes.

"I hope you like my taste," he continued, but as if reciting a speech now. "For me it was the most beautiful one, and I've thought about it a long time, and I really think it ought to belong to you."

He was surprised when she hoisted it up at that point, looking at him like he was about to change his mind and pull it back from her. She pressed it hard in her arms, frowning, her gimlet eyes sending him the warning not to make a move. Something about her had changed.

"I love it," she kept repeating, breathing hard, and though her mouth was closed he could hear her teeth retracting and then re-extending. "I love it a great deal," she repeated, saying it once while the teeth were gone, so that it came out with a very old lady's lisp.

It was a moment of emotion, he felt, seeing the stricken look in her eyes. She had to have a memory of something awful written within, and the split second of despair was contagious. Knox felt overthrown by her, by the figurine, by something.

"You do?"

"Yeah." She held the little man so softly that he looked like he was about to begin melting. "Well, you know what I mean. Really, ever since my first children's book about them, I always liked the precursors, despite what I learned later. Oh, Knox! Can we go back there and get the rest of them?"

It was something he hadn't thought of before. But what is so hard about a second theft, after the nerves and self-awareness of the first? He should have his own figurine, now that he'd given this one away. Start an art collection. Or better, given his attachment, mingled with the death of Illion, he could take it back from her, strenuously perhaps, and let her settle for a different one.

"Of course we can go back," he frowned, looking down at how her legs and hips were lost in her extra large uni, wondering if it would come to their aid as a kind of sail. "I'm the canoeist. The faster one. We can paddle there in little time."

"The sooner the better, I think."

"I like revolutionizing with you."

She unfolded herself an inch, eyes elsewhere, but kept the manikin tight against her chest, so he could also unclench physically, while the mind tightened. The light was prickly and dark in the shadows made by her scalp patterns. The stripes on both their unis glowed brighter.

"He's like time travel," she said. "I mean my toy, my precursor. He has that effect on you. He connects you to...old TV episodes."

"Zelen, us too."

"Hm?"

"Don't you think we coincide? In crime? We were born under the same crime sign."

"I'll tell you only so much. Somebody was attacked."

"Go on."

"My husband got attacked. He was bitten. Chomped nearly in half."

"Oh."

"By me."

"You mean you bit with retractable teeth. So not so puncturing."

"No. That's how I got them. The first panel ruled, after the biting incident, to have my dentition removed, letting punishment fit the crime. So they were removed. On appeal, the second panel said, oh no, that's too harsh, and said I was to have all my teeth back, but by then they'd been lost. So, they arranged for these. Also exile."

"And what happened to your husband?"

"Forman was fine."

"I didn't mean he wouldn't be," Knox said, reddening. "Only if he died. Since you're remarried."

"Forman is my eternal-chain husband. Krell is my metahusband. On Earth the two of us will complete the chain."

It hit Knox then that she wasn't speaking to him, but to the figurine.

"Okay," she went on, raising her eyes, but keeping the artifact close to her throat. "So now your turn to appear before the panel."

"Somebody was attacked," he let out at last, imitating. "Strangulation attack. Some bite with their hands, strike with their mouths. But you knew that."

"Sure."

So at least they had that bond, among others.

He thought she might now place the object to one side and reach out to shake his hand—the hand which he had extended ever so slightly in anticipation. He wanted some form of congeniality. There was a feeling that touching her hand might erase her from him in a way. That physical intimacy could constitute a kind of solitary confinement.

But instead of reaching she shrank, holding her gift tighter, in fact so tight he was afraid she would break it apart.

"I can't believe you," she whispered, but no, again, she was addressing her adoptee. Cooing to it.

What is always needed, he thought, is some kind of crisis, like what had happened with Mhurra, when, the same day as their first kiss, she had almost been killed by the drip train, and after that, they were never apart for long again. But this was nothing like that.

"It took me so long to forget about you," she said in a sing-song, lullaby voice. "And then, and then, here you are again."

He wasn't mystified. She was doing what he had done, instantly turning it into a proxy. She was letting the figure signify.

"Zelen," he murmured, pushing the daypack toward her. "Keep it in here, and don't tell your husband about any of this. We don't want the trustees to know about the ship, or the figurines. They might try to do something horrible."

"They would?"

"Oh, I don't know. Maybe."

"I'll do as you say," she nodded, stroking the cheeks, the arms, the legs, the toes, and finally, hesitatingly, the miniature penis. "Also I'll hold it a minute longer."

A moment later Waugh was standing just outside the curtain, a silhouette.

"Someone's waiting for the room," he hissed. "Are you through in there? I'm asking because you're talking so much."

"Talking always turns into a crime," answered Knox.

But Zelen quickly and silently put her gift away, and stood up. Knox shot upright too, put a hand on her shoulder, more to steady than to express, and they walked out. There was no discussion, no stirrings or queries. Knox had a pain in his forearms, a bone pain, as if his radius and ulna had swollen from thinking, using his imagination to picture, every minute, freedom to return to Earth, freedom to live in stickiness and filth.

No one gains from prison time who avoids meditation, and without the figurine, he found he couldn't meditate. He was free of the burden of it, done with metaphor, but the result was the absence of introspection.

Watching Zelen move away from him down the street, the heavy daypack hanging so far down it bounced against her lower vertebrae, he felt like part of him was forever hidden from his own gaze forever, and that it didn't matter, because it wasn't the Mhurra portion.

This is Earth, nor am I out of it, said an angel in a poem he didn't remember well.

Sometimes Mhurra leaked out of her portion and turned to liquid at his feet, a puddle that perfectly painted her silhouette.

Repeating it made him laugh, and laughter cast a different light on everything.

The rest of the time she inhabited him, was carved into him. Whatever percentage of him that was her was small and naked, with features reproduced in detail, down to the earlobes, down to the spray of stains or freckles along the sternum, the dark Mohawk of pubic hair.

Spiritual figurine.

A gong sounded, so far away that the sound seemed to be reaching him all the way from some actual heaven or hell. In the direction Knox walked, the opposite direction from her, the streets seemed unusually clean and acrylic. It was a high transparency day, and near the bottom of the dome, where it met the ground, there was a mirror effect, as was often the case on such days. This phenomenon made it seem sometimes like the street you walked on was stretching out before you to infinity, except that in the very far reaches of that road you could see yourself walking toward yourself, a figure who looked like a friend coming to meet you from a distant neighborhood. Someone, maybe Fermat, had claimed that the dome was designed this way on purpose, a feature meant to trick us sometimes into a sense of far-flung brotherhood and unity, and thus make us forever forget all our previous friends and angels.

———

That same day, though none of us reckoned it correctly, the third anniversary of our arrival came and went. It had nothing to do with stars or orbits, but there were other ways of measuring. Some of us had excellent biological clocks, still synchronized with home. The question was, had we been sentenced to a year of Earth time or a year of interstellar time? No one knew. If the latter, how long was that? Did the presence of two stars create a year that was three years long? No one understood that either, but worse than not knowing was not caring. Worse was the accommodation some had made, the tendency that certain of the less questioning exiles had of gorging themselves, putting their feet up after meals, patting their squeaking parts, putting down roots, twirling their mustaches.

For the rest of us—some of us—there were Zelen's modestly radical maxims to go by.

We gladly put on manacles and chains, then brag about how shiny.
All comforts are obtained by running away from greater comforts.
The brain is wider than the distance from here to Earth.

The rest of us—some of us—thought every day about departure, about the proverbial lam. To where we didn't know. To outer space. To inner outer space. Like Knox, we sometimes thought or said that it was preferable to self-destruct: to surreptitiously drill a hole, let in the atmosphere, make our dome a quiet killing jar. Round dome, soft round sleep. The horse in the nebula bending his head to note our silence. A wink of approval.

———

The next morning Knox began his new tasks.

And then the morning after that he repeated his tasks. And so on. Canoeist—we called him Canoeist after the fashion of naming on the basis of position—got up very early, in the dark, like an ancient milkman. The hours were difficult to adjust to. When his alarm wand dragged him up to consciousness with its softly insistent birdcall, he would open his eyes in darkness and feel a pair of calloused hands take hold of his stomach, then two other hands take hold of his heart, and so on. Low clouds and darkness all day today, came the inner forecast. There were no sounds of waking or stirring in adjacent cells, and sometimes he had the tendency, left over from youth, to ignore any alarm and rewrap himself in the blanket, like a child in the middle of childhood, floating in velvet space almost to the point of losing the act of breath, but lastly falling dead asleep, only to bolt up a few seconds later to a second round of birdcalls. More hands, more organs. So then upsy daisy, keep his feet square under the breakfast table, lift the chunk, chew and gurgitate. No meditation possible, but at least he could stare into the light, wondering if Zelen might show up at that moment at the door, ready to paddle with him to the ice.

Outside the dome, his procedure was to ease himself into the canoe with minimal rocking and disturbance, to unlash the boat from its mooring point, tear another sterilized paddle out of its shrinkwrap, settle into proper position, spine straight, crown of the head attached by a string to heaven. A tendril stretching away, away. No, not necessary, because there were other tendrils knitting together all parts of him, indigenous and introduced: all equally nuanced, as far as they went, tied together.

Then began the exertion, the bland repetition of the paddle gesture, the same stroke he'd used in the race, then refined in repetition and micro adjustment. Little more than maintenance. At no point did he believe that the assignment was anything other than insult. Revenge of relative order against relative disorder. His very first tests, on his very first day, showed that the water was potable, as he supposed it would be. If he and Krell had succeeded in melting the ice cap, the water would be much worse, full of cheesy elements, but this water that had percolated up from the depths of the lithosphere was as pure as the waters of Earth must have been a thousand years ago. Pure as fire, or light, or fiction.

Nevertheless, he repeated the tests every day, and every day got the same result. So what was the point of sending him out morning after morning? To keep him occupied and out of the way? Presumably, he could stop people from swimming in or otherwise contaminating the canals, but who would try such stunts? Who would bother to go outside the dome? Blister Star had not taken over yet, but still the days were starting to warm, and perhaps if someone had thought of it they might have slipped outside and gone for a quick dip, a dark human body cutting through blue water in the middle of the yellow desert. Knox pictured himself in that episode often. He kept an eye out for Fermat, thinking every day that his friend would appear as a corpse floating face down in the water, or showing up on the edge of the canal to relate the story of his escape, and share his thoughts on how it was to be the first and possible last man in the world.

Meanwhile, no need to keep testing. Everything remained sterile, remained tourist-friendly.

Sometimes he would peer over the edge of the gunwale into the very calm and reflective water and regard his own wet image there, the face of a middle-aged boatman with a hard boatman's mouth, the mouth of a sea turtle, skin dry, nose laced with capillaries, eyes of an octopus, hair standing up straight like Medusa's snakes, or the octopus's arms.

"Where I am I've no wish to be," he'd sing, mouthing the words, moving his feet in the bottom of the canoe in reduced dance. "I am where I'm wished to be. My unknown location is never nowhere."

Other times, staring straight ahead, reaching out the tip of the paddle to trace in the water a figure eight, Knox stiffened, resigning his position, resign himself, pretend that the whole routine got carried out, along with all the test results. Be sure to spend the hours, then, on his back in the bottom of the boat, breath wand like a slender stalk of grass between his lips. He imagined that if he were reduced to only a network of blood vessels, exclusively made of veins and arteries, he would still be recognizable as Knox.

"Be the blood imprisoned not by the body but by the canoe," he'd instruct.

"There was never a stimulus, never a response, and the point is to expand."

Remember that a moment in time exists only in time, he thinks, or would say, if Mhurra were there, and she were dipping down and speaking to him.

He listened more closely and heard a whistling sound, a mind breeze, and understood it was the planet falling through space with a smile, with a whistle, tumbling down the incline of its orbit, and not feeling bad that it couldn't leave orbit and go elsewhere.

———

Finally Knox arranged to meet Zelen at the edge of the canal, early in the morning. She arrived punctually, but he was sorry to see her looking so depressed and exhausted. Surprisingly, all her hair was shaved off, and the Fermat look suited and didn't suit her, revealing the fact that her skull had a somewhat uneven, faceted quality, wax carved with a quick knife. As she walked up to where he stood at the edge of the canal, the dome behind her seemed to levitate slightly. She did that to it. Brittle Star came up, and her head turned brassy, mosaic, trophy-like. Was she regal, despite the missing hair? Yes, she had never been more lost in thought. Her eyes were gray and wrinkled, like wetted fingertips.

"Are we going to go all the way to the rocket?" she wanted to know, frowning, apparently uninterested in the answer.

"It's awfully far," he answered, trying to think of a way to get her to take the ride with him another time. "Let's save it."

She wasn't wearing the daypack, and that was a relief. He offered her a breath wand, but she had one ready, and slipped it between her lips just before his arm reached out. There was a small cloud that came overhead and made a light arch of rain over them, and it was interesting to Knox to watch how the water beaded and trickled on the angles of her scalp, and on his wrists. When it stopped a few minutes later, the air smelled like grass, or chemical grass, and there was a light enchantment for him when he imagined that somewhere, nearby, a weedy prairie or hill of irises lay hidden.

———

There were no difficulties with the canoe. Although designed for one it worked. Knox could paddle awkwardly while she sat awkwardly in what little space was left just behind him. It helped when once or twice she put her hands on his shoulders, compressing them, though then she complained about the tightness she noticed in what she called his canoe muscles.

She might untighten me instead, he thought, and tried to massage his vertebrae without help, by making them rub against one another horizontally.

"The view, the view," he insisted, too sharply, guessing from her silence that she was immune to whatever dumbfounding quality he found in the moment.

She climbed over him then, rocking the canoe perilously, to sit on the other thwart, presumably so she could face him while they proceeded, though at first she didn't face him, just ranged her eyes downward, inspecting only boat, and not planet.

"I love a canoe," she said, leaning back, holding her wand to her tongue as if wetting the point of a pencil. "It's enough to make you fall in love with your own imprisonment. We have canoes."

"I know. But you look so downcast when you say it. I can't tell if you're humoring me."

"I didn't know you could be humored."

"What I wouldn't give."

"You're more engaging as a canoeist than as a dinner guest," she said, smacking her lips softly, barely swaying, as if rocked by doubts. Maybe it was the growing heat. She sat forward, took the wand out of her mouth and pointed it at him like a finger.

"Okay, go ahead."

Her proximity exhilarated him for a moment. It felt like his knees, hard as branding irons, could burn a hole through the bottom of the boat.

"Ahead where?"

"Go ahead and talk about our escape," she went on. "Tell me where Fermat went and if we could go there too."

Knox couldn't answer that, so her told her more about the ice cap. Solid, crystalline, thick as a tropical island, top heavy, possibly tilting the planet out of proper angle at times. White wig heavy on the old yellow head. It was easy to paint a verbal picture of a futuristic city founded on the ice, a city carved of ice, fabulous with spires and bridges, but lacking trustees, lacking guilt. Imagine skating from tower to tower. From room to room. Imagine slipping into unis made of ice, lounging on furniture made of ice, painting pictures in ice.

"I guess so," she shrugged, at the end of this fidgety speech. He had to acknowledge that he'd been a little overexcited.

"But," she added after a while. "There isn't any ice cap. You guys melted it."

"Not."

And he had to tell her the truth of the matter.

"So why didn't Krell tell me all this?" Zelen wondered. "Why did you?"

"We took an oath. I just broke the oath."

"I want to touch the water!" she cried, and leaned over the edge.

"No, don't!" he said brusquely, letting the canoe move forward, as it sometimes would, without strokes. It was an hour since they had begun their outing.

"Why not?"

"When we escape, this is our source of water. Keep it clean."

"But it's as if I have to obey directives."

"Don't you have any maxim about obeying the directives that you could have written yourself?"

"No."

"You know what the others call you now don't you? They call you Zellion. Maybe that means they'd obey you, or your maxims."

"They call me that?"

"Not really. I'd like them to."

"Oh, they do, they do, say they do!"

There was such a little distance between them, but she had a way right then, in the canoe, of wrenching her chin to the left to look at him, as if to decrease their connection by decrease of angle.

"I often think of goodness, you know," she said after a pause.

"Is that another maxim? Too personal, I think."

"Not in goodness as in God the Father. Not like that. Some other kind. God the brother, maybe. Oh, I don't know. God the cousin thrice removed. Don't you think God is removed?"

"All right. But why are you telling me this now?"

But he knew why. She didn't adore him any more than he adored her. This emphasis on an uncomfortable immanence of the holy was meant to push him out, and let something else in.

At that point they were both crying. Their lives, our lives, were always already defined by imprisonment, after all, despite escapes or escapades, and random moments would be tinged with horror. They looked up eventually to examine each other's crying style, and laughed with boatman humor at how horror gets hauled up out of the gut like ballast, like cargo.

When Knox began paddling again he knew something that had been coiled in him was uncoiling, unspiraling like a watch spring. He needed rewinding. Then it felt more like something might separate, precipitate out.

He ended up telling her she could put her hand in the water if she wore a glove, and as soon as he had stretched the silken fabric over her fingers, they ended up taking the breath wands out of each other's mouths and trading them, then sucking in air as if gaining something from each other, lightly at first, then eagerly. Knox held on to some of her extra fabric. Things got unsteady then. Her hand was held out toward him, but in his case there was no extra fabric to seize. Without speaking, he let go and heavily traded places with her again, and they sat for a time without their breath wands, sipping shallowly, staring over the water, her hand sometimes protruding out, possibly to reach his fabric, then drawing back.

Knox thought later, much later, that around that time he'd heard a little splash, as if something had jumped in the water, though he couldn't imagine a fish, or anything like that, and paid scant attention. He paddled on alternate sides of the canoe as if in a greater race than the last one, keeping his elbows level, jerking his shoulders forward with every stroke, away from the dome, or even Brittle Star.

———

He stopped after an interval and they concentrated on silence, on waiting, on letting the planet drift underneath the canoe, rather than the other way around. There was, for him, a kind of victory in everything. He felt that light rays came from his eyes, sweeping across Zelen, sweeping across the landscape, obeying his will, rather than light rays bouncing off everything in the same way and bouncing into his eyes. There came the sound of a toy gun going off, but it was only Zelen coughing, a sound which brought him a little bit back to his senses. Then, mentally, he was adrift again.

She mentioned how she couldn't stop thinking of dancing and couldn't he just start teaching his dance class again.

"Oh no," he said, nearly asleep. "It's one thing at a time. And look at me."

"Hmmm." Her voice had a dove-like moan, or fall in it, and he thought, not for the last time, that if anything could inhabit this planet, it wouldn't be people, but birds.

"Just dance by yourself."

"I will and that will make three things I perform in exile," she said.

"Oh?"

"Can you name them? I'm the maxim reader and... mm, what's the word. I'm some kind of other?"

"You're a dancer."

"Exactly. Like Krell, I'm a dancer."

"Krell," he repeated.

"You mean why did I marry him?"

"I don't know if I meant that."

"Partly the ponytail. Forman had one too. Forman who I attacked. They're similar in more ways than that. It's that marrying Krell seemed at the time like a prison marriage. If I could avoid biting him for a year I could consider myself rehabilitated. So I've been biting myself. Look."

She held out her hand, but there were no bite marks on it that he could see. Then he remembered she could bite without teeth.

"What's the third thing you perform?" he asked, after a silence.

"The third thing is something there's no word for. The figurine you gave me could describe it. What I *am* to him. What I am to *him*. It's what I meant before by believing in goodness, godness. I was afraid to bring him with me today, so can we go back now, please?"

"You're its curator," he murmured, peering through the water, thinking he could see something in it, far below.

When he looked at Zelen again, not that much later, she was asleep. Then he noticed that her breath wand had fallen into the bottom of the boat. He grabbed it and wiggled it gently into her mouth so as not to wake her up, and she took it eagerly in her sleep, like a baby to its bottle.

The thing was, his own breath wand was missing, and wasn't instantly reappearing, even though his hands were frantically exploring every possible spot for it. The only conclusion was that life, in other words the ability to breathe, was gone. What had happened, he had to conclude, remembering the splashing noise he'd heard, is that the wand had fallen, when they were busy rearranging themselves around each other, into the water. Where it sank out of sight.

So why not grab Zelen's wand out of her mouth and throw hers in the water too, just for the sake of romance, just so they could share whatever drama there was in asphyxiation on a distant planet.

Knox refrained, and considered the facts. He'd greedily rowed much further down the canal than ever before, so there was no way to get back to the dome before he had taken in a heavy dose of toxins. There was this fact: toxins kill. And a bad death it would be, an immediate emphysema, a probably livid and purple choking, or auto-strangulation. Maybe a gentle falling asleep and the nicest death imaginable, Zelen singing to him that at least he had found a pair of gentle hands to guide him to some nebula. That's how she would make him comfortable with this style of prison escape.

"Wake up, Zelen," he said, resigned to everything, as he always had been. But when she didn't stir he grabbed her shoulders and shook her hard enough that the back of her head chattered against the gunwale.

"Hey, what is it?" she scowled, stretching up and pushing him forcefully away.

"I have an ending for our story," he smiled, calmer now. "It's death's door. I had to tell somebody. You don't want to wake up and find me dead. I'm letting you know about my death in advance. Can you paddle a canoe?"

———

A few minutes later he curled up on a thwart, and tried to breathe in, taking minimal sips, one milligram of poison at a time as he liked to think. Zelen knelt amidships and awkwardly paddled back in the opposite direction. Nothing was said. She tried to get him to share her wand, but he felt she had to have it to give her the lungs to work the paddle with maximum effort. So she just threw herself into it, her neck so tensed and red that he wanted to massage it, but didn't dare exert himself.

When they got to a Y in the canals she had no idea which fork to choose, left or right, and he sat up to look, but, for the life of him, wasn't absolutely sure. He hadn't in fact noticed the other channel angling in when they were speeding along in the other direction. But now everything depended on making the right choice. Or maybe not. Maybe it didn't matter at all, because there was little hope of survival either way.

"I think the one on the right leads to your distant cousin, God," he whispered, trying to contain himself in every way he knew how: slower movement, slower heart, slower wit. Were there once people called yogis who knew how to deal with this? But all the slowness wasn't really working. His breathing was shallow and quick, mouse breaths.

"And the other one?"

"That one leads to your other distant cousin, Goddess."

That was the one she took. Another hour went by, and they saw no sign of the dome. Tragically, comically, the mountains were looming closer, and they were forced to conclude that they'd picked the wrong bifurcation.

"Just stop here," he said, already standing up and stepping forward in the canoe with perfect balance, perfect tightrope walking. "Let me get out of the canoe. I want to walk around a little bit. I can't stand to die on the water."

As she scraped the bow against the soft edge of the canal and helped boost him up onto the edge, he was happy that one of his last visions in life would consist of Zelen, her lovely mouth as white as custard, her hands wrapping around his ankle firmly and hoisting him upward. There was a boatman who ferried souls across rivers toward some afterlife, and the story was her now. Odd, though, that she was laughing what struck him as an inapropos laugh.

"What's funny?" he asked, as politely as he could, collapsing in the dirt and putting his chin in his hands. Funny. Better. Worse. He pictured himself, in death, head covered in short white feathers. Imagined, also, scarlet wings. Imagined whatever would transform him after death into the appropriate avian, founder of a new race.

"I'm laughing because you're fine," she said. "Look at you, Knox. What are you?"

"I'm a dying bird."

"Me too. Me too and all of us. But you've mistaken the time. You're alive. You're stinky with life. You're at least one picture of vitality. I'd get out and embrace you if I could. Your condition looks contagious."

"Where do you get all this? This vitality idea?"

And, to his astonishment, she pinched the breath wand out of her mouth and tossed it in the water, where it immediately sank.

"Get it?" she asked, arching an eyebrow.

And he did, finally. Curtains parted, red velvet. The maxim on the easel read:

The air is fine, better than fine, and you are an idiot not to be breathing it.

He had been breathing it for a couple of hours, and now that he stood up and consciously breathed, then allowed himself, for the first time, to gulp down breath after breath, all the way in, he felt each lungful fill the rest of him, quaking down through him to the toes.

"Life is giving," he said, open-mouthed. "I mean it's life-giving."

Zelen nodded, and he understood that the atmosphere was not just nonpoisonous, it was air that was as clean as no air, air that was diamond-hard and transcendental. Victory Air.

But it wasn't just that. He had new powers. The low but royal-purple hills that ringed him on every horizon, shifted, as in geological fast-frame, every time he told them to. "Move," he said, and they would roll, as if on wheels, to the right. "Move the other way," he said, and they did. Not many could do more, he thought.

His next idea was to share such discoveries with Mhurra, but realized that she already knew about them, learned them the instant he did, soaking everything in as dizzily as Knox. All of it belonged equally to both of them.

And of course then came the sad but simple meditation on clean air. It was clear that every one of us had been lied to over stretches of time, measured in years, to keep us gratefully contained. Odd to think how we had been purposefully birthed, in rebirth, into fear, in their plan to make us timorous, wee, colonized, hived. But forget about most of that for now. Knox and intoxication had to interpenetrate one another, so he ran along the edge of the canal, holding his lungs out like wings, while Zelen followed in the canoe, so much better at paddling now that it became a new race, with a mutually understood finish line. The two of them collapsed at the same time a kilometer later, ending in a tie, both competitors out of breath, though there was plenty more available to reinflate them.

"So thirsty, too," he gasped.

"Have a little water," she responded, already dipping her hand into the canal and cupping some up to him.

By the time they neared the dome it was nearly dark, and, as cold Brittle Star began to set behind the mountains, it became clear that something was a little different about it.

"It's oblong instead of round," shouted Zelen.

Knox, larger than life, the size of the planet, but still able to collapse from planetary scale when needed, peered at the sun complacently, like an angel studying the face of another angel.

"Yes," he sighed. "What that oblong shape is, is the sign of Blister Star coming back. That's his edge, peeking out on the left and right. He's warming up. He's getting ready to torment us again."

"To cook us."

"But we're dwellers of the arctic regions now."

"Is that still you?" she asked, keeping what felt to him like a nervous distance as they wobbled, still getting their land legs, toward the door to the dome.

"What do you mean?"

"You're grandiose. Is that normal for you?"

But Knox didn't want to think about that just then. In fact, he understood that he was a little too grandiose for such considerations. He had expanded again, and the north pole, undisturbed and unmelted, appeared in great detail in his mind's eye, but from a distance, as if he were looking down from the lofty perspective of both stars. As if he were a third star.

"Think about this," she continued, hearing no answer. "Maybe we could live there, and certainly easily get there, we know now, without breath wands or water bottles. But what would we eat? Just little kids that run away one day and are crying home the next. Some of us ran away, and died. This air is great, but here's a baby maxim for you, baby mine. *You can't live on air.*"

Surprised by her sing-song tone, Knox turned toward her, and saw that, again, she wasn't really talking to him, but to some listener who was very far off.

That night he lay on the floor and, looking up, saw Zelen's body, curled in sleep on her floor. Was she out of bed because she had fallen out, or had had an argument with Krell, or felt chafed by the sleeping platform, or because she wanted him to see her like that? Maybe sleeping on the floor that night made her feel closer, more synchronized. Maybe she took pleasure in the notion that he was awake, and below her, and watching her.

But after a while he turned face down and immediately slept, his mouth wide and loose enough to let out ancient-sounding snores, slack enough to let in draughts of oxygen. But it was stale air, closet air. Even in his dream he knew he'd recently had a taste of the real thing, the air of the gods, and the taste of the sterile dome atmosphere got into the dream and woke him up. He sat upright, remembered the hovering presence of Zelen, then lay back down in order to stare again at his neighbor.

But she was gone.

And there was someone, some other, in the corner of his room.

"Hey," came a voice, and Knox, electrified, leapt to his feet, wrapped his arms around his chest, and patted all around his back and torso, as if his uni were on fire.

"Fermat?"

"Sorry to sneak in on you like this. But I didn't want anyone to know I was in town."

Knox took a few steps toward the corner where his friend was crouched, still clutching at his back, and sat down hard to peer at him more closely in the dark.

Fermat looked good. He was still wearing his uni, his eyes still inky black, but reflective. Still, something was different—the fact that he was no longer bald.

"You can grow it back," observed Knox, reaching out to touch the very short and straight blonde hairs.

"Oh that. No, that's a wig," he said, pulling it off and handing it over. "Pretty good one, isn't it? I think it makes me look wonderfully military."

Knox fingered it, and really it consisted of no more than the lightest of films, or silks, softly bristled, but when he handed it back to Fermat and he put it on again, the realism was startling.

"Where did you get it?"

"At a rocket ship."

"You found the rocket ship?"

"Aha! I wondered if you already knew about it. Krell, too?"

And they spent the rest of the evening trading stories, with Knox finally telling Fermat the whole story, including the ice skates, and the ice skating, the frightening screeches, the discovery of the ship—but leaving out the storage box, and the figurines.

Not yet, not yet.

All this followed by Fermat explaining his escape, and how, at the end of the canoe race, he had paddled for miles, knowing they wouldn't come after him, and how he had hoarded, from his days of trustee privileges, dozens of breath wands, and buried them out on the plain, so that he could stay out for days. Of course he was able to only carry so much food and water, but at least he was urged on to explore as long as these held out, and see if he could possibly stumble across some unknown spot, some island in the sea of lifelessness, where there might be plants or animals or some other revolutionary growth of one kind or another.

"One day," he went on, "exploring on foot, I came across footprints, and realized that a group of people had walked that way before."

"Yoohoos?" said Knox.

"There aren't any Yoohoos! At least I don't think so. I've never seen any. Another hoax, in my opinion."

"Twelve truants, then! Alive!"

"Yes, and they were footprints leading north, following the north canal. I figured that was the route you and Krell had taken, and that they were following your footsteps, maybe thinking that there would be something of value at the ice cap."

"Sounds reasonable, but we never saw them."

"Somehow you missed them. Maybe passed right by them in the dark. At any rate, they led me right to the ice cap, and then right to the rocket. I think they must have been there only a day or two after you."

"So there's another lie. They wouldn't have made it back to the dome then, before we did. And we were told when we got back that they were already dead and cremated."

"What do you mean, another lie?"

"I'll tell you in a minute. First tell me about the rocket."

"Oh," said Fermat, his face lighting up. "It's magnificent, isn't it? I'd like one of those for personal use, as I'm sure anyone would. And I feel bad about this, dear Knox, but my first impulse was to fire it up and take off back to Earth right then and there. I flipped switches, I pushed buttons, I stamped my feet to get that machine going, but it was no good. And of course there's that gaping hole in one of the instrument panels. Bad damage. I figure it must be very old, maybe from precursor times, don't you think?"

"That's what we thought too. And don't apologize. I did the same thing you did. I mean tried to start it."

"Really?" he laughed. "I guess I feel better about being a dope if we're all dopes. Couldn't that be a maxim?"

"Dopes. Dupes. Either way, a good maxim. But go on."

"Okay, so then I start exploring the whole ship in detail. By this time I didn't know where our truants had gone, because the footprints end at the rocket, and it looked as if they'd all gone inside. But no, nobody home."

"You didn't find... anything?" asked Knox, disturbed by the idea that Fermat was about to pull out a figurine, and ask what it could possibly be for.

"Well yes, I did find something pretty interesting, pretty useful, I'd say."

"Tell me, tell me."

"I found food."

But they were interrupted by a sound from the other room. Someone was in Knox's kitchen, and, giving a hush hush gesture to Fermat, he went in to investigate.

It was Krell, sticking his whole head under the faucet to get a drink.

"Now that you're a trustee," said Knox, "you should arrange for everyone to get drinking glasses."

"Sorry to get you up," said Krell, straightening. "But I couldn't sleep, and so thought I'd just wander around."

It was too dark to see anything clearly, but he definitely got the feeling that Krell was putting his hands behind his head and wringing out his wet ponytail like a sponge on Knox's floor.

"That's okay."

"The thing is, I thought I heard you talking in your sleep. Also, from up above, it looked like you were crouched in a corner or something.

Talking to yourself?"

"Well I've always had a tendency to sleepwalk. When I heard you in here it snapped me out of it, and I found myself, as you say, crouching in a corner. I guess I was talking too. Do you know, my wife used to tell me that I said very profound things while asleep. Maxims, really. *From the true opponent, a limitless courage flows into you.* Pretty good, right? Did you catch anything of what I said this time? Because I can't remember it."

"No. Just mumbling."

"Well thanks for checking, Krell. Good night."

"Good night."

But when Knox went back to the bedroom, Fermat was gone.

———

The next day, a day off for him, Knox waited until Zelen came home from work, and went upstairs to see her, to sit around. He thought there would be a lot to say about their discovery out on the canals, and though she was animated when he first came in, full of movement and sarcasm, soon she was slumping in her chair, world-weary and curt. Her complexion was a little off. Not beautiful and not in love.

She was his upstairs neighbor. She made them some ersatz coffee.

Later she got up and made a second cup for both of them.

"Two cups in a row?" he asked, surprised.

"To see if there's any chance of getting a twitch from it," she said. "Some people say you do." And she drank hers down in one gulp, and no, she observed, no twitch, so after that she made them a third cup. And then, after a fourth, perhaps she at least felt something, because by the end of the afternoon she stood abnormally upright, with a smartly military posture, as if the beverage had supplied her with the authority of a trustee. That was funny, sort of, but it only reminded him of her officious husband, now given to spying in the middle of the night.

He got up to leave, but she reached out and grabbed his arm. Her fingers seemed monstrous just then, very red and dry, hard, enlarged, and he hesitated to loosen her grip, for fear her fingers would snap off.

Then he noticed for the first time that there were pieces of creamy writing paper stuck to one of the walls.

"What's with the paper?" he asked, sitting down again, ignoring the pain that her grip caused his arm.

"Oh that. That was my idea. Remember how Waugh has so much paper in stock, but no pens? Eventually I thought, why not use all that paper in the same way he did, to gain some privacy."

Loosening her grip, but still holding on to him pretty firmly, she led him back toward the bed cell.

"And look what I did here."

And he saw that she had woven another plastic-wire curtain, just like the one in the outlet, and hung it in the door.

"Do you not want me to be able to see you?" he asked.

"Oh, I wasn't thinking of you. Just, you know, privacy. You can still see me through the floor. Did you see me last night?"

"Yes, that was nice. Did you see me?"

"Yes, you and Fermat. I'm happy to know that he's all right. Where has he been all this time?"

"Out and about."

At last she let go of his arm, and he rubbed it gently where she had clamped it so hard.

"Did Krell see him too?"

"Yes. He said he was going to come down to say hi to Fermat. He didn't?"

———

The wallpaper idea spread very quickly. Most of us were naturally pretty sick of the beehive-in-a-fishbowl lifestyle. Most craved fewer restrictions, some scraps of dignity, all the time understanding that dignity is like sexual attraction: temporary, contingent, feigned.

There is a primacy to sensation, someone said, not as a maxim, but like a good maxim it made the rounds. We hadn't really traveled to the planet, it was said, but been created here, and furthermore, fashioned by our maker for habits that pertained only here, so no sense in acting fresh-off-the-boat by way of some strict allegiance to the conventions of the old world. Still, we had no stomach for the social disorder that often results from new surroundings. Discipline and caste had been strong on Earth, and now they strengthened. Still, sometimes disorder gains ground through hierarchy. Increased lip service to social norms allowed for unravellings, everywhere, of private norms. Many considered rebellion, not against the trustees, but against far away parents, or deans. Sex became a substitute for resistance. So it is in all societies. What we call freedoms in life are not true freedoms, only amusements we pursue out of fear of the real freedoms.

One day, when Knox went out for a walk, he could see that those same creamy sheets of paper had been pasted up everywhere, without a trace of writing on them.

He couldn't avoid thinking that part of his plan had been spoiled. Those who wanted more privacy might have followed him to the ice cap, he'd been reasoning, because the new buildings up there could be fashioned from ice. You could peer through the walls maybe, but with great distortion. Now with our papered walls we had achieved that, all without comment from the trustees. There is no point to rebellion.

Evaluate. Widen the mind to the size of a small planet, then let it occupy only one corner of the yet wider mind. The aim of it all, Knox knew, was not the pole, but the pole, somehow or other, as the first rung of the ladder home.

Later, at Grand Opening, he found Waugh sleeping or feigning sleep at his counter, two hands on the counter making his pillow. The shelves were bare. The store was sold out of paper, and because privacy is prelude to eros, out of verymouth.

He didn't wake Waugh, but stared out the front window, where a few street dancers had appeared. The vogue in dance, without Knox's guidance, had turned toward animal imitations: chickens flapping wings, horses tossing heads, apes defecating with exaggerated shudders.

As the noise of their dancing and shouting grew, Waugh raised his head.

"There," he said, pointing at the merrymakers. "Have you seen those moves before, Knox? From when you were dance professor?"

The window framed at that moment two men and a woman. They were triangulating, lowering their torsos to the street, hips splayed, hands hovering above the pavement as if to conjure something up from below, then reaching all the way down to drum on the pavement, as if asking something to arise.

"Bravo, students," muttered Knox. "If they were my students. But they worked that out on their own."

"I can't say I'm in favor of it."

"In favor of what?"

"Dance craze. Nothing like that in my day."

Knox turned to laugh at what he supposed was Waugh's studied impersonation of a theatrical type, but then realized from the look on his face that the old man was in earnest. And also looking ill.

"Are you all right, Waugh?" asked Knox.

"I'm alive, aren't I?"

But in the midst of his seriousness Waugh's face had turned a very light shade of green, a celadon, and taken on a hardened look as well, as if subtly glazed and fired.

"Feeling dizzy? Maybe you should close shop and go home."

"I'm fine. And unhappy. Tablets selling out and turning into wallpaper. It was my idea, and now everybody has to imitate. Where am I going to get customers for my storeroom? Would you and your girlfriend at least come back and sit in there and talk, like you used to?"

"Absolutely."

"Look. Look at those two," said Waugh, turning away from him, gesturing out the window again.

Outside a couple of new dancers were at the window, trying some interesting steps: one woman spun in circles while another woman, taller, kept one fingertip fixed at the crown of her friend's head, as if providing an axis for the rapid spinning, and even slapping at her friend's shoulder with one hand to increase the speed, until the spinner was a blur and the slapping girl kept looking around for an audience. Finding none except Knox and Waugh in the window, she pointed at them, then pointed at the blur beneath her finger.

But, thought Knox, taking a few steps forward, aren't both their faces slightly green?

———

His desires, like his youth, ran backwards, diminishing. It would be enough to leap vertically off the ground, in imitation of precursor crafts, face to the stars, spinning, gathering power, chewing thinner and thinner air. Also, to be shot with a bullet, a procedure that precursors, it was said, had invented. Shot from a very short distance, the flesh pierced cleanly, purely, as if by one of their famously religious gunmen. To die and rocket to heaven, the soul carrying something on the way up. Maybe it's a bicycle, and you cycle up in a spiral to find that heaven is the top of the hill, the top of the flight of stairs where he and Mhurra once turned to jelly with witty grief.

One night he lay in bed more in coma than in sleep, with the feeling that he was inflating, but so slowly that years of his sentence might pass before there would be any cause for alarm. His brain was active, and he thought he heard footsteps coming toward him. In the dream portion of his mind the footsteps belonged to Mhurra, and there she was, rolling her eyes, weary of his repeated dreams of her approach. Still she approached, just as she had in the rain, blurry and orange and dogged, one canine tooth caught on a lower lip, her neck strangely bent to one side. She was coming to embrace him, to kiss him, or merely touch his face with a fingertip, but all he could think was how he wanted to reach out and straighten her neck, as it was exactly like a picture hanging crooked on a wall. But the dreaminess evaporated, and naturally enough it wasn't Mhurra, but Fermat.

"Oh, right," said Knox, trying to understand.

"Are you okay?" asked his old friend.

"You're the one to ask about. Are you all right?"

Knox got up and led his guest to the other room, where Knox poured a couple of cups of coffee.

"So you were about to tell me something," said Knox, handing Fermat his cup. "Something about the rocket, about finding food. By the way, Krell knows you were here. Maybe he just wanted to say hello? I don't know. Also by the way, he's a trustee now."

"Krell a trustee? That's funny."

"Yeah. I guess he took over your job."

"Bravo, Krell. What I was going to tell you before he came downstairs is that the rocket is full of food, in a way, and that's what I've been eating out there."

"What do you mean?"

"Listen to this." Fermat took a sip of coffee and leaned in. "I found the storeroom, the pantry. Except it didn't look like that at first. There were boxes and boxes of what I thought were toys."

"I see," said Knox, thinking that this must mean that Fermat had found the figurines.

"So I saw all these different kinds of toys, all miniature versions of animals and vegetables. There's everything, as if they were coming to this planet to build doll houses. There are heads of cabbage the size of marbles, but perfect. Onions and apples the size of ball bearings, but perfect. Chickens and fish in their exact colors and if you looked closely you could see the feathers on the chickens and the scales on the fish. But it was dark so I pocketed a few of these things to look at later. Then, when I got outside again, and took them out of my pocket, and left them for a minute in the sunshine, guess what happened?"

Knox had no idea.

"They expanded. They grew to life size in about a minute. The sunlight seemed to trigger them, and they exploded. Well not exploded, but swelled up, and swelled up, until in the end they were no less and no more than the real deal."

"You mean life-size toys. Now enlarged to scale."

"No, I mean the real thing. I had a real apple, and when I took a bite, it was fine. It was juicy and sweet. I ate it, and I liked it. Do you see? And the chicken? It was strutting around my camp, clucking, flapping its wings. I ate that too, and gratefully. Ditto with the fish. You see what they were able to do in the old days, then?"

Knox did see, vaguely, but he was back for a moment in his dreams of levitation, gunshots, inflation.

"What they knew how to do—" began Fermat, but Knox, eyes narrow, then widening, held up his hand to ask for silence.

"What they knew how to do," repeated Knox, standing up and speaking with his hands on the table, because he understood everything well enough now to teach a course on it, "was to go on long voyages, but not at anything like the speed we have now. It would have taken them decades to get here from Earth. So they needed suspended animation. They needed to shrink themselves, really kind of mummify themselves in a way, along with their food supply, so they could travel for years, and then, on arrival, reanimate themselves with sunshine, or maybe artificial light."

"I hadn't thought of that!" laughed Fermat. "I mean that they shrunk themselves too. But then, where are they? Why is the rocket empty, with so much food still lying around?"

"Okay, listen. You must have gone through the second level down. The one in tatters? With wallpaper or something hanging down in strips?"

"I know the one you mean."

"With a big crate, or barrel in the middle of the room?"

"Right."

"Did you open the lid?"

"No. No need. The lid was on the floor."

"You're sure."

"Definitely, because the light from the upper level was falling right on it. Right in the barrel. So it was easy to see inside. Why?"

———

"I know one thing," said Knox. "I know where one of the preekers is."

And he told the whole story, not omitting his own stupidity for having failed to recognize immediately that what he brought home in his daypack was human, not a representation of the human.

And as he spoke he had a picture in his head of Zelen and the manikin, the mummy, the homunculus, whatever it might be called now, a picture of her taking it out of the pack, laying it gently on the bed in the middle of the day, and watching in fascination and ecstasy as it expanded and lengthened, subtly absorbing water and light from the atmosphere and swelling to its ancient human dimension before her eyes. As it grew, she never took her hand off its leg, thrilling to the sensation of instant organic growth, aroused by the dermal blooms of gold and pink and umber and cream. When at last he opened both eyes, and blinked, he reached out two ultra-strong hands to fold Zelen like a handkerchief and clutch her to his muscled bosom.

"Knox? You were saying?"

So Knox went ahead and told the story, glancing up at his friend almost ruefully at times, of his awkward, tentative entanglement with Zelen, which of course led to an account—and Knox began to get a little boring here—of their canoe trip, their moment of intimacy, and then the accidental and somehow philosophical discovery of breathable air.

"To think," sighed Fermat, "that I've been out there for days, sucking on those stupid wands. Incredible. I just would never have imagined them going to such lengths."

"Fermat, it's a penal planet. They've studied the science of convict control."

"But who are *they*? The trustees don't know about this either. Unless I was the only one who didn't know."

"Somewhere there is the man or woman in charge. Not on this world."

"But why? Why do they need to keep us in a bottle?"

"That's not clear to me, either," said Knox. "They want us to hear the maxims, and improve ourselves, and that wouldn't work if we were all out there wandering around the landscape."

"Right. Look at me," laughed Fermat. "Away from the maxims for days, and I turned into a desperate criminal. I turned into a Yoohoo."

"So there is one, then."

Day was breaking with a nacreous, mottled range of colors, almost paisley, shifting as the suns rose, so that the walls of Knox's cell appeared to be underwater. The two men stood up and, moving from corner to corner, moved like swimmers, revolving their palms before them. It occurred to Knox at that point to peer up through the ceiling, to see if Krell might be spying on them again, or getting ready to come down, but he was surprised, then bitter, then grateful, to see that the view had been blocked by multiple sheets of blank paper, sloppily tossed down, but sufficient for the job.

"Maybe," said Fermat, oblivious to this development, shifting fluidly from point to point, while the oysterish light played on his scalp. "Maybe this is really Earth, and our ship took us thousands of years into the future."

"Or maybe," said Knox, feeling high from the effects of the light, the high of his anger with Zelen, "maybe we traveled to an alternate universe, and our counterparts are doing all these same things on Earth, only with subtle differences, like no exile, no penal colony. Just the two of us floating around our suite, killing time."

Fermat looked funny then, with his dome-reminiscent head and drooping ears. He'd stuck a breath wand in his mouth for comic effect, and started in on a kind of weird dance.

"Everybody's been doing that dance!" exclaimed Knox, finally joining in.

Later, Knox would look back at that conversation and recall that his first fully formed thought about the preekers, once he knew they were still alive, and presumably even wandering about, was, for some reason, one of radiant optimism.

They weren't just convicts, but monsters, he wrote one morning in his tablet. *We sleep and don't think of badness, but it's exactly what's missing here.*

But he kept that second one to himself. He and Fermat went back to lying on the floor, this time without a bottle, as there was none to be had. It didn't seem important anymore, nor did it seem to matter whether anyone would note the presence of Fermat, or care that he was back, or that he'd stolen a canoe and been gone a while. He was back in the hive, if they noticed him, and that's all that counted. Keep the marbles in the jar. Recite sentiments to them. Knox prepared a different maxim for the moment he could take over the broadcast.

"Attention. Your attention please. *The fool's heaven, when examined, looks more like the wise man's hell.* Or something like that."

He sat up after a time, and looking out the window at the labyrinth of buildings all around, realized that his was one of the last cells, or maybe the very last, to remain transparent. The sheets of paper appeared to cover everything now.

"They're out there somewhere," said Fermat, talking to the ceiling. "I mean the truants."

"I know. And as soon as we can get off the floor, we ought to go look for them."

"We're both going?"

"Yes, and Zelen," announced Knox.

"Ugh. I don't know. Why her?"

"Because she's got the last shrunken preeker. Or maybe he's expanded by now. In any event, she can't keep him."

"Keep him?"

"He has to be taken back to his people. The preekers I mean. They'll be wondering what happened. Maybe plotting how to get back to Earth. Don't you think?"

So they rose stiffly to their feet, looked at each other, cupped each other's cheek with the right hand, then offered a coffee toast to the concept of resolve.

"I don't know, maybe we shouldn't be drinking this stuff," commented Knox, staring into his cup. "It's causing depression, I think. Also, look at your hands, or go look in the mirror. There's definitely an off color."

"You have it too."

"I do? Now that I think about it, I don't feel well."

"I'm all right, so here's what I suggest. That I head out now, and make my way back to the rocket. That you get some rest, find Zelen, and the two of you meet me up there. I have the feeling that wherever the truants and the preekers are, we'll find them somewhere around there. And somehow all together."

Knox sat down heavily on the floor again. His head was swimming.

"Wait a minute," he said. "Don't you think that they'll head down this way?"

"Who?"

"The precursors."

"Oh, them," sniffed Fermat. "But why would they come here?"

"I don't know. I guess I just wish they would. I'm enjoying the prospect of them marching right into town, monstrous and ancient as they are, and how the trustees would first fall out of their chairs, and second, worship them as gods. Become their slaves. You get what I'm saying? Imagine the value, tourist-wise. I mean, if this place were inhabited by actual men from another millennium."

"Planet of the Preekers."

"Exactly. Though for some reason that doesn't sound right. I picture them as tremendously wise. As very deep. As gurus."

"But what do you mean, inhabited? You mean as replacements for us?"

"I guess so. Yes! Imagine this town, all preekers."

"Preekertown."

"Preekerworld!"

"But how would they replace us? You mean kill us? Or do you mean send us home? Remember they were famous for their brutality. It could be that we'll have to find a way to kill them."

"I don't know, Fermat. I just have this funny faith in them. That somehow they won't let us down."

Alone, and back on the floor, Knox kept thinking about all the years of history the preekers had missed. All that folly. And how would they feel about returning to the story now? Wouldn't they wonder what was the point, when anyone who knows human beings could conclude that any given future would be no different from the present? They'd swelled too soon, too soon. Thousands of years later would be more interesting. A hundred thousand. Lifting his hand to his eyes, confirming that the yellowish green tint or yellowish blue tint on the back of his hands was slightly stronger than it had been before, he drew his arms and legs in tight and experimented with willing himself to a smaller, mummified state. They had it right, and I spoiled it, he said to himself. I brought them back to life before humans turned into some new species. Bird species. At the same time, his refrain kept repeating. *They will save us.* But how? Probably naked, probably disoriented, their ship unable to take off, they would eventually stand up straight, and laze around like everybody else, waiting for the tourists to show up, waiting to hitch a ride back home—back to a home they might not recognize, but would easily thrive in, maybe reconquer.

Alone with such thoughts, Knox succumbed to lethargy, to darkness. He was unable to leave his suite for days. Zelen might have come by, but didn't. Did she ever peek through the papers on the floor? He didn't notice. Was the city still inhabited? There was no way of knowing. Krell dropped in once, but apologized and left as soon as he saw Knox solemnly flopping around on the floor like a baby.

Of course the maxims kept up, though without anything near the frequency of the early days. Still, he didn't know whether they were being broadcast live from the little dome, or simply being played back. Some of them sounded familiar but his brain wasn't operating quite right during his mental lapse.

"Just be yourself and really enjoy yourself," her voice rang out, in her most harmonious and persuasive tones. Really, she was getting pretty good. Clearly it was a maxim she'd written herself.

During the time of his illness certain others reached his consciousness.
Sensation is primary, thought secondary.
Burn always with a hard, blisterstar flame.

We have the right to be whoever we want to be, but have no right to be who we were.

Well that was it, wasn't it, the ur-maxim, known to all, and now finally spoken out loud.

And now he saw that with one other maxim, if he could get Zelen to broadcast it, as he was sure she would, the revolution would be complete.

The air is healthy and clean. Yes, it is. The water in the canal is delicious. Our sentence is up. Go outside and enjoy the suns and the breezes. The truants are already out there, and they're probably fine. When the tourists arrive, that's when we'll go home.

But Knox couldn't get well. And then he did. Some strength returned. He stood up, walked around, even tried a few of the old dance steps. There was one called a saltarello that he tried, a brief leap into the air with a witty scissoring motion of the toes, and he could still do it, though with less elegance perhaps than in the past. Afterward he stood on a chair and pressed an eye up to the ceiling, trying to peer through one of the gaps between sheets of paper, but saw nothing. Finally he ate something, drank something, and felt well enough to go find Zelen, wherever she was.

His first guess was Grand Opening. And there she was. Alone. The first thing he noticed was that she was wearing a daypack. She winked, turned sideways, pointed to the bulge in the pack, and Knox took all of it as a good sign. The little preeker had been in the dark all this time, and could remain there, he hoped, for the time being.

"Are you all right?" he panted, out of breath.

"Yeah, but what about you?" frowned Zelen. "You don't look well."

"You don't look so hot yourself."

It was true that she had the faint green tint as well. But the top of her head, where she was bald, was still as pink and milky as the day she shaved it, and in fact it looked like she must have shaved it again recently. The effect was that the green was rising in her, giving her body a thermometer effect, an idea of mercury slowly rising from below, not yet reaching her head.

Then he noticed something else. This new color of her skin bore a striking resemblance to the color of her uni.

"Zelen," he said, cautiously. "Tell me something. When you picked your uni, did you pick celery or celadon?"

"Celery, why?"

"Look at your hands. What color would you describe them?"

"They are," she said, in the tone of one picking colors for a bathroom remodel, "the same color as my uni."

"Now look at my hands and my uni. I picked the celadon. And my hands are celadon as well. It's a subtle difference between the two colors, isn't it?"

"I'm not sure what you're trying to say."

"I'll spit it out for you. The unis are doing this. The uniforms are turning us green."

"Because they're so cheap? Crummy dye job? That doesn't make sense to me. They're so nice."

"It's on purpose. They're poisoning us, or dyeing us, or something. Somebody planned this, and I'm afraid to think why. Although I know why."

And Knox grabbed the zipper pull near his shoulder, pulled it diagonally across his torso, and stepped cleanly and adroitly out of his costume. That was that. He was free of it. Then there was nothing to do but stand naked before her. He recalled having done it once before, or at least having done it in front of the whole colony, when we changed our clothes on that very first day, and because it was not a big deal then, he was determined not to view it as a big deal now.

But, for a moment, the nakedness prevented him from knowing what to say, and then he realized that it had silenced her as well.

"Take yours off too," he said. "There might still be time to undo the effect. Unless you want to promote a lasting celery tone. Unless you want to turn Martian."

She was eying him up and down, with the expression of an important scientist.

"Please put it back on, Dr. Knox. Not because I'm embarrassed, though maybe there's a hint of that. Just put it on because we're in town, under the dome, and you don't want everybody stopping you to ask what's going on."

"But I do! Everybody must get theirs off, and the faster we convince people, the better. Starting with you."

"Listen," she whispered, and, grabbing him by the arm very tightly, as she had done before, pulled him into the storeroom and spoke to him softly and articulately in the relative dark.

"Let's think this through. I've seen you before. I mean I've seen a naked man. Every man. But a naked man is a revolutionary. And I just want to take this one step at a time."

All the time she spoke she held her hand above her eyes, not to avoid seeing him, but as if some light from above were preventing her from seeing him better.

"Okay," he said, this time in a more submissive tone.

"I'll take my uni off too, Knox. Eventually."

"I see."

"Only to test your hypothesis. Maybe we can get everybody to do the same, though I think that's going to be hard. Now, are we still going to take the canoe and go up to the ice cap, as promised?"

"Of course."

"Let's go now. I'm for it. As far as Krell and I are concerned, that's over."

"Did you bite him?"

"Don't be stupid. Of course not. It's more like he bit me. Not literally. It seems that trustees prefer to be with trustees."

Considering all this, nodding eagerly, Knox put his uni back on, slipping into it with disdain, as if it were a tuxedo, or a gorilla costume. Then he explained to her about the maxim she should broadcast, leaving it to her to word it exactly, but making her promise to include the new information about everyone shedding their uniforms.

Zelen was agreeable to that. That could take care of step one, and why not.

Then, step two, Knox suggested, would be to meet at the canal, get out of town fast, like fleeing bank robbers, jump in his canoe, and take off in pursuit of Fermat, who must be now already be at the rocket, looking for the truants.

"The truants?" she asked.

Oh yes, the truants, the defectors. Alive, maybe. He hadn't filled her in on all the details, but he did now.

Zelen listened to everything he knew about the truants, but he held off on the story of the preekers, including their suspended animation, their miniaturization, the whole thing. He'd save that story for the trip. Best to let out one revelation at a time, because he wasn't at all sure whether she would exult at the news, or crumple, or simply hand the preeker back to him in its bag.

The next day they walked out to the canoe again, naked this time, both having shed their unis upon exiting the dome, thus losing the protection of the magic fabric. At the same time they put an end to the discoloration process that must have been working on them and all of us since the day we put them on. Zelen's shaved head stretched higher on its neck than normal, and then higher still, as if some force, some filament, were pulling her up by the crown of her skull. Her nudity gave her an air of sharp attention, as if seeing through compound eyes, absorbing everything, everywhere, in great detail, borrowing the naked hauteur of a preying mantis, or a green parrot.

Their mutual exposure gave a prelapsarian quality to the evening as well. The distant mountains were sharp in their outlines as if recently engraved there, and the yellows of the soil, the blues of the canal, all seemed to have been engraved there recently by the hand of some benevolent aesthete. The air was as intoxicating as before. Knox's lungs felt charged with thought, with animal spirits, as if they had turned into a pair of brains. Complicated issues of liberty and obedience came to mind. What were they free to do? What duty bound? Starting over like this, what was the whole idea? Why are humans the only animal that laughs, that cries?

But it seemed unlikely that they could talk about any of this. Their nudity suggested silence and, once in the canoe, Knox simply got back into his familiar position, his Hiawatha crouch toward the center of the canoe, and the paddle went to work, tossing off its spray, a bouquet of silver drops at every stroke. Zelen sat behind him again, still shy, though when she massaged his shoulders, as she had agreed to do to help keep him paddling as long as possible, her breasts inevitably pressed into his scapulae, which might have seemed erotic except for the fact that some buckles on the straps of her daypack sometimes scratched painfully against his ribs.

They advanced, at first, at a reasonable speed, but later things didn't go as well. One of his hands swelled a little, and he could think of nothing except the difference in size, and for that matter, color (the swollen one, as the skin stretched, seemed less green), and whether or not it was permanent. Meanwhile, Zelen kept moaning, stretching her head up to peek over the edge of the canal, as if she feared they were being watched, and while at first Knox grew tired of her vigilance, he then began to believe in it too, however faintly, and started glancing behind every few minutes, watching for another canoe to appear, possibly in pursuit.

But they were not pursued.

Eventually they argued over speed. She wanted to move quickly, and he calmly explained that he could go no faster, due to the swollen hand.

Yet in the end, he could and did increase his pace, finding that the less he thought about her the more he could put himself into the act of paddling, the more he felt the creakiness of his upper arms turn into easy, fluid strength. After all, he was Canoeist. Canoeist was he. At one point the paddling became so automatic, and her arms draped over his shoulders felt so relaxed, that he wanted to start talking, and tell her about a certain dream he'd had during his period of extreme lethargy. In the dream he took her out in the canoe and, because of an argument, pushed her and her daypack overboard, only to come back later and find she hadn't drowned but instead had been rescued by the homunculus, who had stayed small but turned into a kind of water snake, or lizard, and was swimming back to the dome with her, keeping her head above water. But he didn't tell her, and discovered that, after all, her arms were hanging over his shoulders so flaccidly because she was asleep.

And that made sense. Zelen was always, in a way, out of earshot, always somewhere far beyond him, awake or asleep, forever negotiating a connection to someone who was not exactly Krell, not exactly him, not exactly anyone. Or was it the case that all this muddle with her was due to his own clumsy way of dealing with the world, any world, and that he had awkwardly changed things around, rearranging all of his nature and elements, convincing himself that there existed some tremendous surplus of feeling without an object, so how and where to bestow it, when the answer was simply to bestow it in every direction, every dimension, at once, in heaven, hell, Eden, Mars, wherever. *To be a free inhabitant of the cosmos,* he wrote, old-style, with the pen of the mind on the paper of the brain, *is to dangle from a filament, but not from such a long filament as to drop out of the cosmos altogether.*

"Oh by the way," he said after a while, speaking over his shoulder as he stroked. "There aren't any Yoohoos."

That woke her up.

"Huh?"

"No Kangaroo Men."

"Who are they?"

"Characters in an old piece of fiction. And it was fictions that kept us under thumb. Under foot? Which is it? Anyway, do you see? Poison air, poison water, murderous neighbors. All chapters in the same novel."

"Well, there could be Yoohoos. How do you know there aren't?"

"It just fits the pattern. Seen any?"

"Hard-to-find doesn't prove nonexistent. We'd have to scour the whole planet first."

"Go ahead and scour."

"What I'd like to discover is that they really are out there, and that they're not so bad after all. Rather polite. Anxious to be good neighbors."

"Maybe that's why they made you the maxim reader," said Knox. "You bleed for all of us. You even bleed for the Yoohoos."

"Not that much. A little. I bleed more for the ones back in the dome. By the way, I left that last maxim on loop, and they will have heard it dozens of times by now. Do you suppose anyone has walked out to breathe the air by now?"

"The more I think about it," he said, cheerfully, "the more I doubt it."

———

Two days later, at the rocket, there was no sign of Fermat, or the truants, or anyone. However, Knox did volunteer to enter the ship, look around, and retrieve some food if possible.

Once inside, he soon located Fermat's larder, and filled a box with miniature steaks, cheese wheels, coffee beans, and pies, then proceeded to the wallpapered chamber, fingering the hanging strips, noticing for the first time that they bore a patterned, cartoonish repetition, as in a child's room, of space ships and planets. There was Saturn with its rings, Jupiter with its red spot, and of course Mars, with its canals and ice caps, all swimming against a deep indigo background, and though he had never been to any of those worlds, the sight of them was saddening, because everything is relative, and in some sense those planets were home, or at least close enough to home to make him cry a little.

Then, moving to the center of the room, staring into the storage bin, confirming its emptiness, he concluded that the time was at hand to let Zelen in on the secret of the entity in her daypack, about how in fact it didn't really belong to her, and that now was the time to take it out and let the poor fellow expand.

And so, outside, first showing her the pantry items he'd carried out, and explaining the preekers' method of preserving themselves through the long years of slowpoke space travel, he walked her through the whole story, as he and Fermat had worked it out between them.

To his surprise, she seemed to find the story gratifying.

"What's inside my pack then," she smiled, "is what I should have, I guess, inside my womb."

"That's one way of looking at it. A very weird way."

They stood face to face, by this point unaffected by each other's nakedness, such as might occur after a few days in a naturist colony. However, given the growing heat of the new Blister Star season, and their lack of unis, they had mostly traveled by night, and had had little occasion to really look closely at one another. Even then it had been uncomfortable. What they did each morning, before it got light, was to drag the canoe out of the water, invert it, and sleep underneath through the day, unavoidably rubbing up against one another in the dark of the canoe, but removed now from eros or even a goodnight kiss, though one evening he woke up to find she had entwined her fingers in his while sleeping.

It was morning now, painfully bright, and they stood in the shadow of the rocket to keep out of the sun, just as we all had stood in the shadow of the *Antibody* on that first distant day. As she twisted to remove her daypack he saw how her face filled with that subtle, silent animation he had once found so attractive, a kind of waking R.E.M., a vivid expression of the cerebral flickerings under the skull. Then, despite certain compunctions, he allowed himself to take in the angles and depressions of her body, which did remain celery-tinged. Her breasts and sternum were dyed the darkest green of any part, a watermelon green, with the freckles on her sternum nearly black in contrast. It struck him that, again like a thermometer, the level of green had dropped, and her face was largely free of it now.

"So what," he asked, "do you want to do?"

"Think, think, and think," was all she said, sitting down heavily on the ground, putting on the daypack so that it hung in front instead of behind, then burying her face in her hands.

"What about we eat?" Knox suggested, spreading out on the ground the tiny banquet he'd brought down, and sitting down across from her to wait for its expansion in the light of day.

———

Sometimes it was possible to bleakly admire the advantages of exile. Knox, positioned where he was at the horse head of the universe, sometimes felt like the universe, or at least the horse, had fallen in love with him. At night, looking up at the stars, there was no longer the familiar feeling of insignificance. At that distance from home, it was just the reverse. The pitiable inhabitants of Earth looked up to see *him*, and felt abashed. His little penal planet, having further shrunk, now expanded. And that, it was clear to him, was the reason to keep the world unnamed, unlabeled—to let it enter everywhere. That way, when he got back home, he could keep Blister and Brittle inside him, like two saints shining out from him at the same time.

———

All planets tilt on their axes. Therefore they seasonally angle away from their suns, just as with Earth, and that angle promised Knox and Zelen a day of lesser heat at northern latitudes. They climbed slowly up the canyon, the direction the truants had to have gone, their footprints ending at the rocket because there the ground turned to hard flat rock, pavement free of traces. The morning sky, medicinally purple in the east, turned black inside the canyon, and the stars came out again between threads of cloud. Below, at shoulder level, the rock walls were layered cream and cinnamon, alternating.

Knox aimed for a mood of forgiveness and reception. The human machine breathes itself forward. The brain sends the brain back, one beat out of synch, one step behind the body. You see more that way. "Order yourself into disorder," Mhurra would say, scanning the air for frickling flies. She was good at mentally structuring what she saw into numbered zones, then randomizing the zones, and she did that habitually with people too. At least so she confessed. Today the trick of it came easily to Knox, and he made his rhythmic, chaotic advance, sticking to canyon shadows when possible, stumbling at times. He felt sure they were closing in.

Eventually his two minds merged, and two plans formed. The thing to do when meeting the preekers, he decided, would be quick apology for waking everyone up accidentally. Maybe they'd understand how things were, how it was now a world of civilization, incarceration. They had their suspended animation while we had our general blurriness, and look at the similarities: they in their bin and we in our dome, all waiting for an alarm to go off. Knox didn't know much about the society the preekers came from, but he thought it impossible that they would fail to understand first the benefits and then the limits of our modern babyishness.

By mid-morning they were far up the canyon, flagging. There were still no footprints, everything gravelly underfoot and hard on the naked soles of the feet. After a time they walked in tempo, matching strides, silent for the most part. She still wore her daypack in front, but it didn't seem that she did it that way for the sake of modesty, because she had loosened the straps in such a way that the bag hung low, below her widely separated breasts, bouncing slightly on her stomach, and she cradled it there in her hands like a swollen belly.

"If you're going to be pregnant like that," he said at last, "you might as well let me have him back. Any man could do that too, you know."

Zelen only laughed, then swore at a sharp rock underfoot. He thought there was a new dullness in her eyes, the dullness that comes from masking the self, and saving a stored-away brightness for somebody else.

"It's not because I'm female," Zelen said at length, drawing the unborn closer to her gut, as if afraid he really would reclaim him. "It's because I'm wiser."

And all of it was all right. No facts in her life, or his life, were sour enough to scour him down to zero. What he had was a compact, if that's what it could be called, with himself—an agreement that rattled and cracked, but prevailed.

The canyon opened up, and they began threading their way through a field of boulders, egg-shaped stones as tall as they were, and if they hurried from shady side to shady side, the heat wasn't so bad.

"Look at this," he said, pointing to the ground. "Prints again. A lot. The truants, or the preekers, or both. Some group definitely came this way."

"Good, good. But, please, Knox, can we rest for a minute?"

They found an especially large boulder, and sat down on the ground in its egg-shaped shade.

There, Zelen whispered into her daypack for a while.

Then she brightened, and talked about the way the planet might look in the future, and Knox learned that she had lost all hope of returning home, but hoped for a better world under the administration of the preekers. Knox nodded, and expressed his own belief in their superior intelligence. Zelen believed they would make the planet fertile, fecund, green as celery and celadon, and maybe even more loving at the same time. So great were their powers, she speculated, that they would build multiple cities, but then reduce the world to a size where it would be possible to visit any loved one in a matter of hours.

"By canal, you mean?"

"Oh yes, by canal! And they'll have speedboats! What I picture is a kind of electrified kayak, and it goes on top of the water and underwater as well. A really fast submarine, with portholes."

"Zelen, it's as if you're thinking of staying here."

"It's as if you think there's somewhere to go."

"But just listen to yourself," he scowled. "You want a green paradise, but you also want speedboats? You're worse than Krell."

"Not that bad!"

"What makes you think," he continued, "that the preekers could pull off any such thing? We've got to think about how they'll help us get out, help us get on that tourist ship. That's all."

"Oh," she said, slowing down. "I can't say I believe that the tourists will ever come. All I know is that I'm worried about Fermat."

"He has a way of showing up."

"I decided that it's okay for you to carry this for a while," she said, slipping off the daypack.

Knox was surprised.

"He's very heavy," sighed Zelen. "As of course you know."

"Are you sure?"

"Yes, of course. And you are, in a way, the father."

For the first time since they took their clothes off, Knox became humiliatingly aware of his nakedness, his rounded stomach, his graying pubic hair, the peculiar organs hanging below. His fatherness.

"That may be true, in a way. But think how much older he is than we are."

"Knox, listen, if we could reduce ourselves like that, and hibernate, and stay here for years and years, wouldn't you do it? Wouldn't you want to wake up in the future?"

"So I can wake up and see what humans have done to this place? I guess not. The odds are against me liking it."

"Then you don't like us."

"There's today's maxim for you. That's a good one. *Don't like us.*"

"All of the green is gone," she said, and for a moment he thought she meant Earth. But she was examining herself, checking every inch of skin. He also noted that her hair was starting to grow back, though at this stage it looked more like a stain on her scalp, an ink spill.

"And me?" he asked. "Is mine gone too?"

"Yours too."

———

They walked on through more boulders, now spaced closer and closer as they advanced, until they were forced to squeeze, one at a time, through the spaces in between, while the boulders themselves were by that point the size of houses, so that it seemed like they were walking through a cramped, stone-age suburbia.

"At least you can't say anything negative about a man who hasn't been born yet," she said, maneuvering sideways ahead of him.

"You mean reborn. We might find that this precious little boy of ours used to be one hell of a character."

"Give him back to me now, please," she commanded.

And though Knox was sort of enjoying the weight and bounce of the little fellow on his stomach, he didn't dare say no.

Still, they traded the heavy daypack a couple more times as they progressed.

When at last they emerged from the maze of rocks, they found themselves at the edge of a flat and empty area, round in its outlines and surrounded on all sides by boulders. It felt like a plaza, or a field where different kinds of sporting events could be held.

But here also, not exactly in the center, and at first mistaken for a collection of boulders, they found a town. Perhaps it would be called a village, an impoverished one, since it was only a collection of rock shelters thrown together in a precarious way, with roofs fashioned out of what looked like random stretches of fabric.

"It must be where they live!" whispered Zelen, dancing backward and dragging Knox by the arm with her.

They got out of sight behind a rock and watched in silence, not sure what move to make. They were frozen, full of speculation. A breeze came up. There was a welcome coolness seeping from the ground into the soles of their feet.

Then they could both make out some movement. Two figures emerged from the dark interior of one hut and stepped out into the full light and dust of the day, a man and a woman. Nothing seemed at all threatening about them, especially given that they also were completely naked, but not green. So Knox, despite Zelen's grip on his arm, stretched out his other arm into open space to make himself visible, waved it wildly, but didn't manage to attract their attention.

The two figures merely crouched together in the heat and scratched one another enthusiastically, as if scratching were forbidden indoors and they had to get all of it out of the way this minute. After a time their skin began to glow red and rather hideous, but they remained as absorbed with one another as early hominids or some other unexpected prodigies.

"Hey," said Knox, not very loudly, not sure of and not caring too much about what contacting them would lead to, and he waved his arm some more.

"Hey."

Still no response. Still they scratched, and laughed gently as they did so, and Knox wondered guiltily if this was a moment of itchy eroticism that he was trying to intrude upon. There was some question in his mind at this point whether they were truants or preekers.

"Do you want something else to yell at them?" asked Zelen from behind him, where she hung back in the shadow of the rocks.

"I'll take whatever you've got," he exclaimed.

"Yell out, *Attention, your attention please.*"

"Oh. Are you sure they're truants? How can you tell?"

"You just can. They're not magnificent enough to be our ancestors."

"All right, so what do you want me to broadcast?" he asked, inching back towards her, pleased to have become, at least for the moment, the new Maximist.

"Well, I don't have one. I was trying to be funny. But it might work."

"How about, *Rare as true love may be, it's never as rare as true friendship.*"

"Fine, I guess. But Knox, I don't really care about truants. Let's get out of here."

"No, no. I'm anxious to talk to them. Get some answers."

"If you ask me," she said, gently patting the daypack, "all the answers to all the questions are right here. Whatever's going on in Renegade Village here, whatever it's called, I think we already understand it."

"Maybe."

"Come on, Knox, let's just go somewhere and give birth. Don't you want to? And think about it. None of the toil and trouble of early childhood. You'll have a grown son within minutes."

But the answer was probably no. Nothing was the same for him as for her. They were spending a lot of time together, but were essentially alone in the world. This particular world. So boldly enter the village? Or go with her, let the preeker self-inflate, and see if he might have some sort of deus ex machina resolution for them? See if he might build them a cool speedboat?

"I do love you," he said, and meant it, in a way. On one level. What it was was a kind of goodbye.

"I love you too," Zelen smiled, though her attention was elsewhere, the phrase automatic. And that was also a goodbye.

There was one way they were like each other. Both had difficulty with decisions, with decisive actions. So they waited. It was comfortable standing in the shadow of the rock, leaning their bodies against its chill surface. They could observe without being observed, and the two people they were watching, after scratching a while longer, did seem to move toward more erotic gestures, but for some reason stopped. Then, looking about stealthily, they ran straight toward Knox and Zelen as if fully aware of them, though in fact it became evident that they too were simply looking for a cool hiding place among the rocks.

It was at this point that Knox realized with a start of pleasure that the young man was none other than Maxim Illion.

He was a little older looking now, more masculine, but also more savage in appearance, with dark leathery skin, short hair, and long dirty nails. Still, his face had that same quality of the unknowing know-it-all that had drawn Knox to him in the first place.

"Illion," he hissed at the two of them, the two naked villagers, as they approached, and they stopped running just a meter away. "Illion," he repeated. "It's me, Dr. Knox. It's all right. I just want to make sure it's you. Is it really you?"

The two young people stepped into the shade, gently and fearful, hunter and gatherer, and Knox, peering more closely, could see that Illion had not only grown, but suffered, since their last meeting. There was something dissipated, something shiny and more criminal glazed onto his skin, maybe put there by rebellion and heat. His face looked private, as if it had the relevant answer to everything safely stowed in it, a wealthy man's cabinet, never to be opened.

But by whom? The truants had put their hands over their genitals, despite Knox's and Zelen's nudity, and acted as if they might dash off again. But something changed, and the young man dropped his hands and boldly stepped up to Knox.

"My name isn't Illion," he sneered. "It's Shoe."

"Illion or Shoe. It doesn't matter," smiled Knox. "I knew you back in the dome. Do you remember me?"

"Sort of."

"Look, Zelen, look," said Knox, turning toward her. "The dead come back to life. Two of them, anyway. You must remember Maxim Illion."

Zelen stayed back a few feet, wrapping her arms like warning tape around the daypack, and said nothing in return.

"Illion," continued Knox, resting a hand on the kid's shoulder, noticing as he did that the skin was thin and fragile to the touch, a dry drum head. "Tell me what happened. Is everyone here? Everyone alive?"

"We're all right," answered the boy, staring back with a mixture of surrender and sarcasm. "What's great is that we don't have to live in your stinky dome anymore."

Knox was already breathing hard, a little panicky. Things weren't going well, despite the discovery. There was something wrong about both of them, but he wasn't sure what it was. The woman, somewhat older, smug in a way, didn't seem to want to speak, and went off to spread and curve her alarmingly emaciated body against a neighboring boulder.

"Now please," said Knox. "Tell us the story. Tell us how on earth you escaped."

"It's not like it's any big deal," said Illion, finally, reluctantly, returning one hand to shield his penis. "Because we're *very* happy that we left. One of the trustees was nasty, and a bunch of us decided to get back at him."

"What do you mean?" asked Knox. "What did he do?"

"It was stupid. He sent a dozen of us outside to polish the surface of the dome. Polish it and polish it, he said, until it gleams like the outside of a jellyfish. And when he saw that we could only polish the very bottom, because we could only reach so high, even on tiptoe, he made us stand on each other's shoulders to reach higher, and then form human pyramids to get even higher. So we just kept rubbing and polishing in that crazy way, all day. Then, when our breath wands were probably going to run out, we noticed that the trustee wasn't around anymore, but no one came out to hand out new ones, and we jumped off each other's shoulders, and tried to get back in, but the portal was locked. So we just lay down in the dirt, thinking we were going to die."

"And then you found out that you didn't need the wands."

"Right! That was amazing! You know about that too, right?"

"Obviously."

"Right. Obviously."

"Go on."

"Yes, okay, so we just looked at each other, and we all thought it was a good idea to run away, and see if we couldn't at least camp out temporarily, until we ran out of food. It wasn't like we could be punished for it, because we were already being punished, if you see what I mean. I mean by being here. On Pissworld."

"Pissworld?"

"That's what we call it anyway. Because of the color. Or Deadworld. Because we thought everything was dead at first."

Knox, taking all this in, couldn't help but notice that Zelen was barely paying attention. Her hands were nervously in action the whole time. She kept fiddling with the zipper of her daypack, or digging little holes in the loose dirt with her toes, or alternately bringing one finger slowly to the tip of her nose, as if to check her depth of vision.

He lost his own concentration and began to imitate her, pointlessly he thought, but unable to do otherwise, stretching out a foot to start digging a hole in his own dirt, listening but not listening as Illion went on in an uninteresting way about some theory of his that the core of the planet was actually made of rubber, like the core of a golf ball.

And at this moment, for a moment, a recent dream came back to him, the memory of it prompted by the act of digging.

It had been more of a nightmare, really.

He was on his knees in his cell, trying to dig a hole in the floor. Someone came in to say that he would never get off the planet that way. It was Krell, and a moment later they were playing ping-pong, but Krell had developed a new spin shot, based on the lesser gravity of the planet, where he would hit it over the net, just barely, and then when it hit the table surface *it wouldn't bounce up at all,* but just roll forward, completely unplayable.

"That's how you get off," said Krell in the dream. "By not bouncing."

In the waking world, Knox turned to Zelen to see if the hole she was digging was deeper than his.

But she wasn't there anymore.

What an odd time to leave, he thought.

Meanwhile Illion had returned to telling the story of their expulsion from the dome, and was just getting to the good part of the story, but speaking more rapidly than ever, and explaining breathlessly how the twelve of them had followed Knox's and Krell's footsteps all the way to the rocket ship, and inside it there were people, naked people whom they'd never seen before.

"Full-sized people?" asked Knox.

"Full size? What does that mean?"

"Never mind."

"And they were real nice, and gave us—all of us—plenty of this really amazing stuff to eat. And it was real food, not chunks. Delicious food."

"Stop," said Knox. "Hold on with the rest of the story. I want my friend to hear this."

"Who?"

"My friend. The woman I was with."

"What if she's not coming back?"

"Oh, she'll be back."

But this was wishful thinking. He understood that she had gone off to a private place to give birth, just like the females of many species do. Her baby was about to be born, and she wanted that moment to herself. For Zelen, it would be the birth of an extraordinary being who would turn into—at least Knox was convinced that she saw the future this way—a grown child who would fit her definition of love, of family cheer.

"He doesn't want to tell you the worst part," said Illion's friend, moving forward and speaking for the first time. She was light as dust, wary, peering through the rocks, keeping an eye on the village.

"What's the worst part?" Knox prompted her.

"The monster part. The bad part. They yell at us if we don't do things."

"Don't do what things?"

"I don't know. Build these shelters, for one thing, and run all kinds of stupid errands for them."

This nameless and naked but now voluble woman wouldn't look at him as she spoke, just kept her head turned away, eyes glued on the village.

"Maybe we should escape again," she said, fiercely. "But you can't escape twice. Or escape once, even. Not when the bad part of the world consists of assholes, and the good part consists of dessert."

"You mean desert."

"No, I mean dessert."

She wiped away some sweat on her face, or maybe it was tears, and finally settled her gaze on Knox. But he didn't like the look at all; it was wistful and whiny, the look of a child peering up skeptically at a mild-mannered father.

"Unless," she added, "you know how to do something to make everything better around here."

"I've got to find my friend," answered Knox, looking at Illion, who was now on his knees, digging in the sand very aggressively, as if planning to escape underground.

"Hold on, hold on," hissed the woman, who had turned back to keep an eye out. "A few of them are coming outside, Shoe. They must be wondering where we went."

Knox peered around the other side of the boulder to see what she was looking at. And sure enough, there they were, marching their way. Three of them. Three of the beings that Knox, leaving the lid off the barrel all those weeks before, had brought into the world. They were moving, very much alive, very human, and as naked as everyone else on the planet at the time.

One difference was that they moved forward rather awkwardly, groping with their arms, more like swimming than walking. There was no particular direction to their movements, just a drifting, a random bouncing off each other. There was a stretchiness to them, a pliability. When they did collide they didn't seem to like the contact, and rebounded away, randomly, like molecules in a gas.

The surface of their skin, Knox noticed, as they got closer, was the same as it was when they were small, that is, brown and puffy, like fresh bread crust, so that color-wise they stood out against the yellow dirt, but were almost the same color as the boulders. In fact when they came very close, among the boulders, they were camouflaged, even transparent looking, like wraiths, neither near to him nor far away.

"What are you doing?" whispered Illion, furious, and Knox realized only then that he'd been waving to the group. Just a reflex! But now Illion went rather limp, and stood with his head down.

"Hello there," Knox said out loud to the preekers.

"I'd like to stay and speak with you," he went on, trying to insert some note of practiced charm into his voice. "But I'm worried about my friend. I have to go find her. And guess what! She has your missing comrade with her."

They showed no sign of comprehension. Knox took a step backwards, as if to finally be on his way, but found himself surrounded then by others. Maybe because of their way of blending into the landscape, more preekers had emerged from nowhere without warning, ten or twelve of them, and they now formed a tight circle around Knox and his two young friends.

Taken as a whole, their naked bodies were unappealing, male and female alike. Something was wrong, and Knox wondered if they had always been this way or if the process of compaction and then reconstitution had not really worked out all that well. If, in some ancient era, they had been truly violent, or horrible, they seemed nothing like that now. For one thing, their necks were long and not very firm, so that each of them had his or her head tilted to the side, the way a dog will do when inquisitive, except that they seemed to have no other way of holding themselves. Their lips were rubbery or loose, protruding in a kind of kissing expression, yet smiling at the same time. Everything, including the nudity, gave the impression of an intense and erotic curiosity. Or a pompous appraisal. All of it took Knox back in memory to his crime, to how the dean's neck had felt thin and plastic when he grabbed it, how the dean's lips had sputtered out a blubbery protest. And now here were these ancients with their preeky necks that simply begged to be throttled, maybe because in fact they had been, in their own time on Earth, not too different from college deans.

"Well! What happened to you?" Knox asked, sympathetically, kindly, stretching and tilting his neck to make them understand what he was talking about. He still assumed, as he had always assumed, that they were going to help out in some way, or ask him to celebrate their rebirth, or punish him for it, or do something sweet and civilized, or surreal, it didn't really matter what. Now that he could see them up close, he had absolutely no idea what contribution if any they could make. Perhaps it would be better to throttle them all immediately, to free up that much more food supply for the colonists to eat while away from the ship, as well as to release the truants from what sounded like just another sad imprisonment. How hard could it be to at least neutralize them in some way? With their skewed heads and their too short arms—almost dinosaur arms, strangely reduced, with large but delicate hands—they had an air of disability, of pained because meaningless amiability.

"Oh wait," he said, putting on his friendliest possible smile, as one of them seized him by the arm in a spongy grip. "Wait," he repeated, speaking very loudly, as if that would help them understand his language. "I'm not planning to stay here a minute longer."

The preeker peered at him closely. It was clearly a she, her sex revealed to him through her frank nakedness, as his sex was revealed through his, and when she spoke, it was in a lyrical, somehow articulate voice, in a language that surprised him with its degree of movement—tongue moving rapidly, skipping from tooth to tooth, protruding. It was a language that seemed to rely a lot on a kind of quick licking of the lips. But there was also a neutral tone to it, a lack of affect, as if she were reciting something from memory to him. Maxims? It was undoubtedly an Earth language, but not at all possible to understand. These were human beings, he had to remind himself, but strangely altered, alien, with crust-like skin, kissy lips, lightly clamping fingers, and in all cases, men and women, a short crop of blond hair, though he had to guess that they were all wearing the same kind of wig that Fermat was wearing when he came back to the dome.

Knox tugged his arm away, but not strongly enough for his new acquaintance to let go her ever firmer grip. In her other hand she held a mass of some glistening and creamy substance, tapioca pudding maybe, as if she had scooped a big handful out of a bowl and, again, gently, she appeared to be trying to convince Knox to take a taste.

But he recoiled. Something in him told him to refuse this food at all costs, even though he was hungry by then for something. Looking around he found Illion and his friend unpleasantly slurping up the pudding from the hands of their respective captors, oddly equine in the way they bent down to gobble and smack, and when they stood up, their faces smeared with it, he felt sickened. In their startling paleness and greed they were the ones, despite the relative perfection of their naked bodies, who came off as less than human.

"Oh, just look at yourselves," he cried, with some passion, his contempt for the truants rising in proportion to his sense of how little power the preekers actually had. True, it was an impressive achievement, putting themselves into a state of semi-mineral suspension for all those years. But what of it, if in the end, emerging from it and turning human again, they were both distorted and authoritarian, and could do little better than persuade others to perform menial tasks in exchange for gobs of rehydrated foodstuff? Given the way he and Zelen had idealized them, secretly or not so secretly, given how they'd hoped that the preekers would change everything for the better, they were a bruising disappointment, and he was sure that, wherever she was by now, face to face with her own full-grown version, she was experiencing the same let-down.

Meanwhile, Knox's preeker only brought her kissy lips closer to him, uttered some syllable, and brought her handful of pudding up to his face again.

Again he turned away, shook a finger at her, and shot another look of disgust at his comrades.

"How can you eat that stuff?" Knox asked.

"Whose food have *you* been eating?" asked Illion, wiping smears of pudding off his mouth.

That shut him up for a minute.

"If you come with me," Knox said at last, "we'll figure something else out. There's tons of food in the ship. They're just rationing it out to you. You don't have to stay here."

And, as if to demonstrate the procedure, he knocked his captor's hand away, took a few steps backward as if to depart, and somewhat rudely pushed aside some of the preekers who had formed a circle.

"Okay, then," he called out. "I've got to go find a friend. My friend I mean. Maybe we'll both come back and rescue you later. Got that?"

But it felt like leaving children with babysitters reputed to be abusive. The preekers looked on with an expression of milky sweetness mingled with regret. "Stay here," Knox cried over his shoulder as he walked several steps away, not sure who he was talking to. "If you move somewhere else, leave us a way to track you down. A note or something. Please."

———

The final stage of any fantasy is the deactivating of it, our faces turned up to the slowly falling drops of acidic realism. The book ends, the movie rolls its credits. Time twists itself back to where it was before our long, sweet reverie, our time of belief.

Still, despite his new incredulity, it was hard for Knox to walk away from the frozen tableau of preekers getting ready to abuse truants. As failing as any of them, he let go of linearity. What good had it done him. The hairs on the back of his body felt like steel wires. His thoughts were only of pudding, and the sense that every offering of it was a whirlpool. He kept one hand above his head, not sure where to point the finger, but meant it as a goodbye. Later, not remembering how he got to where he was, he stood stock still, deeper in the maze of boulders. The texture of the rock had changed from dustiness to crystal, chocolate brown and as sharp as if worked by jewelers. Zelen was possibly a few feet away, possibly farther. Knox could have called out her name. Where are you my dear, my Doctor, my Zelen?

Love is drunk from an inner cup, says a maxim from another planet. *Love is a cup for the inner drunk.*

Or this: *The dust of love forms a sticky spoon, which covers itself in dust.*

———

He wandered among the indigo boulders and soon enough came, not unexpectedly, upon Dr. Zelen. Came upon Zelen and her companion. But it was not a sight to light a smile. Her preeker had expanded with the same difficulties as all the others, and Zelen was trying to straighten his neck with one hand and lengthen one of his arms with the other, offering words of encouragement and kisses on the cheek at the same time.

Meanwhile her charge leaned back against a rock, pouting with the already familiar expression, oblivious to her exertions, blinking rapidly. Finally, when the full expanded figure caught sight of Knox, he gave him a critical look and uttered something in their language, which again reminded Knox of music, but music from the future, not the past.

Zelen stopped tugging at the little arm, and turned around.

"It's no use," she said, gasping a little, but also showing some sense of humor about it. "He just won't come out quite right."

"They're all like that. Maybe that's what's normal for them. Their food and their animals came out all right, so maybe that's what they looked like before they shrunk themselves. We just can't be sure."

"He was so beautiful when he was small."

"Weren't we all."

"And what is he saying? It never occurred to me there'd be a language barrier."

The preeker was still going on, more eagerly now, making a series of interestingly rounded gestures with his hands.

Knox, as if subtitles had appeared, immediately caught the gist of it.

"I know perfectly well what he's saying. He's asking us to help him get back to Earth."

———

Some days later, Knox lay asleep within the rocket, inside the wallpaper room, curled up on a carpeted platform he found that might have served as a preeker's bed at one time. He dreamt, and in his dream, Mhurra, not for the last time, was walking toward him, her shoes tapping closer across the floor.

She was about to crouch over him, lay her pale wrist on his shoulder, whisper something melodious and spare, something about the myriad surfaces of love, and in this way wake him into a world that contained her and whatever it was she contained. Labyrinths and illuminations. "Everyone gets stirred and spilled," she said succinctly in the dream, stroking the back of his neck as she had a thousand times. "Atoms swerve. The world is stained with secret blots. Don't think there's something special about me."

"It's not the stirring that I miss," he said, and because he was waking up he could hear the self of the dream, who seemed like an entirely different person, continue speaking.

"It's the tendrils," said this dreamer.

And Knox awoke coldly, completely, flat on his stomach, to find not her wrist on his shoulder, but a bird.

It was a pigeon that had flapped up to roost there, and in his sharpened wakefulness, he felt a tremble of blood, as if charged with the same electricity that powers genius.

But then he realized it was a pantry squab, reconstituted. He stirred, and the bird flew off, and perched on someone else's shoulder.

Knox was a little puzzled to find another person there, this one also lying on his stomach on a similar platform across the chamber, sleeping. Whoever it was must have come in during the night, and either chosen not to wake Knox or not noticed he was there. But, from the bald head and droopy, muscular limbs, Knox understood pretty quickly who it was.

"Oh, Fermat."

And his friend moaned, rolled over slowly with one eye barely open, and the pigeon fluttered off.

"What did you say?"

"Just your name. I said, *Fermat*."

"But you said something else just before that. You said the word tendrils."

"Talking in my sleep."

"Wonderful to dream of tendrils."

"Wonderful." He couldn't be sure if Fermat was kidding, and thinking about it, almost went back to sleep.

"What about Zelen?" asked Fermat, after a time.

"Oh," sighed Knox, then unfolded himself upwards to stand his feet. Still naked, he was colder than he'd been in a long time, but there was an iota of warmth in the carpeted sleeping platform, and he lay down again and stretched himself out flat to maximize the effect.

"Zelen came along," he said. "By now she must be living with the preekers, staying in their village, I guess. You been there? Have you tried the pudding?"

"I have. I've hung out with preekers. Obviously you have too, if you know about the pudding."

"Briefly, briefly."

And Knox sat up and rubbed his face hard, and went on to tell the story of his last few days, ending with Zelen and her now fully grown companion, and his limp goodbye to them as they walked back into the maze of boulders, back toward the rocky village.

"They do have a lot of food up there, I think," observed Fermat. "It seems that when they woke up they all had a tremendous craving for pudding."

"Yes, so there's a fair amount of food still here. We could hold out for a while, and maybe fight them for it, if you think it could come to that."

"As enemies go, they don't show me much to be afraid of."

"No, but you know, all food exhausts itself eventually."

"Just how secure in your dream of yourself are you feeling now?" asked Fermat. "I mean could you crawl back into the dome? Could you grovel for chunks? I'd choose to die a long time before that. Wasn't that one of the first ones?"

"First what?"

"*I'd rather die first.* First maxim."

"I don't think it went that way."

"Anyway, you wouldn't crawl."

"No," whispered Knox, "but at the same time imagine fighting with preekers over food. Somehow we've got to figure them out. Be human to humans."

"I've done all the figuring necessary," answered Krell, taking apart a tangerine, chewing up sections, lazily spitting the seeds onto the floor. "To me, they're just ancient trustees. More savage."

"Seeds," said Knox.

"What?"

"You spit out seeds. We could plant the seeds. Also, think about this. We could mate the animals."

"That makes you the god of this world, doesn't it?"

"What?"

"Farmer god."

"Oh, look at you," said Knox, just then realizing that Fermat was naked. "You're not green anymore."

"Neither are you, Knox. In fact you're turning leathery. I predict your leatheriness will become fashionable."

A few minutes later, outside, soaking up some welcome heat from the just risen sun, they made coffee, real coffee, with fried eggs, and toast smothered in oily chunks of salmon roe. Could they raise salmon in the canals? Maybe, maybe.

"So I went back to the dome," said Fermat, sipping.

"And you found it empty, or you found everybody packing, getting ready to march here to join the rebellion."

"Sorry to disillusion you."

And Fermat went on to tell his part of the story starting from where they'd all planned to meet at the rocket. He had, according to plan, gone there right away, and waited in the canyon for several lonely days, unaware that Knox had fallen ill. In the end, he chose to paddle all the way back to the dome to find out what, if anything, had gone wrong. The two canoes must have passed each other, what with Knox and Zelen paddling at night, and Fermat paddling during the day, still wearing his uni because he hadn't noticed yet that it was making his skin turn green.

But when he got back inside the dome, and into the center of town, it was to discover that nothing whatsoever had changed. The maxim that Zelen had left on auto-play was still going, still repeating itself, but within a few hours of Fermat's arrival it stopped, and the loudspeakers began blaring music, ancient glissandos and heavy chords and such, like Knox used to put on during dance lessons.

And there, in the main plaza, he found almost every convict. Most of them were dancing. It was the gala that had been promised months ago, back when they were all solid citizens, playing their parts under the dome. And here they were, still cooperating, remembering their dance steps very well. They weren't going wild, like at a crazy party, but dancing politely and smiling, executing some of the little leaps and scissorings that Knox once taught them, while others stood and watched, chatting, chewing on food chunks, guzzling politely from bottles. There was Chemo, still wearing his tie, collapsed in a chair and looking a little ill, and there was Krell, one of the dancers, his tie hanging loose so that it streamed out behind him as he leapt.

"The only difference," concluded Fermat, "was that they were all, of course, a little bit green, like me. That includes Chemo, who I expect to be the first to rip off his uni as soon as he understands what's going on."

"But he does understand! They all do. Like you say, the maxim was repeating for days."

"Then they must prefer to turn green."

"Did anyone see you?"

"No, I was careful. I don't think there would have been a big welcome. Especially once I stripped. So I slipped away, leaving my uni behind, and came back here."

They sat in silence, nibbling at the remains of their breakfast. Clouds were gathering overhead, and what warmth there was quickly drained away.

"Here's the worst possible scenario," said Knox. "The tourists show up, look around, enjoy their stay, tour the canals, get back in their ship, go home. Will there be security guards watching their ship in the meantime? Seems likely, doesn't it? And right now there's just the two of us, unless we can convince some of the truants to help us out. And even then..."

"I know. In fact there might be a lot of security. There might be a full military escort. On our side we need an army, ready to scare off tourists and whoever they've brought with them. Give them the *Antibody*, trade our ship for theirs."

"And fly home," said Knox, but as he said this he really couldn't picture Earth anymore, just a wet, brown sack of tornadoes, a whirlpool of assaults, a point in space to point spaceships at, and say, "Ignition."

"If only there were a way," said Fermat, "to pour some sense into bottles that are already full with something else. You have to empty the bottle first."

"Or break the bottle. Somebody already thought of it. Was it you? Somebody thought that a good thing to do would be to blow up the dome."

"Or maybe just make a hole in it. Throw a rock through a window. Sound of tinkling glass. Here come the suns, and so on."

"Hmm. Or melt it."

"If only we had a big enough rock."

"Fermat, I think we do."

"Excuse me?"

"I happen to know where there are some thermal devices."

"Some what?"

"Thermal devices. Meant to melt the ice cap, once upon a time. Stick them on the outside of the dome, and I guess they'll melt that just as well."

————

Imagine, then, how we could pull off our successful rebellion, depending on who we are. Imagine the tourist ship landing some months later, its arrival timed to coincide with the Brittle Star season and its cooler temperatures, only to find, surprise, the highly hyped city, so beautifully depicted in the in-space magazine, in ruins, the dome mostly blasted away, and the town itself just a runny, melted mass of towers and blocks, an ice sculpture left out all day. Imagine the disappointment of those who traveled all those weeks to fulfill the dream of a Martian vacation, complete with excursions on picturesque canals, while tinted "aliens" attend to every need. Standing next to their travel trunks, staring up at the ruins, they understand that the rooms they booked, at astronomical rates, are collapsed, or entirely gone, and discover further that the Martian staff, expected to greet them, pamper them, bow to them, is nowhere to be found. Where is the concierge, the maid, the cook, the bellboy, the manager, the fitness trainer? Where's the dance master, the ethics instructor, the gondolier for the excursion on the canals? The planet, in fact, looks deserted in every direction. The least they could have done was put up a "Resort Closed" sign. But there's nothing for it but to get back on the ship for the long and bitter ride home. At least the canals are there, picture-perfect, even real, if by real you mean simulacrum.

However, a second later, the tourists, along with the security detail that has accompanied them—this is, after all, a former penal colony—freeze where they are, for now, on an agreed upon signal, *we,* whoever *we* are, make our entrance, emerging from the ruins like dogs, unorganized and stumbling, completely lacking in the discipline that armed insurrections long for but seldom attain. But look at us! We are wide-eyed, shouting obscenities, but also coolly civilized in our sunburnt, alarming nudity.

Next we are running, sprinting as best we can, converging, surrou[nd]
and there are those among us, all running their fastest, who are old,
Dr. Waugh, or young, like Maxim Illion, and even a few whose heads
droop strangely sideways on their slightly too long necks, but who scre[am]
obscenities in a dead language, appalling to our enemies' ears. Everybod[y]
is armed with a single metal knife, a classic penitentiary shiv fashioned ou[t]
of the materials at hand, a weapon that resembles nothing so much as an
ice-skater's blade, and we are simply making a dash for it, heading straight
for the gleaming, dripping ship, ready to intimidate, or cut, or even kill
anyone who tries to stop us from reaching our goal.

And then there we are, crammed into the ship, strapped into our seats,
hurtling and dripping through the ink of space, our backs turned to both
Brittle Star and Blister Star, course precisely plotted for love star and
violence star.

Or imagine an alternative. We come under fire immediately from the
security guards, armed in this case with powerful death wands, and they
vaporize, that is, murder, any number of us as we charge. Moments later
the horrified tourists are herded, all screaming and weeping, back up
the ramp of the ship. Then, with a shudder of horror, the ship seals itself
and lifts off, leaving us ragged survivors behind, each one staring ahead,
realizing that no ship will ever be caught dead there again. Imagine us,
imagine Knox, cut off, excised forever from Earth's drippings and feasts
and dangers. As he sits on the ground, head in his hands, he hears, far
away, one loudspeaker stuttering back to life, crackling and humming until
a human voice comes on, not Illion's or Zelen's, but, miraculously, his own.

Attention. Your attention please, intones Dr. Knox, voice so smooth
you'd think he'd been promoted to Maximist.

Not once can you be exiled, he pronounces, *from exile.*

And looking around him at the landscape, breathing it in—the
sparkling canals, the royal-purple hills, the fractured light, his leathery
hands raised in front of his face—he is able to say yes, he does more or less
love it all. Or will. And that's the more successful rebellion.

nding,
like

m